RETURN TO
CRUTCHER MOUNTAIN

Cedar Hollow Series, Book 2

by

Melinda Clayton

Thomas-Jacob Publishing, LLC
USA

RETURN TO CRUTCHER MOUNTAIN

by Melinda Clayton

Copyright 2013 Melinda Clayton

Published by: Thomas-Jacob Publishing, LLC
ThomasJacobPublishing@gmail.com

Cover Art: Clarissa Yeo, Book Cover Art:
http://www.bookcoversale.com/#

ISBN-13: 978-0-9895729-1-0

ISBN-10: 0-9895729-1-9

Third Edition

First Printing: July 2013

Printed in the United States of America

Dedication

This book is for my brother, Sam, who has inspired and influenced all of us more than he'll ever know. This book wouldn't exist without you.

Janie

Acknowledgements

I would be remiss if I didn't thank my parents for their patience, input, and advice throughout the writing of this book. It wasn't until they gave it the seal of approval that I was ready to submit it for publication.

Thanks also to Dennis Roe, the very first friend I ever made, for reminding me that no story is complete without a handsome Dennis somewhere within. Forty years after our first meeting in a Leigh's Chapel cow pasture, Dennis is still giving good advice.

And always, to the loves of my life: Donny, Caleb and Isaac, thanks once again for putting up with me while I holed up in the office, hunched over the computer tapping away on the keyboard.

RETURN TO
CRUTCHER MOUNTAIN

Cedar Hollow Series, Book 2

by

Melinda Clayton

How to Talk to Grownups

You can't be too smart.
They don't like that.
It makes them mad
because they like to think they know the most
about everything.

They won't understand you anyhow,
so it doesn't really matter how you say stuff.

Sometimes one will understand
and not care about feeling stupid,
but that is very rare.

I have only known one or maybe two
like this, and not at the same time.

I keep looking for more, but maybe that is not fair.
The first one I knew was too special
for anyone else to be like him.
The second one I am still not sure about.

Tracy R. Franklin,
author of *Angst, Anger, Love, Hope*

Chapter 1

Monday

The day it began started like any ordinary day. My first thought upon being jarred awake by the blaring alarm clock was, *Oh, no. Not again.* My first reaction upon realizing my first thought was to wince. This awakening thought was a relatively new one, creeping uninvited over the past few weeks into my fuzzy brain when defenses were down, before the routine of the day asserted itself and wiped out the cobwebs. I didn't know the reason behind the thought, and I put no effort into discovering it. Instead, I banished it from my mind.

I briefly considered turning over and going back to sleep; I was, after all, on vacation. But I needed my morning run, not only because I'd put on five pounds over the last few months, but because without it, I had a tendency to fall into a mental funk. Running was one way of keeping disquieting thoughts at bay.

Reluctantly, I dragged myself out of the tangled warmth of the bed, gathered up the trailing sheets, and tossed them back onto the sleeping form of Michael, who snorted and rolled over under the added weight. I paused for a moment, studying him as he slept. Six months into the relationship I still had no idea where it was going. There had been plenty of men in the years since the divorce, but none I cared to know beyond a few shared dates and fun evenings.

Michael Bell was a respected independent film producer, well on his way to the top. I met him at Sundance, shortly before he won his first award. Having once been an independent film producer myself, I knew the talent showcased at such events and made it a point to attend as many as my own hectic schedule would allow. Michael had been an unexpected treat. He was a nice enough guy—too nice, probably—and extremely talented in his field. We certainly had common interests, and conversation came easily.

Taking in his muscled back and broad shoulders as he sprawled across my bed, I had to admit that he was also quite handsome, with his salt and pepper hair and dimpled chin. But handsome older men are a dime a dozen in Los Angeles, even for middle-aged women such as me. All in all, Michael was turning out to be a decent guy. More than decent. Still, I found myself slightly annoyed that he was snoring in my bed.

Shaking the troubling thoughts out of my head, I stumbled across the dark room and flipped on the bathroom light, squinting in the sudden brightness, and peered at the face staring back at me from the mirrored medicine cabinet. I had a fleeting and not at all pleasant memory of my mother, not the one who had raised me, but the one who had birthed me and then abandoned me at the age of ten.

In the memory my mother is clothed in a tattered blue polyester housecoat, sitting at a scarred and pitted Formica table in a ramshackle cabin in the mountains of Appalachia. She's swigging coffee and puffing on a cigarette, as she is in most of my memories. Her bleached hair is wild about her head and sleep lines scar her cheeks.

Jessie, she is saying, closing her eyes and delicately rubbing her temples with the ring fingers of both hands, cigarette held precariously between the first two fingers of her left, *git the baby. He needs changin'.*

My mother had been young when she left, not even thirty, but she'd lived a hard life that had aged her beyond her years. At the age of forty-seven, the resemblance I saw in the mirror was irrefutable. Strange how I'd never seen it before.

I leaned closer to inspect my face. I'd made a lifelong habit of avoiding bouts of introspection, but I found myself oddly curious about this sudden resemblance to my birth mother. I hadn't thought about Lindy in years, and it was somewhat shocking to see her image reflected back in the bathroom mirror at six o'clock on a Monday morning.

I tilted my head to the left in the light from above the mirror. In spite of the mark of years, mine wasn't a bad face; it was angular, the nose a little too sharp. Deep lines were just beginning around eyes that were green with specks of gold, the color highlighted under the glaring bathroom light.

Overall, it was a respectable face, some had even said a beautiful face; it just wasn't the one I wanted. This face belonged to someone else, someone in a dingy blue polyester housecoat sitting at a scarred and pitted table drinking coffee and smoking cigarettes while a baby screamed in the background. I felt no connection to this face.

I didn't blame my mother for leaving. Lindy's husband, my stepfather Roy, had been an evil man. Drunk more often than sober, he had terrorized all of us, me, my mother and my half-siblings, keeping us isolated in a tiny little hunting cabin high in the mountains of West Virginia. No, I didn't blame my mother for leaving. I blamed my mother for leaving *me*.

You can fend for yourself, but the little ones cain't, she'd said. *Lenny Sue ain't but six and Leroy's just a baby. Besides, someone needs to look after your stepdaddy.* She had paused to spit-wash a spot of dirt from Leroy's face, creating one clean spot on the otherwise filthy infant.

Roy done raised you all these years, she'd said, rubbing the baby's face raw while he tried to squirm away. *I reckon you owe him that.* Then she was gone, dragging my half-siblings behind her as Lenny Sue reached towards me with her grimy little hand, her eyes never leaving my face. That was the last time I saw them, either my half-siblings or

3

my mother. In the words of my mother, I reckoned I had paid him what I owed, and then some.

Lost in thought, I pulled my hair back from my face for a better look. Unlike my mother I kept my hair natural, the dark waves falling to my waist, tangled from sleep. In the harsh reflection of the lighted mirror I saw with dismay that the strands of gray noticeable at my temples seemed to have multiplied overnight. The vision of my mother's stiff, bleached hair flickered again in my memory. A cut, maybe, or a hat, or even a chador. But no dyes, highlights or bleaches. Period.

Impatient and uncomfortable with my wandering thoughts, I turned away from the mirror, bypassing the scale altogether (this was obviously not a good day for *that* exercise in torture) and dressed for my morning run.

An hour and a half later, fresh from the shower and dressed in a faded red flannel robe, I stood in front of the open refrigerator peering past day-old takeout Chinese food, hoping for something quick and reasonably healthy to eat. I envied women who turned cooking into a form of art, but I'd accepted long ago that that would never be me. I ate because I had to; the style the food came in made little difference to me.

Michael was gone now, after having given me a perfunctory peck on the cheek. "Call me later," he'd said, "if you want to meet for dinner." I wouldn't call. I never did. Although Michael seemed intent on denying it, he was just one in a string of men that I found temporarily interesting. Reckless? Maybe, but safer for me than the alternative.

While he was nice and undoubtedly intelligent, I had no intention of committing to anything that might resemble a relationship with Michael. Relationships did not work for me. I wasn't sad about that fact, nor was I angry. I knew the blame was solely my own. I also knew that at my age, I was no longer willing to attempt to be someone I wasn't. It never worked, and it was misleading to whatever man I happened to be entertaining at the moment.

Finding a pint of relatively fresh strawberries in the refrigerator, I grabbed a fork and stepped out onto the balcony of my Los Angeles condominium. It was late fall, and my unit overlooked the private gardens of the Association. Oleanders swayed in the gentle breeze, their colorful blooms faded in the heavy smog of Los Angeles' morning air.

Traffic sounded in the distance, impatient horns blaring and an occasional squalling of tires. The temperature was cool, low sixties that early in the morning, and I pulled my faded flannel robe close around me. *Nothin' like flannel to beat the cold*, I heard echoing through my memories, and I smiled. Billy May.

At forty-seven, my life had been anything but easy. Indisputably, climbing the entertainment ladder in any part of the world would be difficult, but much more so in the entertainment center of the world. Yet I had done it. As a renowned producer of big screen historical dramas, I had a well-earned reputation as a hard-nosed perfectionist, a take-no-prisoners workaholic. Many of my colleagues considered me detached. Still others considered me cold. I, however, simply considered myself a survivor.

The product of a teenaged mother and an unknown father, the victim of horrendous abuse dished out regularly by my stepfather, I had finally found safety one stormy night in an ancient hunting cabin on top of Crutcher Mountain, just outside the tiny coal mining town of Cedar Hollow, West Virginia.

Since then, I had used the challenges of my past to build stepping stones to a future, and if that made me seem cold and callous, so be it. I had not only survived; I had succeeded. By all modern measures of success, anyway. I pulled my robe closer, burying my nose in the soft, cottony smell of flannel. *Jessie girl*. Billy May's voice echoed in my head, and the sorrowful tone disturbed me. *Bí comforted,*

5

beag amháin. Be comforted, little one, a remnant of her father's native language. I blinked away sudden tears, angry with myself.

Billy May Platte, the half-Irish, half-Cherokee mountain woman who had rescued me from a lifetime of abuse had died eight months ago, and I had yet to come to grips with her passing. Los Angeles was about as far as I could get from the memories of my childhood, both literally and figuratively, yet every glimpse of the Santa Monica Mountains reminded me of home, and the warm smell of flannel propelled me instantly into the arms of Billy May.

Billy Momma, I had called her. It was a torturous exercise, this inhalation of flannel, but I couldn't help myself. Since her death, I'd both craved her nearness and pushed away her memory. My ex once told me, during one of his many moments of frustration, that I'm a woman composed solely of opposites. In that, he was right.

Standing on the balcony overlooking the garden, I set the pint of strawberries onto the patio table and swallowed against the lump in my throat. While the world I had created for myself was built on calculated indifference, my world with Billy May had been anything but. No genetic history had bound me to Billy May, yet she had been my mother, both in my heart and in her actions. The loss of her was still fresh and raw, sneaking up on me sometimes, summoned by me other times. Just as the sadness reached out to overwhelm me, the phone rang.

I entered the warmth of the condo, leaving the strawberries behind, and snatched the cell phone off the counter, impatient with the intrusion. Who could be calling this early in the day? I was enjoying a rare break in my usually hectic schedule after celebrating the release of my latest film, and I had hoped the frantic early morning phone calls regarding funding crises and wayward actors would cease, at least until the next film. The older I got, the more my work bored me, the outrageous antics of spoiled actors and actresses no longer titillating but simply vulgar.

Irritated, I glanced at the screen. A 304 number. I stared, frowning at the display; goose bumps pimpled my arms. Cedar Hollow was calling.

Chapter 2

I gripped the handle of my wheeled luggage and ran through LAX, the Los Angeles International Airport. The 12:45 to Huntington Tri-State Airport was on time, but I was decidedly not. Although my close friend, John Johnson, had offered to drive me to the airport I had declined his offer, opting for a taxi instead.

John hadn't been happy. "Let me drive you, Jessie. My mother will kill me if she finds out I didn't see you safely onto the plane." But I had refused. I was already a bundle of nerves at the thought of returning to Cedar Hollow. Being with John would have only made it worse.

Good old John, Hollywood director, friend since childhood, co-conspirator against all things Cedar Hollow. John's mother, Corinne Johnson, had been Billy May's best friend for decades, and John and I had known of each other since both of us had been washing the coal dust of West Virginia off our barefooted heels, though John was older than I. By the time Billy May had taken me in, John was already in California, modeling for a clothing company. He had eventually worked his way into directing and had pulled me along after him as soon as I'd graduated from college.

John alone knew my past and my roots and accepted me as is, scars and all. I loved him for that and for many other things as well, but I needed to spend my last hours in Los Angeles preparing myself for the onslaught of emotions I knew I'd feel as soon as I stepped off the plane in Huntington. I couldn't do that with company, particularly not company that shared so much of my history.

Corinne and Billy May, his mother and my mother-substitute, best friends and more, I thought, as I tripped through the airport on my Manolo Blahniks, cursing myself for wearing such ridiculously high-heeled shoes on a day of endless travel. On the day of Billy May's funeral, John had informed me that our mothers had been more than simply friends. "Who better than I to spot a clandestine love affair?" John had asked, glancing across the cemetery towards his partner Steve.

While I was comforted by the thought that Billy May hadn't been alone, I couldn't help but feel somewhat slighted for having been left out of such an important part of her life. No matter now, since it was too late to do anything about it. Not that I would have, anyway, but still it hurt that she hadn't confided in me. Why hadn't she told me?

The overhead speakers blared that flight 52 to Huntington Tri-State Airport was boarding. I paused to rip off my ridiculous shoes, clutching them in one hand and sprinting to the gate, dragging my suitcase behind, just in time to board. I found my row and stuffed the carryon into the overhead, already crowded with bags. A full flight. I was disappointed. I had hoped for a quiet flight with little chance of interaction.

Squeezing in past an older man in a business suit and a woman in brightly colored gypsy garb, I collapsed into the window seat and buckled my belt, exhaling a breath of relief as the flight attendant launched into his speech regarding safety protocol. I stashed my laptop under the seat and leaned back against the headrest, crossing my arms over my chest and pointedly staring out the window, discouraging any attempt at small talk from my seatmates. I wanted time alone to think about the conversation I'd had with Dr. Nora Wright.

Blocking out the drone of the flight attendant I gazed out the window, absently watching the orange-vested grounds crew members as they motioned planes in and out of various gates. Nora, the clinical director of the Platte Lodge for Children, hadn't given specifics but she had shared enough to cause me the proper amount of concern to ditch my responsibilities for the week and fly to West Virginia.

I met Nora shortly after Billy May's funeral and I knew her to be a no-nonsense woman. Just a few years younger than I, with a Ph.D. in psychology and a couple of decades of experience, it took a lot to shake Nora but that morning she had sounded shaken. "I'm sorry to bother you, Jessie," she had started out, "but I think it's time to pull you in."

I had listened with growing concern as Nora recited the events of the past few weeks, beginning with an injured horse and ending with a fire in the common area of the Lodge. "Luckily, we were all out on a hike and the fire never really took hold, but you can imagine how frightened the kids were when they saw what had happened. Thank goodness the groundskeeper, Richard Huffman, smelled the smoke. Otherwise, the whole place might have burned down before we've really even gotten started."

The Platte Lodge for Children was capable of housing up to a dozen children at a time, all with developmental disabilities. The children were divided into groups depending on gender and age, and were treated to a weeklong wilderness experience, as stated in the brochures.

I had to admit as cheesy as the brochures made it sound, it was a phenomenal program, run by experienced clinicians who had the proper training both in the various therapies involved and in wilderness survival techniques. The program was a dream come true not only for the residents of West Virginia but for residents across the country, and a scant two months into functionality the waiting list for families seeking such services for their children was already several months long.

As the plane taxied to the runway to prepare for takeoff I closed my eyes against a wave of sadness. Billy May would have loved to see the end result of her deathbed wish. I had barely managed to make it to Billy May's bedside in time, thanks to delayed flights, rental car frustrations, and general traffic difficulties outside of Huntington. Entering the hospice at a sprint, I'd nearly run over a nurse in my haste as I desperately tried to find her.

Following the little nurse's directions I had run to the room and, pausing in the doorway in an attempt to collect myself, had had a single, panicked moment of fear, thinking that after all that, I hadn't made it in time. The room was dark, and the tiny figure in the bed hardly resembled the strong mountain woman I had come to consider my mother. Then she had opened her eyes, as black and glittering as always, and I had nearly collapsed from relief. I'd made it.

I spent the last few hours of Billy May's life stretched out next to her on the hospital bed as she drifted in and out of consciousness. "My mountain," she had whispered at one point, and I leaned close to hear. "That mountain is a healin' place. It needs to keep on healin' folks." Billy May had inherited Crutcher Mountain decades before, and before rescuing me she had lived for nearly thirty years in isolation in the tiny cabin up on its summit.

I hadn't understood it all at that time—I was, after all, barely thirteen years old when I first met Billy May—but I did know that as a teenager Billy May had been attacked by a group of thugs down in the town. My stepfather had been one of those thugs, a calling he never outgrew. Following the attack, Billy May had chosen to live a quiet life on the mountain, removed from Cedar Hollow.

After I literally stumbled into her life that frigid winter night, Billy May left her mountain home, knowing instinctively that in order for me to heal from the trauma I had experienced, I needed the support of the village. Every so often over the years Billy May had leased the little cabin on the mountain out to one wealthy family or another, people who wanted to spend their weekends or summers getting back to nature.

Those families never lasted long, life on Crutcher Mountain being wilder than they had anticipated. At the first sighting of a bear or the first screech of a mountain lion, they hightailed it back to the safety of the city, where the muggers and bank robbers were at least a known danger and presumably not as frightening. For the majority of the last few decades, aside from those times Billy May and I returned for a few days at a time, the tiny cabin on top of Crutcher Mountain had sat vacant.

"Talk to the pretty little nurse," Billy May had instructed me in those final hours. "Starlette. She's got a youngun's got somethin' wrong with her. Got some kind of disability, ain't got enough help for her. Poor woman is plumb wore out, workin' all the time and takin' care of that little one. Said they need...what did she call it? Let me think a minute." Billy May had taken a moment to catch her breath. I smoothed her hair back and wiped the sweat from her face with a cool cloth, giving her time to rest.

"Respite care," she said finally, her voice wheezy and thin. "Said they need places for them younguns to go to learn things, fun places that can teach 'em things and give their parents a break." She paused, wracked by coughing. When the fit subsided, she looked at me and squeezed my hand, her grip startlingly strong. "Let 'em use my mountain, Jessie. That mountain can help 'em. You talk to 'em and let 'em use my mountain."

To my surprise, it had been easier than I'd imagined. A phone call to the West Virginia Bureau for Behavioral Health and Health Facilities had started the ball rolling. In the end, I had found an established, licensed facility in Huntington that needed room to expand their respite program and that was very interested in adding a wilderness experience to their list of services offered.

A small state grant was able to provide some minimal funding for initial staffing and programmatic issues, and my wealthy acquaintances were able to provide even more. Celebrities, I knew from my years in Hollywood, loved to have their name tied to a charity, particularly a charity aimed at helping vulnerable children. The promise of publicity photos was all it took for wallets to open.

With the funding secured, I was able to provide the place. I had flown out for the ribbon cutting ceremony back in August and the first round of children, including Nurse Starlette's young daughter, had come for a week long stay in September. And now, thanks to a series of mysterious and unsettling events, everything appeared to be in jeopardy.

Chapter 3

"Your color is not good."

I awakened to the husky voice of the woman beside me. Opening my eyes, I was startled to find the woman nearly on top of me, scrutinizing my face, her peppermint scented breath an unwelcome breeze against my cheek. The woman waved a long finger at me, the nail a vivid shade of red. Her turquoise bracelets clanked with the movement. "Your color is very bad."

Taken aback, self-conscious, I leaned towards the window, moving away from the woman's uncomfortable examination. "I haven't had enough sleep," I found myself explaining, pushing my hair back out of my face, defensive.

The woman interrupted. "Not that color," she shook her head impatiently, dangling silver earrings brushing against her shoulders. "Your psychic colors. Your aura."

I sat up, rubbing my eyes, my defensiveness giving way to irritation. "With all due respect," I began, my mouth dry, stuck to itself, "if you're looking to do a reading, or whatever it is you call it, I'm really not interested."

I turned to the window and tried to orient myself as the plane banked and the pilot announced that passengers should prepare for landing. I felt unsettled from the time change and the flight, and the nonsensical rambling of the gypsy woman beside me wasn't helping matters. Behind me, the woman laughed, a pleasant, melodious sound, incongruent with her husky speaking voice.

"No, Seniorita," she said. "No readings. There isn't enough to read." The woman faced forward, checked her seatbelt and, as directed, raised her seat to the upright position.

Against my better judgment I turned back to the woman, insulted by her comment in spite of myself. I saw that she was really quite pretty, the primary colors of her outfit highlighting the tanned color of her skin. She was smiling at me as she adjusted the bright yellow scarf she had knotted at the back of her neck.

"Okay," I said, securing the snack tray to the back of the seat in front of me and leaning towards the woman. "I'll bite. What's wrong with my colors?"

The woman's smile broadened, revealing straight, white teeth. She leaned back, folding her hands across her lap as the plane touched down. "Your colors are too dull," she said, as if that made some sort of sense. "You've turned them off."

When she said nothing more, I sighed, holding the back of the seat in front of me for support as the plane taxied to the gate. "That's it?" I swayed against her with the movement of the plane. "They're dull? I was really hoping you could do better than that."

We rolled to a stop and I felt under the seat for my laptop. Before I could stand, the woman reached out and touched my arm with one long fingered hand. "Seniorita, wait." This time her expression was solemn. Annoyed, I waited, uncomfortable with the coolness of her fingers against my skin. I didn't like for people to invade my personal space, but this woman seemed intent on doing it.

"Be careful, little girl," she said softly, her grip tight on my arm, her dark eyes intense. "Turn your colors back on. The universe is talking to you, and you must listen." With that, she stood and pushed her way out into the aisle, lost in the throng of people impatiently waiting to exit the plane. For the second time that day, goose bumps prickled my flesh. The woman's words sounded exactly like Billy May.

I didn't see the strange woman at baggage claim, nor did I see her as I made my way to the rental car area. By the time I'd signed all the paperwork and headed south on I-64, I'd nearly decided she was nothing more than a crazy woman looking for attention. Nearly. But not quite.

The night was a cold one, crisp and tangy, and I lowered my window slightly and inhaled the fresh scent of the mountains, clearing my head of the long flight and the lack of sleep. It was almost midnight. The mountains were dark shadows all around me; for a fleeting moment I felt claustrophobic, as if I might suffocate under their weight.

Beside me on the seat of the rented Subaru Outback my cell phone buzzed. I glanced down to see that it was Michael. He'd left a couple of messages since that morning but I hadn't had the opportunity to return them. Along with half a dozen work related calls from my assistant, John Johnson had also left a message, still annoyed with me for not allowing him to drive me to the airport. His mother, Corinne, had called too, asking me to stop in as soon as I got to Cedar Hollow.

I'd call Michael when I got settled into a hotel. I hadn't even told him I was leaving, and I supposed I owed him that. Corinne could wait until morning; it was much too late to call her tonight. Work could also wait; I trusted my assistant to handle anything that came up during the short time I'd be gone. As for John....I found myself smiling affectionately. I'd call John tomorrow after he'd had sufficient time to get over his tizzy.

I signaled my intention to take the exit ramp leading to a Hampton Inn and yawned loudly, exhausted from the long day. I'd have to complete the trip to Cedar Hollow, and Crutcher Mountain, in the morning. It was much too late to disturb the elderly owner of the only boarding home in Cedar Hollow, and it would be foolhardy to try to make the drive up Crutcher Mountain in the dark, in spite of the narrow, winding road that had been paved several months ago. I pulled into the nearly vacant lot of the Hampton Inn with relief.

Twenty minutes later, showered and hungrily munching on a pack of stale crackers from the vending machine down the hall, I climbed wearily onto the king sized bed and reached for my cell. I didn't want to call Michael; I wanted to crawl into bed and put the day behind me, but while I'm a guarded person, I'm not a cruel one, so I scrolled to his number.

I'd barely pressed the send button when Michael's voice sounded in my ear. "Where in the world are you? I've been trying to reach you all day."

I popped the tab on a can of diet soda and washed a mouthful of crackers down before answering. "I'm in West Virginia."

"West Virginia! Has something happened?" Knowing that I had been raised in West Virginia, Michael's tone changed abruptly from irritation to concern.

"Possibly," I responded, "but I'm not sure. I'll need to be here for at least a week." I paused, unsure where to begin. "I'm affiliated with a children's facility here, a respite program that provides a wilderness experience for children with disabilities."

I was much too tired to explain all of that to Michael at such a late hour. "It's a long story. Anyway, the clinical director called this morning to tell me about some strange things happening at the Lodge. We've only been operating for a couple of months, and it's important that we get this all sorted out as quickly as possible."

Michael didn't speak right away and I could picture him weighing the information, pacing through his condo, measuring his words before answering. "I had no idea you were involved with a children's facility," he said finally. "Some days, I feel as if I don't know you at all." Silence again, and then, "Is it something I can help with? I could fly out tomorrow."

Sitting up on the bed in the hotel, I found myself frantically shaking my head. "No. There's nothing you can do. I'll call you later in the week. Good night, Michael."

I ended the call and leaned my head back against the pillow. Michael was right; he knew very little about my past, only the basics, such as where I'd grown up and that I had no living relatives, at least none that I knew. Explaining my past was something I had no desire to do.

The only person I'd ever attempted to share my life story with had left me for another woman years ago. In the early days of our relationship, when everything had seemed possible, my ex-husband, Charles McIntosh, had assured me that whatever demons I faced we could face together. He'd been wrong.

In the end, when he'd finally realized the battles never ended, he'd left me to fight the demons on my own. *Inanna* he'd called me the night he left, after the Sumerian goddess of war and discord, a goddess known for her ambiguous paradoxes. I didn't blame him for his description of me. Nor did I blame him for leaving; the battles were indeed exhausting. What he hadn't understood—couldn't understand—was that the external battles were insignificant. It was the internal ones that caused all the damage.

Chapter 4
Robby

Hi my name is Robert Justice O'Brien and I am ten years old and people say I am retarded. The counselors here get very mad at me when I say that word. They say I have a developmental disability called Down Syndrome. They say, "ROBERT! You have a developmental disability caused by chromosomes. Do not say that you are retarded." It makes me laugh when they say my name that way. People only call me ROBERT when they say it loud. The rest of the time I am just plain old Robby. Ha!

The only one who never got mad at me when I said that word was Grandpa. He didn't call me ROBERT. He called me Now Robby. "Now, Robby," he would say, "you know that is not a nice thing to call yourself. Why are you trying to get everybody all riled up?" And he would wink at me and then we would laugh at everybody getting all riled up.

I tell them it isn't me that says it. It's everybody else. Maybe the counselors should tell everybody else not to say it. "Other people don't know any better," the counselors say. "We have to teach them better." But when I try to teach them better they don't listen.

I have Down Syndrome but I am High Functioning. That is what the counselors and teachers say at Staffing. Staffing is when they all get together to talk about me. Sometimes people think I am Low Functioning because I don't talk right but I am not. Dr. Jiang says I have a narrow pal...pal...palatal vault. I do not know what that means except that it means sometimes people don't understand my words but maybe they are just Low Functioning. My words are not hard.

Tiffany from down the street is the first one who told me I am retarded. She told me that all the way until she graduated high school. She was my babysitter sometimes when my mom had to work before we moved in with Grandpa. She was very pretty and very mean. Nowadays when she comes home from college to visit her family she is not mean. I don't know why not. She is still pretty though. Nowadays she is very pretty and very nice. My mom says thank The Good Lord the little slut finally grew up. I do not know what a little slut is but I think it is a good thing. Nowadays Tiffany is a nice pretty grown up little slut.

Mrs. Jamison from church said that my mom was a crackhead when she was pregnant with me and that is why I am retarded. She said, "Robby, honey, it isn't your fault you're retarded. You can't help what your momma is." The counselors here say that Mrs. Jamison is very wrong. They sigh and sound mad when they say it. They say my mom didn't have anything to do with it. They look at each other and say, "For Pete's sake, can you believe this?"

I don't know who Pete is but I know that Mrs. Jamison is right because she is a Christian. That means that she tells other people what is wrong with them and then she prays for them to get better. She has The Lord's Ear. That scared me until she told me it just means he is listening to her. I would not want somebody's ear even if it belonged to The Lord.

At first when she said that about my mom I was mad because my mom does not have a cracked head but Mrs. Jamison said crackhead means my mom did a lot of drugs when she was pregnant with me. She said it like it was a bad thing. She had her face all wrinkled up and she used that voice like my mom uses when I don't wash myself good enough.

Mrs. Jamison prays a lot for herself too because she has arthritis and she is asking The Good Lord to fix it for her. She takes a lot of drugs for her arthritis so I guess she is a crackhead too. She is a Christian crackhead. I guess if you are a Christian crackhead with The Lord's Ear instead of a pregnant crackhead that is okay. Whatever.

I don't mind having Down Syndrome. I get to do a lot of special things like coming to this place. They call it the Lodge. This place is very cool. It is the only time I have had fun since Grandpa died. That was a very sad time. It is still a sad time so I will not talk about it.

I get to stay at the Lodge all week. We get to be with horses and we get to go hiking and be in the Wilderness. The people here love the Wilderness. In the mornings we have Group with Dr. Wright to talk about Important Things like Friendship and Trust and Bullying. The people here love Group even more than they love the Wilderness.

When we got back from the Wilderness yesterday the Lodge had smoke in it. The counselors acted like they were not upset about the smoke but I know that they were. The fire department had to come and it took a long time for the fire engines to climb up the mountain. If the fire had still been here the whole mountain would have burned down before they could help. I think it is kind of stupid that the fire trucks are so far away. And people say I am the retarded one. Ha!

Anyway after dinner last night we got to roast marshmallows over a fire pit outside. I helped Stacey roast her marshmallows because she is in a wheelchair and she cannot hold the stick. I helped Marcus too because he is Low Functioning. He just laughed and laughed at the fire and did not even eat the marshmallows. I had to eat them for him so they would not go to waste.

Waste is a bad thing. My mom says, "ROBERT! Do not waste your food! There are children starving in Africa!" I do not know where Africa is but I tell her she can give them my spaghetti if she wants to because I do not like spaghetti. But I do like marshmallows.

Anthony did not get to roast marshmallows because he was Over Stimulated after the fire trucks left and he needed to Take Space. My counselor Mr. Paul tried to tell jokes to make us laugh and not think about the smoke in the Lodge but the counselors all kept looking at each other like they were scared and they whispered to each other when they thought we didn't see them.

When you have a developmental disability other people talk in front of you. I guess people think if you have Down Syndrome you cannot hear what they say but I can still hear. Sometimes people say very strange things around me. Like one time Ms. Hill the librarian at school called someone on her cell phone and told them she wasn't wearing any underwear. If I forget to put my underwear on my mom gets mad.

When I was in third grade my Staffing put it in my IP that I would wear underwear. My IP is my Individual Plan that I have because I am special. Everyone who is special has an Individual Plan. I guess Ms. Hill does not have underwear on her IP. But maybe she doesn't have an IP because maybe she isn't special. She does yell a lot. Anyway she must not get in trouble for forgetting her underwear because she was laughing when she said it.

Last night in the Lodge some Grownups were saying strange things in front of me. All of us kids were in bed but I wasn't asleep because Anthony rocks back and forth and he is in the bed on top of mine. Sometimes he rocked so much I was afraid the bed would fall down on me. That scared me and I could not sleep. "ANTHONY!" I told him. "Stop rocking or the bed will fall on me!" But he didn't stop. He just rocked and rocked.

Grownups talk weird and sometimes they don't make sense. I did not understand all of the things they said last night but I did understand some of them and they were not good things. Now I have a secret but I don't know who to tell it to. I wish I could tell it to Grandpa. He always understood my words.

Chapter 5

Tuesday

The sun was just beginning to rise over the mountains, reflecting off the reds and golds of a West Virginia autumn, when I pulled up to Mr. Smith's General Store in Cedar Hollow to top the Subaru off with gas and pick up some coffee creamer for Corinne. The time was barely 5:00 a.m. when my phone rang, Corinne on the other end. "I figured you'd be up early, wantin' to get a good start to the day."

I had, in fact, been up early, already loading the car for the fifty minute trip to Cedar Hollow. "Come on by for breakfast," Corinne had ordered. "I got everything you could want, except creamer. I remember you never did like your coffee black. Better stop by the store and pick some up on your way. They'll be open."

No sooner had I turned off the ignition than a stooped older gentleman in a plaid shirt and khaki work pants made his way slowly out the door, pulling his wheeled oxygen tank behind him and shuffling towards the car.

"Jessica Russell McIntosh," he said with a wheezy smile. "I heard you was comin' to town." My spirits lifted at the sight of him.

"Good morning to you, Mr. Lane. I see news in Cedar Hollow still travels faster than the speed of light." I climbed out of the car to bend and hug the old man. Darryl Lane had been a friend of Billy May's and had always been kind to me. He cackled and patted my cheek, just as he'd done when I was a young girl.

27

"You know Corinne. She was so excited you was comin' she told near about the whole danged town as soon as she heard. Then again," he paused to adjust his oxygen, "it don't take long for word to spread among two-hunnerd-sixteen people."

"Two-hundred-sixteen, is it now? We've grown. At Billy Momma's funeral the sign said two-hundred-twelve."

Mr. Lane nodded. "You know them Pritchetts. Always makin' more." He removed the gas cap and inserted the nozzle, shaking his head with disgust. "Like we need more Pritchetts. Course," he said, pulling a handkerchief out of his back pocket with his free hand and mopping his forehead in the cool morning air, "if we hadn't lost Raymond, it'd have been two-seventeen." He replaced the kerchief and turned his attention back to the pump, facing away from me.

"I was sorry to hear about his passing," I said quietly, placing my hand on Mr. Lane's bony shoulder. "He was a very dear friend. He'll be missed by all of us." Raymond O'Brien had been a childhood friend of both Billy May and Darryl Lane.

When I let myself think of such things, it frightened me that the people I loved most in the world were growing older and passing on. It was much easier to deny things in the busy chaos of my hectic life in Los Angeles. Coming back to Cedar Hollow was always difficult, on many levels. I'd barely been in town five minutes and my emotions were already threatening to get the best of me. I drew a deep breath, reminding myself to stay focused on my reason for coming.

"He was a good man," agreed Mr. Lane. "There ain't too many like him. I reckon he was ready to go on and be with June. Lord knows, worrying about that girl of his took years off his life and just plumb killed June. That girl was a handful, she was. I hear she's takin' some kind of treatment now. Maybe it'll take hold, for the boy's sake if nothin' else.

Just too bad it wasn't sooner, but there ain't nothin' to be done about that now."

He cleared his throat noisily and reached for the handkerchief again, loudly blowing his nose. "Goin' to be a nice day," he said abruptly, gazing at the lightening sky and stuffing the limp kerchief back into his pocket. "Chilly, but nice."

I nodded in agreement, grateful for the change of topic. "You know, Mr. Lane," I said, watching him fill the tank with gas, "this may just be the only place on earth where a person can still get full service."

"Is that right? Well that's a cryin' shame, ain't it? The world sure is changin', and it ain't in a good way, either. Wars ever'where, prices skyhigh. Can't hardly afford to live no more." He turned back to the pump, muttering under his breath.

Hands on my hips, I took in the front of the store. The suspended sign was as it had always been, the wording in dark green paint against a white background hanging over the door, although the Smith family hadn't owned the store for many years. The last Mr. Smith had died the night Billy May saved my life.

After his death, Billy May bought the store and we lived in the upstairs apartment until I went to college six years later. Throughout those years we never spoke of the events that occurred that night on Crutcher Mountain. Instead, we concentrated on making a fresh start and blending into the life of the town.

As the years passed, I sometimes wondered how much of what I remembered had really happened, and how much had grown—or shrunken—in my memory over time. I didn't know, and I didn't want to know. I was most content when I completely blocked that night from my mind. *You've turned your colors off*, I heard the gypsy woman say, and it was true.

The sign swung gently to and fro in the early morning breeze, and I remembered how the squeaking sound of the swinging sign had often been the first thing I heard upon waking each morning. Instead of annoying me, it had comforted me. It was a sound that had become enmeshed with the feeling of home.

Billy May kept the store, continuing to live in the upstairs apartment even after I graduated college and moved to California. That's where I had visited her several times a year until her death eight months before. Now, I owned the store.

Mr. Lane followed my gaze and reached out to pat my arm with his gnarled hand, giving it a little squeeze. "It's hard, ain't it little girl? We're all gettin' old." His voice was rough. "But she was happy; I know that. She had good years, even after all them bad ones. You brought back the good years for her."

Before I could reply a younger man, in his thirties, wearing jeans and a green Thundering Herd baseball cap, stepped through the doorway of the General Store. Smiling, he held out his hand. "Jessie," he said with a broad smile. "How are you?"

"Good, Dennis." I gave his hand a firm shake. "Just visiting with your dad while he tops off the tank. You're looking well." I took in his trim build. "Marriage must be suiting you. How's business these days?" I nodded towards the store.

"Steady as always." Dennis turned to look at the front of the store along with me. "It's a nice way to put the marketing degree to work." He crossed his arms over his chest and rocked back on his heels, glancing sideways at me. "You decided whether or not to sell yet?"

I shook my head; this was not a topic I liked to think about. "Not yet. Maybe soon. When I do, you'll be the first to know. In the meantime, I really do appreciate you taking care of it for me." The lump had returned to my throat. I didn't know what in the world I would ever do with a little store in the middle of Cedar Hollow, West Virginia, but I couldn't bear the thought of giving it up. It hurt me to see it, but it would hurt even more not to.

"It's been my pleasure, Jessie." He studied my face, and I turned my head, pretending to watch the flipping numbers on the gas pump. Vaguely, I wondered how many little towns still had pumps with flipping numbers. It certainly wasn't a sight I'd ever seen anywhere else, not within the last twenty years.

"There's no hurry," Dennis said quietly, watching me. "I'm not going anywhere. Now then," he said, turning towards the store and briskly rubbing his hands together, sensing my need to get back to business, "what else can I get for you?" I followed him into the store.

Fifteen minutes later I was pulling into the gravel drive leading up to Corinne's house, a cheerful home painted a bright white, with flower boxes and shutters of hunter green. I killed the engine and opened my door just as Corinne came trotting down the steps, arms open wide, surprisingly spry for a woman in her eighties. Her hair, long and gray, was tucked into a bun on the back of her neck, and her eyes were as blue as I remembered. Her face creased in a smile.

"Jessie girl, it's so good to see you!" She reached up and clasped my face in her hands, planting a solid kiss on my cheek. Funny, I thought, how my fierce protection of personal space went by the wayside every time I returned to Cedar Hollow. But these people were my family, as much a part of me as if we shared DNA. I smiled and bent down to the tiny woman, returning the embrace. "It's good to see you too, Mrs. Johnson."

"How many times have I told you to call me Corinne? No matter. Come on in here; I've just started settin' it all on the table." Corinne pulled me up the steps by the hand, leading me into a warm kitchen fragrant with the smell of sizzling bacon. "Get your coat off now," she ordered. "Make yourself at home. Coffee's over there. Did you get you some creamer? You know where the spoons are."

I draped my coat over the back of a chair and made my way to the utensil drawer, as familiar with Corinne's home as I was my own. Pouring two cups, I added creamer to one and a spoonful of sugar to the other, setting them on the table as Corinne turned off the burners and untied her apron, hanging it on a hook by the stove and smoothing her blouse. "Better eat it while it's hot," she said, tucking an escaped strand back into the low bun. "And tell me about what's goin' on up at the children's place. John said there was some trouble." She settled herself into her chair, spreading her napkin over her lap.

I scooted my chair in and reached for the platter of eggs, my mouth watering. My half-shriveled pint of strawberries from the morning before couldn't compete with the breakfast Corinne had prepared, and I'd had little since. I was famished.

"I'll need to hike up the mountain to work off all this food," I told her. "Thanks for breakfast, Corinne. It's good to see you again." Sitting there with Corinne in her cozy yellow kitchen, the sun slanting through the window warm on my shoulders, I almost felt as if my life were a normal one. It was a nice feeling, one I'd only ever felt in Cedar Hollow. If only the place that brought me peace didn't also bring me pain. I'd never been able to figure out how to reconcile the two, and that was the sad irony of my life. A woman composed of opposites, whose yin and yang had never meshed, forever at war.

Corinne waved away my compliment. "It's always good to see you, too, Jessie. Now tell me what's goin' on up on Billy May's mountain."

I spooned blackberry preserves over my toast and thought about the phone call from Nora. "Nora seems to think someone has been playing pranks on the staff," I said finally, resting the spoon on my plate and reaching for the salt. "Apparently, strange things have been happening since it opened, but she didn't take it too seriously until now. The pranks, if that's what you could call them, have gotten more dangerous."

In the beginning, it had been easy to dismiss the incidents as coincidence, or even as careless accidents on the part of the staff. The pasture gate had been left open and the horses had escaped, but the gate was notoriously difficult to latch securely. Once the horses were recovered, one with a pronounced limp, a secondary latch had been installed and the veterinarian had been summoned. Thankfully, the injury wasn't severe and the bruised horse was on the mend.

A week or so later, the storage shed had been left unlocked and cleaning solutions had been poured all over the floor. As potentially dangerous as that was, there was no proof a human had been involved. After all, the wildlife in the area was the basis for the program, and leaving a door open invited woodland visitors. Staff had been given a stern safety lecture following the incident and an incident report had been filed.

More recently, the office had been ransacked, but everyone knew that Virgil Young, the van driver, had been let go the week before, per policy, after receiving his third traffic ticket in three years. He hadn't gone quietly, and it wasn't beyond the realm of possibility that he was somehow behind the vandalism. True, he didn't have a history of violence, but tough economic times can bring out the worst in people.

Sitting across from me, Corinne delicately wiped her mouth and placed the napkin on her plate. "Well," she said, pushing herself slowly to her feet and reaching for the coffee pot, "I can see how they might be able to convince themselves all that stuff was just accidents and coincidence, I reckon, though it does seem a stretch to me."

She poured more coffee into my cup and replaced the pot on the counter. "But what happened to make you fly all the way out here, Jessie? What you've already told me is concernin' enough; what is it you ain't tellin' me?" Corinne lowered herself back into her chair, falling the last few inches with a soft grunt, and waited.

I added cream and stirred while pondering the best way to tell Corinne about the incident two days ago. Deciding direct was best, I leaned back in the chair and looked at her. "A fire," I said. "There was a fire in the Lodge."

"Oh, my goodness." Corinne's hand fluttered to her throat. "When? Was anyone hurt?"

"No," I shook my head. "No one was hurt. It happened Sunday afternoon, shortly after the kids arrived for the week." I placed my napkin on the plate, my appetite gone. "Luckily, the staff had taken them for their first hike, so they weren't there at the time. Just the housekeeper and the groundskeeper. It was the groundskeeper who discovered the fire and put it out before any real damage was done. Policy dictates they call the fire department for any evidence of fire, so they did, but it wasn't needed."

Corinne sat quietly for a moment, mulling over all that I had told her. "And they think it was arson? Couldn't it have been faulty wirin' or somethin'? It's all so new up there, the electric and all. Maybe they didn't wire it up right."

I took a sip of the coffee, set it down slowly. "It does seem it was arson." I paused, rubbing my hand over my face. I was already tired, and the day had just begun. After the chaos of yesterday, five hours hadn't been nearly enough sleep. "There was a note."

"A note!" Corinne leaned forward, her own coffee forgotten. "What kind of a note?"

I placed my utensils on my plate alongside the napkin, stalling for time. "A note addressed to me." I cleared my throat and met Corinne's stare. "A note telling me to come back."

Chapter 6
Robby

Hi it's me again. Robby. Remember? Well we had to get up early this morning to do Group because the lady that owns the mountain is coming for a visit. Mr. Paul said she is a very very nice lady who lets us use her mountain for free to do Groups and see the Wilderness. I didn't know people could own mountains but I guess they can. I thought God owned the mountains but I guess I was wrong. I will have to ask Mrs. Jamison about that when I get back home.

I think Ms. McIntosh is very nice to let us all use her mountain. If I had a mountain I don't think I would let Anthony use it because he does not let me sleep at night. For two nights now he has been Over Stimulated and he rocks and rocks and rocks at night and I know his bed is going to fall on top of me.

I would let Stacey use my mountain though because she is pretty. I like Stacey. I think I am in love with Stacey but don't tell my mom because she will say, "ROBERT! You are too young to be in love. Look where that got me!" Whatever. My grandpa said love makes the world go 'round. But I don't want to talk about Grandpa because that makes me sad.

Mr. Paul is always asking me questions about Grandpa. He wants to know how I am feeling. That is a silly question. Grownups ask silly questions. He says it will help me to talk about it but that is silly too. It does not help me to talk about it. It makes me sad to talk about it.

I don't know why but counselors always like it when people cry. Then it is a Breakthrough. "Oh," they say at Staffing, "he had a Breakthrough!" I don't want a Breakthrough. I want Mr. Paul to stop asking me silly questions. I like Mr. Paul but I think he is Low Functioning.

In Group this morning we made cards for Ms. McIntosh. Mine is the best one because it is the only one that doesn't have a mountain on it. Why would she want a card with a mountain on it when she already has a real mountain? Duh! Mine has me on it. I used a brown crayon to draw myself. I am not brown but they don't have a tan one. They never have tan ones. I don't know why not.

I used a blue crayon to draw my clothes because I am wearing blue jeans and a blue t-shirt with Platte Lodge for Children on it in yellow. I used an orange crayon to color my hair. People always say my hair is red but I know it is really orange. They say I got my grandpa's hair but that is a silly thing to say. He had his own hair and it wasn't even orange. It was gray. See? That is what I mean about Grownups not making sense.

Now we are just waiting for Anthony to stop screaming so we can start our Morning Work before Ms. McIntosh gets here. Mr. Paul says we want everything to look nice for her visit. Anthony does not look nice right now. I think if Anthony would just sleep at night maybe he wouldn't be so cranky in the mornings.

They are trying to hurry us up and make us get our jobs done but they can't make Anthony hurry up. He is running around outside and he will not come back in. Mr. Paul and Ms. Janice are trying to talk to him but he is not listening. "Go get his jacket," Mr. Paul tells Ms. Janice. Ms. Janice is a counselor for the girls but I guess she works with boys too when they are Over Stimulated.

All of us are just watching everything because it is kind of crazy. Marcus is laughing and laughing but Marcus always laughs. Joseph is not laughing. He is kind of crying and saying, "I'm scared, I'm scared," because he does not like it when Anthony screams.

Joseph is a cool kid and he also likes *Teenage Mutant Ninja Turtles* just like me. He even has a *Teenage Mutant Ninja Turtle* jacket on but it has Leonardo on it and I like Michelangelo because he is funny. I don't want Joseph to feel scared.

"It's okay," I tell him. "Anthony is just being loud but he is not going to hurt you." Stacey smiles at me and I know it is because she is happy that I am so nice to Joseph. I smile back at her because I am in love with her and then I hear a car coming so I look to see who it is.

It is a big black car and it pulls all the way up to the office and then a lady with very long hair jumps out and then it gets *really* crazy.

Chapter 7

As I wound my way up the newly paved blacktop on my way to the Lodge, I thought about my visit with Corinne. It was hard, since Billy May's death, to see Corinne without thinking of John's revelations after the funeral. I had spent the last years of my childhood surrounded by the Johnson family. Since I had no known relatives of my own, Corinne comfortably fit into the role of favored aunt. The information John had shared required a shift in thinking, and I wasn't quite sure how to make the shift.

The issue wasn't Billy May's sexuality. I had always believed in a live and let live sort of lifestyle, assuming everyone involved was a willing participant. In my view, love was elusive and successful relationships even more so; kudos to anyone who could make it work.

I wasn't quite sure what the issue was, but for some reason I felt betrayed. My life had been an open book with Billy May, but Billy May had apparently had a separate life about which I had had no clue. My feelings were difficult to categorize, but something about the unknown, unperceived distance that had apparently existed between us hurt me deeply.

Standing in Corinne's driveway, preparing to leave, I had been tempted to ask Corinne about her relationship with Billy May, but I hadn't. I didn't know how to approach the subject, and looking down at Corinne, her hair forever slipping loose of that bun, blue eyes looking up at me in a smile, I doubted I ever would. Instead, I'd bent down to wrap my arms around my favorite aunt.

As she hugged me back Corinne had pressed something into the pocket of my jacket. Remembering the pressure of her hand as I steered the car carefully around the curves of Crutcher Mountain, I reached under my seatbelt to fish around in my breast pocket. As soon as I pulled out the small leather pouch I knew what it was, and my breath caught in my throat. Billy May's trinkets. Unable and unwilling to deal with the knowledge at that moment, I shoved the bag quickly back into my pocket. This was not the time.

Rounding the final curve leading to the Lodge, I forced myself to stop thinking about the past and focus on the task ahead. I rolled to a stop under a towering maple, brilliant orange in the fully risen sun, just outside the little cabin that now served as the office for the Platte Lodge for Children. Taking in the sight in front of me, my attention immediately snapped back to the present, all other thoughts shoved aside. I couldn't believe what I was seeing. *What the hell?*

"What on earth are you *doing*?" I shouted, throwing open the car door and jumping to my feet in one swift movement, crunching through the fallen leaves. "Get that off of him immediately!" I strode angrily towards an older man who turned to look at me in surprise. Just as I reached him, a younger woman rushed in front of me, holding out her hands in an effort to stop my progress. Both the man and the woman blocked my path, refusing to let me get any closer to the boy, who appeared to be restrained by some sort of straightjacket-type device and who was screaming bloody murder.

"How dare you!" I yelled. "Get out of here immediately, both of you! We don't allow such treatment here. I'll be reporting both of you to the Department of

Human Resources. Where is Dr. Wright? You'd better believe she's going to hear about this."

"I'm right here, Jessie." The doctor appeared in the doorway of the little cabin and stepped quickly forward. "Paul, Janice, go see to Anthony. I'll explain to Ms. McIntosh. Jessie, let's go in my office."

For a moment I simply stood, dumbfounded, before noticing the group of giggling children peering at me through the doorway of the adjacent Lodge. Confused, the first stirrings of embarrassment seeping in, I looked back at Nora, who smiled. "Come on," she said to me. "I promise it will all make sense in a minute." She took me by the arm and led me inside.

"I feel like such an idiot."

Dr. Wright laughed. "I can only imagine how it must have looked to you. How could you have known? Trained professionals often have the same reaction the first time they witness a patient using a weight jacket."

"So the child *wants* to use the jacket to cut down on *unwanted* stimuli." I shook my head. "Fascinating."

"Mmm," Dr. Wright nodded. "It is, isn't it? Studies indicate that children with autism experience stimuli much more intensely than most of us, whether it's visual, auditory, or tactile. The jacket is one way of cutting down on troublesome tactile sensations. Anthony brought the jacket with him, and we have a clinical order in place that allows him to use it when he feels the need."

"Well," I grinned sheepishly, running my hand through my hair, "I suppose I owe everyone an apology. As soon as I work up the nerve to face them."

"They'll understand. Besides, it's always nice to run into someone willing to fight for the rights of our children." Dr. Wright smiled. "We like that around here. Now," she changed the subject, "how was your trip?"

41

I pursed my lips and released a tired breath, leaning my head back against the upholstered chair. "Weird," I said. "That's probably the best way to describe it. I love Cedar Hollow, but it's painful to be back. Even this," I gestured around the office. "It's hard."

In the interest of preserving the authenticity of the place, the Platte Lodge for Children had kept the main cabin—Billy May's cabin—to use as the main office. Although the cabin now had running water and electricity, they'd done a wonderful job maintaining the feel of a rustic hunting cabin. The stove still took center stage, the very stove Billy May had used that long ago night to boil water and herbs to heal my injuries.

It must be worth a fortune now, I thought, though to us its worth had stemmed from its functionality and from the comfort it brought. A braid rug was spread across the floor, much like the one Billy May had had, the one Old Mongrel had lain on, keeping guard and protecting us from the evil he had known was coming. Dear Old Mongrel. He'd passed away our first winter in Cedar Hollow. Billy May had buried him—without permission or even knowledge from the town—adjacent to her own burial plot.

The long counter across the back wall now had drawers underneath and cabinets above. File cabinets lined the wall where Billy May's bed used to be, and Dr. Wright's desk, flanked by cushiony office chairs on either side, was against the far wall, where the homemade table and chairs had once stood. The cabin was different, yet it wasn't.

Billy May's presence was all around, so much so that it was hard to believe she wouldn't come clumping in at any moment, dropping split wood into the box behind the door and wiping the sweat off her brow with her sleeve. I shook my head to clear it. I simply could not function if I allowed my grief a way in. I had spent the last eight months holding it at bay, but being there, in that town, on that mountain, in that cabin, was nearly more than I could bear.

Dr. Wright watched me, her expression inscrutable. It was unnerving to remember that she was, in fact, a psychotherapist. I wondered what she must think of me. Her mannerisms were purely professional, her black pantsuit nicely fitted, her dark hair cropped in a sensible bob. It was impossible to see anything other than empathy in the gray eyes behind the scholarly glasses, yet I had the feeling I was being dissected and filed away somewhere in the database of her brain. I was sure I could provide plenty of material for future study, but today wasn't the day to do it.

I shook my head again. "I can't allow myself to dwell on any of it," I said, sitting up straight and crossing my legs, all business. "Let's talk about what's been happening here."

Dr. Wright nodded a quick nod and reached into a desk drawer, withdrawing a single sheet of paper. "As you know," she began, "I've been concerned about some of the potentially dangerous things that have happened the last few weeks." She set the paper on the desk. "At the risk of seeming paranoid, I couldn't help but think these things were done deliberately, as much as we tried to rationalize them away. But this," she gestured at the paper, "this proves that something, or rather someone, is deliberately doing things to undermine the Lodge." She picked up the paper, reaching across the desk to hand it to me.

It was a copy, scanned, I assumed, from the original. "The police have the original?" I asked.

"They do, but I managed to scan it before handing it over." She grimaced and looked away for a moment before making eye contact again. "They don't know I scanned it. I suppose I should have told them, but I worried they wouldn't allow it, and somehow it seemed important to have you see it."

"I think you did the right thing," I said, searching through my purse for reading glasses. "If it's me they're asking for, whoever 'they' happen to be, it seems only fitting that I view the invitation." Slipping the glasses on, I held the paper out for a look.

The message was typed, short, and to the point. "Dear Jessica McIntosh," I read aloud. "What a nice thing you've done, providing a retreat for all the little disabled children." I stopped at Dr. Wright's snort and looked at her over the top of my glasses.

"Sorry," she apologized. "I know it's silly, but they aren't *disabled children*. They're children who happen to have a disability. There's a difference. Pet peeve of mine. My apologies. Continue." She sat back against her chair, pressed her fingertips together, and waited.

Adjusting my glasses, I picked up where I'd left off. "It would be a shame if the program were unsuccessful. If, for example, someone got hurt or it burned to the ground. For that reason, we insist that you come back to Cedar Hollow. Your presence will safeguard against any number of tragedies just waiting to occur, and we're quite certain, given your affluent Hollywood lifestyle, that you can afford the trip. We look forward to seeing you. We have unfinished business to conduct." I looked back up at Dr. Wright. "No signature, of course."

"No," she agreed, "but we can always hope the original has fingerprints. I handled it very carefully for the scan."

"So, now what?" I held out my arms, palms up. "I'm here. Am I just supposed to hang out and wait for something to happen?"

"I wish I had the answer to that." She removed her glasses and rubbed her eyes. "My hunch is that the responsible party will make him- or herself known fairly quickly. Otherwise, why summon you? They obviously want something from you."

Replacing her glasses, she looked at me. "Do you want protection? I haven't yet told the sheriff's department that I called you, but I'm sure they'd be willing to set up a patrol outside the Lodge. As it is, they've said they'll make a trip or two up the mountain each night just to check on things until this all gets sorted out. They're also checking into Virgil Young, the van driver I had to let go. Supposedly, he gave them an alibi for the time the fire was started. It seems he was having the van serviced, but they'll chase down all the leads and make sure."

I shook my head. "I don't think protection will be necessary. This place is like a fortress when it's locked up tight. We'll just need to exercise caution and make sure we keep it locked." I stood, eager for a tour. In anticipation of future visits, I'd undergone all the necessary background checks to volunteer for the program, and I was actually quite excited about participating. "If it's okay with you, I'd like to take a look around. I haven't seen the program in action."

"Of course." Dr. Wright stood as well. "And let's get you settled in. You'll be staying in the south end of the Lodge, across from Mr. and Mrs. Huffman. The day therapists go home after dinner, but we have night counselors that clock in when the day therapists leave. The night counselors do fifteen minute checks on the children throughout the night so there will be some activity, but as you know, the residents are housed on the north end, across the common area."

I brushed away her concerns. "I'm sure it'll be fine. I'm used to city noises, remember? If anything, it may be too quiet for me."

Dr. Wright hesitated, a small smile playing at the corners of her mouth. "We can certainly hope that's the case, but I sort of doubt it will be," she said. "Anthony has a way of making sure it doesn't get too quiet around here."

Chapter 8
Robby

Hi it's me Robby again. Well today was fun but boy am I tired. I hope Anthony will let me sleep tonight. We went on a Scavenger Hunt in the woods today and I found an owl feather and a shiny pink rock and best of all a snake skin! A real live snake skin can you believe it? It is so cool!

And the mountain lady? Ms. McIntosh? She came with us and she wasn't even scared of the snake skin. She held it and she said, "Isn't that pretty? Look at the head of it. It's small, see? And there aren't any pits, or little holes, between the eyes and the nostrils. I'm not a snake expert, but I don't think this came from a poisonous one."

And then she gave it back to me and she didn't even say, "ROBERT! Throw that nasty thing away!" like my mom would have said. She is nice and she is cool for an old lady.

She is the one that Mr. and Mrs. Huffman were talking about the night after the fire but they didn't call her Ms. McIntosh. Mr. Huffman is the one who fixes things around this place and Mrs. Huffman is the one who cleans up after all of us. Especially after Marcus because he is wearing a diaper and sometimes he makes a mess in his chair but he doesn't mean to. Marcus is nice he is just Low Functioning and he can't help it. Nobody around this place gets mad at him not even Mrs. Huffman. She just says, "That's okay, honey. I will get this cleaned right up." And then she sprays stinky stuff all over it to make it smell better.

The night they talked about Ms. McIntosh they called her Jessie. I was awake because Anthony was rocking and Mr. Huffman was in the hallway with his tools fixing the wall banister where the fire was because Marcus and Stacey have to have a banister and the police took the old one. I don't know why they took it but they took it right off the wall and stuck it in a big bag and took it down the mountain with them.

Mrs. Huffman was cleaning up the mess Mr. Huffman was making and she said, "When are we going to tell Jessie?" And he said, "Maybe never. I don't know that it matters." And then they talked some more about Jessie but I did not know who Jessie was.

Now I know it is Ms. McIntosh because today I heard Dr. Wright call her Jessie too. Dr. Wright took her around to everybody and said "Let me introduce you to Jessie McIntosh." She even took her to Mr. and Mrs. Huffman and said, "This is Jessie McIntosh," and they pretended like they didn't know her but I know that they are lying. I thought they were nice people but it is not nice to lie. Ms. McIntosh acted like she didn't know them either. I wonder if she was lying too. I hope not because I like her but I don't think I can like her as much if she is lying.

Mr. Paul says we have to wash up for dinner and then have Evening Routine. We are having hamburgers for dinner and I am very hungry and I love hamburgers. Anthony loves hamburgers too and he is not Over Stimulated tonight. When he is not Over Stimulated he is an okay kid. He likes Pokémon just like me. He has an Articuno card that has a picture of a big blue bird. It is one of the three rare bird cards but I have Moltres and I think that is better. I will sit with him at dinner if he can stay On Task.

Chapter 9

I was beat. It had been an exhausting couple of days, first with the travel and then with the kids. They were amazing, but they'd certainly given me a run for my money. A couple of groups, a trust walk, lunch, an equine therapy session, and finally a scavenger hunt. More excitement than I'd had in years, and my respect for the staff had tripled throughout the day as I'd observed their skill with the children.

I ate dinner in the cafeteria with Nora, bypassing the hamburgers in favor of a salad and fresh fruit. As we sat observing the kids at their scattered tables, my circumstances felt surreal. I was unable to fathom any threat of danger in such a therapeutic place. The mountain was peaceful, of course, as it had always been, but it was more than that. The staff had done an exemplary job of creating an atmosphere of acceptance and safety, and it showed in the open faces of the children. I was beginning to learn the kids' names, their personalities, and even more I was beginning to develop a fondness for each of them.

There was Marcus, systematically picking his food apart and dropping it on the floor, cackling the whole time. And Anthony, quiet now, his beautiful face angelic, leaning slightly away from Robby, listening intently to something Robby was saying. And Stacey, in her chair, smiling at Joseph as he spread mayonnaise on her hamburger bun.

I still had no idea, really, why I was even there, and I felt rather silly for having dropped everything for the earliest flight to Huntington. The whole scenario seemed foolish now, like an overly dramatic practical joke. Barring any incidents, I thought I could change my flight home and leave early, making it back to Los Angeles by Thursday at the latest.

I didn't need to remain on Crutcher Mountain any longer than was necessary. The last thing I wanted was to fall under the spell of the mountains. Grieving as I was, vulnerable, I couldn't survive the sorcery of Appalachia. Already, I could feel the mountain seducing me.

The children finished with dinner and staff guided them into the common area for closing group while Mrs. Huffman bustled about, tidying up the cafeteria. I had seen both Mr. and Mrs. Huffman several times throughout the day, and though we hadn't had a chance to speak, I'd been impressed with their work ethic and their apparent devotion to the children. Mr. Huffman had obviously expended an enormous amount of effort ensuring that the forest paths were cleared well enough to allow even those children with limited mobility access to group wilderness activities, and Mrs. Huffman, though noticeably tired, cleaned Marcus' thrown food from the floor without complaint.

"They've been quite a blessing," Nora remarked, noting my observation of Mrs. Huffman. "Lost most of their retirement when the stock market took a nosedive," she said, shaking her head in disgust. "Can you imagine? You work your whole life and when it's time to retire, you can't."

She pushed back her plate. "The plan is for them to stay here year round, even during January and February when we're closed. They'll look after the place, and in exchange they'll receive room and board and a small salary. They seemed as grateful for the accommodations as we are to have them. They're alone, no children or grandchildren. From what they tell me, Mrs. Huffman wasn't able, which was heartbreaking for both of them. That's why they've spent the majority of their lives working in one sort of children's facility or another."

I hesitated, reluctant to ask my next question, but it needed to be asked. "Mr. Huffman was the one who found the fire, wasn't he?"

Nora nodded. "I know where you're going with this, but they've both been through extensive background checks. They're so clean they're boring."

She shoved back her chair and stood, stretching her arms over her head and yawning loudly. "I'm about ready to call it a day," she said. "I've got to be back here early in the morning. I'm going to go wrap up a couple of things in the office and then I'm heading home. Do you need anything before I go?"

I shook my head. "I'm about to turn in myself." I stood as well, groaning at the stiffness already evident in my thigh muscles. I'd forgotten how hard it was to climb mountain trails. My morning runs just couldn't compare.

"I don't remember the last time I hiked so much." I bent over, reaching towards my toes to stretch out my leg muscles. "Drive safely, and I'll see you in the morning." We returned our dishes to the kitchen, greeting Mrs. Huffman as we passed through, and went our separate ways, Nora to the office and me to my room for a shower and change of clothes.

As I tried to make my way unobtrusively down the hallway to the south end of the Lodge I could hear the counselors wrapping up the final group session of the day, sending the children in pairs to complete their evening routines. "Robby," I heard Mr. Bryan, the night counselor, say, "Thank you for sharing your concerns about the bunk beds. Anthony, thank you for being willing to switch places. As soon as we find Mrs. Huffman, we'll get some fresh sheets on there and get you two settled for the night."

I'd been pleased to see Robby O'Brien at the Lodge. I'd known that Raymond O'Brien's grandson had Down Syndrome, of course, though I'd never met the boy. It had frequently crossed my mind that he might enjoy the services offered by the program, and I had even mentioned it to

Raymond when I'd been in town for the ribbon cutting ceremony.

I wondered if it had been Raymond, before his death, who had arranged for Robby to attend. I decided that it most likely had. Raymond's daughter, Isabelle, had a rebellious history both as a daughter and a mother, but Billy May had mentioned several times that Raymond absolutely adored his grandson and often cared for him when Isabelle was unwilling or unable. I wondered how Robby was handling the loss. I wondered, too, if Isabelle would finally be able to pull herself together enough to be a mother to the cute little boy. I certainly hoped she would.

Dimly through the dark hallway I caught a sliver of light as the shadow of someone, Mr. Huffman I thought, passed through the doorway into his room, across the hall from mine. As his door closed, I realized mine was slightly ajar. I was certain I'd closed it, not out of any particular concern that someone would steal from me; after all, as Nora had reminded me, the staff had all undergone mandatory criminal background checks and the external doors to the Lodge were locked. The counselors were taking no chances in light of recent events.

But I knew I'd left it closed. I've always been an intensely private person; closing and locking my door is second nature. I was more than a little irritated at the thought of someone entering my room without my knowledge or permission.

Reaching the open door and snapping on the light, I was somewhat appeased to see that all appeared as I'd left it, unpacked suitcase on the bed and toiletry bag on the bathroom counter. Perhaps Mr. or Mrs. Huffman had needed access for some reason, to bring extra soap or oil a squeaky door. I made a mental note to ask Nora to speak with them about checking with me before entering my room. I didn't want to be difficult, but I was adamant when it came to maintaining my privacy.

I'd jumped into the role of volunteer so quickly that morning that I'd never had a chance to unpack. I eyed the suitcase, briefly tempted to arrange my clothes along the hangers in the closet before deciding to leave it as it was. The feeling that I'd overreacted to Nora's call continued to grow. I didn't plan on being at the Lodge long enough to warrant unpacking.

There was a reasonable explanation for all of the strange things that had happened. New programs were bound to have a few bugs to work out. As the staff grew more confident and experienced, I felt sure the carelessly unlocked doors and forgotten latches would be a thing of the past.

I also couldn't help but wonder if maybe Corinne had a point about the fire. The investigation was still open, and it wasn't beyond the realm of possibility that the new wiring was at fault. As far as I was aware, the initial suspicion of arson hinged solely on the note addressed to me.

The note I could not explain. I had no idea who could have written it or why, but the sheriff's department had it and I had every confidence they'd get to the bottom of it. If the investigation validated that the fire was indeed intentionally set by someone, presumably the same someone who had written the note, the matter became a criminal investigation, outside of my control.

In the meantime, I felt rather foolish hanging around and waiting on the mysterious note-writer to contact me. Barring any further contact, I fully anticipated catching a return flight to Los Angeles no later than Thursday, which meant I'd only have to live out of the suitcase for a couple more days.

Satisfied with my decision, I kicked off my hiking boots, bending down for a moment to rub my aching feet, and rummaged in the suitcase for a pair of sweats. As I shed my clothes on the way to the shower, my hand brushed against the hard lump in the front pocket of my jacket. Billy

May's trinket bag. I'd done a good job of pushing it out of my mind throughout the course of the day.

Stopping in my tracks, one leg still caught up in my jeans, I reached into the pocket and gently drew out the pouch. Made of worn leather and closed with a drawstring, the bag fit comfortably in my palm, the contents clinking softly as I held it. I knew what it contained without looking.

A handful of stones. Pink quartz. Billy May had called it rock crystal. I had seen the stones glittering beside the creek bed in the setting sun one nightmarish evening when I'd run away from my stepfather. They had been my first gift to Billy May. I hadn't known who she was at that time, other than that she was an elusive angel of mercy who left food and blankets in the little cave I used as a hiding place.

Inside the bag, mixed in with the quartz, was also the last gift I'd given Billy May, an early Christmas present from the year before. Coquina shells, in every imaginable shade of blue, yellow, pink, orange, even purple, collected by the two of us on our walks along Paradise Cove the previous September.

I could still see her clearly, facing out to sea, her white hair, cropped short as always, ruffling in the wind. Her jeans were rolled up to her knees and in true tourist spirit she proudly wore a Paradise Cove Beach Café t-shirt, ocean blue, the tail un-tucked and too long on her tiny frame, hanging halfway to her knees.

She held a pair of white Keds sneakers in one hand, her bare toes wiggling in the wet sand, waves washing over her ankles. In her other hand she held a Coquina shell, the first she'd ever seen. She turned it over in her hand, the marbled pink shining in the light from the sun. *It's like holdin' a little piece of the rainbow, ain't it?*

Most of all I remember her expression, filled with wonder. *I never knew, little girl,* she was saying, looking again out to sea, watching the waves break apart. *I never knew of anythin' like this.* She turned to look at me and her dark eyes sparkled. *It's the most beautiful sight I ever seen. It's...well, I just never knew of anythin' like it.* I'd answered with a smile, content in that moment, a rare feeling for me.

Billy May had laughed with pure delight when a squawking flock of seagulls swooped around her in search of food. It always annoyed me to see people feeding the gulls, precisely because it created the bold behaviors they were then exhibiting. They were a nuisance. In that moment, however, they were magical. Billy May had read about seagulls, but until that moment she'd never seen one.

Look at that, Jessie, she had said, pointing to a particularly brazen gull. *It's Jonathan!* A reference to the gull created in the imagination of author Richard Bach. *He's come to see me.* Her voice was one I'd never heard before, young and weightless. Time shifted for just a moment and I had a glimpse of the girl she must have once been. She was beautiful.

Billy May had always been fascinated with the ocean, and I'd tried for years to get her to come to Los Angeles for a visit, but she'd always refused. *I reckon if I was meant to be in California, I'd have been put in California.* Underneath her bravado, I'd assumed she was afraid. The furthest Billy May had ever traveled from Cedar Hollow was the fifty miles to Huntington, and that only after I enrolled at Marshall.

I didn't know what had made her finally agree to the trip, but I wondered if she had known it was the last opportunity she'd have. She died eight months later. Standing there on Crutcher Mountain, clutching her trinket bag to my chest, I couldn't open it. I simply couldn't.

Billy May was everywhere; she was all around me, surrounding me. Yet she wasn't. Therein lay the heartbreak. *Bí comforted,* she whispered again in my memory. *Be comforted.* But I wasn't.

Chapter 10
Robby

Hi it's me Robby again. Well I got done with my Evening Routine early and so I got fifteen minutes Free Time before bed. Everybody got Free Time because we all had a very good day. Well Anthony did not have a good day this morning but he did since then so he got Free Time too.

They all wanted to watch SpongeBob SquarePants in the common area but I did not want to because he hurts my ears. I asked Mr. Bryan if I could sit outside because Grandpa said there is nothing like the clean night air to make a body sleep good and I am tired and I want to sleep good. At least Anthony will be on the bottom bunk tonight so his bed will not fall on top of me.

Mr. Bryan said I could only go outside if I had someone to supervise me but who could that be? He opened the door and looked outside and said, "Oh, Ms. McIntosh, I didn't know you were out here. Would you mind keeping an eye on Robby? It'll only be for about ten minutes or so, then you can send him in."

I did not hear what she said but I guess it was okay because Mr. Bryan said, "Stay on the porch, Robby, okay?" And then he held the door open for me to go outside and I saw Ms. McIntosh and I knew she had been crying because I had seen my mom with that look lots of times.

But she didn't say anything about it. She just said, "Hello, Robby. It's good to see you. Are you enjoying yourself?" I really liked her voice because it was nice and

57

different from the voices I was used to so I went to the steps and sat down beside her. She smelled good and I could tell she had finished with Evening Routine because her hair was wet like she'd been in the shower. When I sat next to her she looked at me and smiled and I thought maybe she wasn't that old after all. She had a nice smile.

"Uh-huh," I told her. "I like it here." I really hoped she could understand my words because I liked her a lot. But not as much as Stacey.

I guess she understood me because she said, "Good. I'm glad." Then she surprised me and hurt my heart a little bit because she said, "I knew your grandpa, you know. You look a lot like him." I just looked at her because I didn't know what to say about that. I was proud to look like Grandpa but he looked old and I do not and I don't want to talk about Grandpa.

"He was my mother's best friend," she told me. And then I could tell she had tears in her voice but she didn't have any in her eyes. I knew I would have tears in my voice too if I tried to talk because they were also in my eyes. Grandpa was my best friend too. I didn't say anything though. I just looked out at the stars. There were a lot of them. She looked out at the stars too.

After a minute she reached out and put her hand on my hair. Grandpa used to do that sometimes. The tears in my eyes got bigger. "I know it's hard, Robby. It's always hard to lose someone you love. But he's still with you, in your heart. Do you understand?"

I did understand that he was in my heart but I wanted him to be here in the world with me. I looked at her but I did not know how to tell her that but I guess she knew what I was thinking because she smiled but her face stayed sad and then she said, "It isn't the same, is it? I still miss my mother every day. And I know you miss your grandpa. It isn't the same at all." And then I saw that the tears were in her eyes too and we just sat there for a while to let them dry out.

Then she took a deep breath and she said, "So, Robby. It's time for you to go in, but do you know where I can get a toothbrush? I seem to have forgotten to pack mine."

I was glad that she asked me for help and glad that we weren't going to be sad anymore that night. I took her hand to take her inside and show her the storage closet where all the toothbrushes and stuff are for the kids who forget to bring their own. And for the Grownups too I guess but I didn't know Grownups forgot stuff.

She picked out a green one which is my favorite color and then she said, "This one is perfect. It looks just like the one I forgot at home. Good night, Robby, and thanks for your help. I'll see you in the morning." And then I don't know why I did it but I hugged her before I ran to bed. She hugged me back too and it made me feel happy.

Chapter 11

Wednesday

After a restless night's sleep I awakened both cranky and sore, desperately in need of my morning run and a cup of strong coffee. A run would be nearly impossible on the mountain, so I settled instead for a brisk walk along the trails. Double-knotting the laces of my running shoes, I let myself quietly out the front door of the Lodge, locking it securely behind me. The children were still sleeping, and I could hear the faint murmuring of night staff as they tidied up and finished chart notes, readying things for shift change.

The air was cool, still misty as the sun fought its way up into a pale sky, and I enjoyed the sharpness of it as I inhaled, crunching my way across the fallen leaves on my way to the trailhead. Living in L.A. as I did, it was easy to forget the simple pleasure of a lungful of clean air. As I entered the woods, I caught a glimpse of movement over towards my right, behind the storage shed, and turned to get a better look.

Mr. Huffman, dressed in a red hunting jacket and khaki work pants, stood at the back of the shed, propping one hand against the rough logs, facing my direction. In his other hand dangled a pair of clippers. He was obviously getting an early start, making sure the trails were clear before whatever wilderness activities the staff had planned for the day got underway. In spite of that, I had the distinct impression he was watching me. Upon catching my glance he startled and threw a hand in the air in a quick wave before disappearing around the building. I stayed put for a moment, but he didn't return.

As I started down the trail, puffs of breath steaming in the cold morning air, I admitted to myself that I was somewhat put off by the Huffmans. I didn't want to be, because they sounded like wonderful people, but I couldn't seem to help it. According to Nora, the Huffmans came with glowing recommendations and years of experience, but something about them made me uneasy.

It wasn't simply that Mr. Huffman had been the one to discover the fire. There was also the fact that Mr. Huffman, as groundskeeper, was the one responsible for locking the storage shed and keeping the cleaning chemicals properly stored. I assumed fitting the pasture gate with a functional latch also fell under his job description. Lots of coincidences, enough to make me wonder. But even more than that, the memory of Mr. Huffman disappearing into his door just as I discovered that my own was open troubled me. And why had he been watching me?

I'd speak to Nora more about it after my walk. I knew I was being overly suspicious, but given the childhood I'd had, I paid attention to my instincts. The Huffmans might not be responsible for the strange happenings at the Lodge, but something was off, of that I was sure.

When I returned to the Lodge an hour later, sweaty and invigorated from my walk, the children were already up and dressed, participating in goal-setting group in the common area before being taken to breakfast. Several of them glanced my way and Robby offered me a shy smile. I waved at the group and returned the smile, trying to be as unobtrusive as possible as I turned down the hall towards my room. I was pleased to see that this time, my door remained shut.

I showered quickly, dressing in jeans and a sweater, and caught my hair up in a ponytail before throwing on a lightweight plaid jacket and stepping back out into the morning. I made a quick detour through the cafeteria to pick up yogurt and coffee on my way to Nora's office. Stepping across the little porch, I knocked once and poked my head in the door.

Nora looked up from her desk and motioned me in, leaning back in her chair. "Just the person I wanted to see." She removed her glasses and gestured towards the chair across from her. "How'd you sleep?"

"Good, actually." The office was warm, and I took off my jacket, draping it over the back of the chair before sitting. "All was quiet. I think you wore them out yesterday; I didn't hear a peep." I held up my yogurt cup. "Do you mind?"

Nora smiled. "Of course not; help yourself. I'm glad you slept well. The nights up here can be somewhat unpredictable." She picked up a stack of papers on her desk, dropped it back down, and blew out a frustrated breath. "I just got off the phone with Sheriff Moore. We seem to be at an impasse."

I paused, spoon halfway to my mouth. "An impasse? In what way?"

Nora ran her hands impatiently through her hair before linking her fingers and resting her arms on the desk. She studied me for a moment before answering. "There's no doubt the fire was set intentionally. The burn pattern makes that evident. The accelerant has even been identified."

I swallowed a mouthful of strawberry yogurt. "So how is that an impasse? It sounds pretty clear to me. Who did it?"

"That's where the impasse comes in. For one thing, there were no unaccounted for prints on the banister. Mine were on there, of course, as were the Huffmans' and the rest of the staff. Many of the prints were child-sized. Short of printing all the children here, which we obviously don't want to do, they're left without viable prints." She stood, clearly agitated, and began to pace around the little cabin, chewing thoughtfully on the earpiece of her glasses. I waited.

63

Finally, she perched a hip on the corner of the desk in front of me and sighed. "In spite of all the progress that's been made, so many people still have the wrong idea. Tell them you're running a program for children with developmental disabilities and they immediately jump to certain conclusions."

I placed my spoon carefully into the yogurt container and set it on the arm of my chair. I had an idea where this was going, and I didn't like it one bit. "Such as?"

"Oh, you know." She rubbed her eyes with her thumb and forefinger. "They equate a mental disability with a propensity for violence. They're afraid of differences; they don't understand that different doesn't mean bad. As you know, we had some resistance to the program in the beginning. 'Not in my backyard' and all that. I thought we'd gotten past it, though. Overall support has been phenomenal, but I suppose there will always be some who don't understand."

"Are you saying that the Sheriff thinks one of the children set the fire?" It was my turn to stand and pace.

Nora nodded, replacing her glasses. "That seems to be the thinking."

I felt a wave of anger. "Did you explain to him that the children weren't even *near* the Lodge when the fire broke out?" My tone was harsher than I meant for it to be, but I was incredulous at the Sheriff's stance on the matter.

"Of course, but his mind is made up. There's little I can do at this point. His exact words were—and I quote— 'There's no evidence of any outsider coming in and starting trouble. You got kids already up there that have a history of stuff like this.' Apparently he did some investigating into our current group of kids and found Anthony's old records."

"What records?" I sat back down.

"Anthony has had some violent behaviors in the past. He doesn't like to be touched, especially not by strangers. That's not uncommon for children on the Autism Spectrum.

Anyway, a couple of years ago some poorly trained staff tried to physically maneuver him onto the school bus and he struck out at them. One of them ended up in the emergency room with a broken nose. As a result, Anthony spent a little bit of time in a residential facility before being discharged back into the care of his mother."

"That's hardly an indication that he's responsible for setting a fire two years later," I said. "I'd say it's more an indication that staff needs to undergo proper training before working with children who have special needs."

"I agree, but the Sheriff doesn't."

"How does he explain the letter?" I myself had trouble explaining the letter. I was curious as to how the Sheriff would do it.

"He hasn't, yet. It's still being tested for prints, but he didn't seem overly concerned about it. As he pointed out, there were no specific threats made, meaning that even if they find out who wrote it, if they can't prove that that person also started the fire, there isn't anything to charge them with."

Nora returned to her seat behind the desk.

"Now what?" I asked, unwilling to accept the Sheriff's explanation. "What about the van driver, the one you let go? What was his name? Virgil?"

"Virgil Young, yes. That seems to be another area of contention."

"I can hardly wait." I sipped at my coffee, motioning for Nora to continue.

"It seems Virgil does have a history with you. Unfortunately, he also has an ironclad alibi."

I nearly choked on the now cold coffee. "What are you talking about? I have no idea who Virgil Young is. I've never met the man in my life." I set the cup back down.

Nora looked down at the desk, fidgeting with her pen. "You probably wouldn't remember this," she said slowly, "but he claims he knew your stepfather, Roy Campbell."

I felt the blood drain from my face. Nora didn't know all of my history, but she knew enough. I sat speechless.

"Take a deep breath, Jessie," instructed Nora. "Breathe in through your nose to a count of eight, and release through your mouth.

I waved away her instructions. "I'm fine." I wasn't, obviously, but I didn't feel like listening to psychobabble at that moment. "I think you'd better tell me what you know."

Nora cleared her throat. "Well," she said, "Sheriff Moore tracked Virgil down yesterday at Peggy's Diner down in the town. According to the Sheriff, Virgil had quite a lot to say, and a great deal of it wasn't very nice."

"If he was a friend of Roy's, I'm sure it wasn't," I interrupted. "Roy didn't tend to hang out with nice people."

She ignored my interruption. "Virgil was at Peggy's Diner when the office was trashed. Apparently he's a regular there at that time of day. You know Kay?"

I did. Kay was Peggy's daughter. She had taken over the diner when Peggy died years before. Kay's son owned the diner now, but Kay remained active in the running of the place.

"Kay vouched for him," Nora said. "She remembered clearly that he'd been there that day because he'd been cursing both of us, me for firing him and you for opening this place to start with. Several other regulars backed up the story. If he was as obnoxious as it sounds, I suppose he was hard to miss."

"All right," I conceded, "maybe he didn't trash the office himself, but I don't think his alibi absolves him completely. He could have had someone else do it. With the amount of anger he apparently has towards both of us, isn't it possible he got someone else to trash the office and set the fire? And what about the day the horses got out? Or when the chemicals were spilled? I can't believe the Sheriff would let it go so easily."

"I asked the Sheriff those same questions," Nora replied. "He said they'll check into it and they'll let me know if he has alibis for those times and if his prints turn up on the letter. Until we hear back, all we can do is wait. But Jessie...."

I raised my eyebrows. "What?"

"There's more."

"Then by all means, let's hear it." I somehow knew that what was coming wouldn't be good, would, in fact, be quite bad.

She took a deep breath and released it. "Virgil told Sheriff Moore that as long as they were in the mood to investigate, they should investigate you. He implied that you'd been involved in a murder."

Chapter 12

I hadn't thought about that night in years, but upon hearing Nora's words I was immediately transported back to a time I'd hoped never to revisit. How to describe it? It overwhelmed all of my senses.

I could feel the cold against my skin, brutal cold, blowing through the door in spite of the quilts under which I huddled. I was leaning against Mrs. Johnson—Corinne—and I could feel her heart beating against my cheek, her arm tight around my shoulders. The bed was soft, I remember that, feather soft, but still I felt pain, horrible pain that threatened to swallow me whole.

I smelled the soft smell of Corinne, something fruity and warm, and then her fragrance was overtaken by the smell of gunpowder, and then corn whiskey and sweat. And blood. I smelled blood, too. Whose? Mine? Or someone else's? I didn't know. My stomach lurched with the odors.

I heard cursing, awful cursing, damning us all to hell and back, calling us filthy names, vile and disgusting words. I heard gunfire and I pressed myself further into Corinne, covering my ears, and then I heard myself. I was crying. In my heart I was crying for my mother, but even then I knew it was a hopeless cry.

I tasted my tears, mixed with the bile in my throat. Most of all, I tasted fear, sour and coppery against my tongue.

And I saw...what did I see? Nothing. Only Billy May's face, pale and drawn, her dark eyes glittering, looking at me with a promise. I believed that promise more than I'd ever believed anything in my young life. I saw nothing else. I did not.

Chapter 13

"Jessie." Billy May? No. No, it was Nora's voice. "Jessie, breathe with me." But I didn't want to; I was so tired. There's a tired that happens when you've had a hard week, a tired that results from too little sleep, too many hours awake, too much stress at work.

And then there's the tired I felt in that moment. It's a completely different tired, one that encompasses not just the body—and you must understand that I hate this expression— but the soul. Soul weary. It's a terrible cliché, one I caution against in every movie I've ever produced, but for those of us who have experienced it, we know it's true.

Being soul weary is close to being dead, in a spiritual sense, anyway. Once you've passed through sadness and worn out anger, given up on hope and embraced apathy, you've arrived at soul weary. One step in the grave, as Billy May would have said. Maybe even a good step, I sometimes believed, although I knew Billy May would have chastised me for that thought. *Hush that talk, little girl. You just hush that talk right now.*

Once, when I was about sixteen years old, I'd made a similar statement. I knew by that time that I couldn't have children. I also knew I was damaged goods, no matter how hard Billy May worked to make me believe otherwise.

I don't remember exactly what it was that brought on my bout of self-pity that particular day. A spat with a friend, maybe, or a rejection by some long forgotten boy. Whatever the reason, I didn't, at that time, have the life experience to realize that those things were just a part of life. In my mind,

71

everything was tied to what had happened to me. I was tainted, soiled, and other people knew it; I felt like Hester Prynne must have felt, except that my scarlet letter was invisible. I couldn't imagine ever having a normal life, and I said as much to Billy May.

"Maybe you should have just left me there."

It was the only time I ever saw Billy May angry with me. She stopped in the middle of taking inventory, counting eight penny nails, if I remember right. She set down her tablet and walked over to the register, where I'd been sorting money, to peer into my face, her black eyes boring into mine. I was taller than her by that time, by at least three inches, five in the clogs I was so fond of wearing back then, but that didn't faze her. She reached up and took my chin in her calloused fingers, forcing me to look at her.

Don't you ever let me hear you say such a thing, she'd said. *You are a beautiful girl, a smart girl, and you got all kinds of things you can give to this world. Little girl, it ain't about what* has *happened to you; it's about what* can *happen to you if you'll let it. I am livin' proof of that. Ain't nobody got the power to destroy you but you. Don't you never forget that.*

"Breathe, Jessie," Nora was saying, and my body betrayed me and I did. I felt her cool hands rubbing mine. I was afraid when I opened my eyes I'd see not the cozy office Nora had created, but Billy May's cabin from that long ago night. That was not something I wanted to see. I kept my eyes closed and concentrated on breathing.

I sensed Nora moving away before she placed a cup of water into my hand. "Drink," she ordered. "And when you're ready, we'll talk."

I drank, and the world slowly came back to me. I heard the chattering of squirrels in the clean morning air outside, and under that the voices of the children readying for a walk in the woods. I felt the sun reaching my shoulders through the small window by the door, and I was grateful for the warmth. The taste of strawberries and cold coffee was still on my tongue. No gunfire, no bitter cold, no taste of fear. I drank again before opening my eyes to Nora.

She was crouched by my side, her eyes penetrating, much too close for my comfort. Instinctively, I leaned away from her. Sensing my discomfort she quickly stood and moved to the chair behind her desk, where she continued her appraisal of me. "Better now?"

I sat up, straightening my sweater and adjusting my jeans, embarrassed. "I'm fine." I was also angry, I was surprised to discover. So much for apathy. My hands shook as I set the cup of water down, and I worked hard to control my voice.

"You tell Sheriff Moore to investigate anything he'd like. I was barely thirteen years old when Roy disappeared and I thanked God that he did. That man tortured me, raped me on a daily basis. Quite frankly, I don't care what happened to him; I only hope whatever it was, it hurt like hell. Given Sheriff Moore's apparent lack of investigative skills, I don't think I'd have much to worry about even if I *had* killed the son of a bitch."

I was surprised to see Nora smile. "Anger is good," she said, and she looked very much like a proud parent looks when a baby sits up for the first time. "It's a very healthy reaction. I'm glad you're feeling it." I rolled my eyes, and she laughed aloud, breaking the tension in the room.

"If you're done psychoanalyzing me for the moment, I'd really like to join the kids on their walk."

"By all means," she waved towards the door, still smiling. "Oh, I almost forgot. Jessie," she stopped suddenly, the smile gone, "I'm really sorry, but when Sheriff Moore learned that you were here he asked me to see if you'll stick around for a few more days. I doubt very much it has anything to do with whatever garbage Virgil is spouting off. I think it's more so that he has access to you if he has any questions about the Lodge. Will you be able to stay?"

My heart rate jumped for a second before I got it back under control. "I had actually planned on trying to fly out in the morning," I said. "When do the children leave?"

"Friday around noon. We'll have a light breakfast at seven and wrap up with a closure group from eight until nine. Parents and caseworkers are invited to come and tour the program from nine until ten. After that, we'll provide a nice brunch, and everyone should be packed up and gone by eleven-thirty or so."

"I'll arrange to fly out Friday afternoon." I stood and shrugged into my jacket before remembering the reason I'd stopped by in the first place.

"Oh, before I go, I actually came in to ask you about the Huffmans."

"What about them?"

I sat back down. I had wanted to press her on their histories, but after the intensity of the morning I no longer had the desire. Instead, I mentioned finding my door open the night before. "Would you mind letting them know I'll ask if I need anything? I'm just not comfortable with people in my room."

"Not a problem; consider it done. Have fun on the walk. I believe the topic today is 'The Healthy Expression of Feelings.' You might enjoy it." She looked down, busying herself with the papers on her desk in an attempt to hide a smile.

"Good God, you people never give up." Damn therapists. I let myself out.

Chapter 14
Robby

Well it's me Robby again. I finally got some good sleep last night because I am on the top bunk and now when Anthony rocks the bed will not fall down on me. We had pancakes for breakfast and now we are going to go on a walk in the woods. Mr. Paul said that while we are on the walk we will stop sometimes and talk about what we are feeling. That's pretty cool I guess unless I am feeling something I don't want to tell people and then I won't tell them and they can't make me. Ha!

I hear a door close and I look up and see Ms. McIntosh coming out of Dr. Wright's office. She is zipping up her jacket and I wonder if she is going on the walk with us. She comes over to stand with us and she is! I like Ms. McIntosh and I can tell that Marcus does too because he is going crazy banging on his chair and laughing.

Mr. Paul tells us the safety rules and then he gets behind Marcus' chair and Ms. Janice gets behind Stacey's chair and we start down the trail. Mr. Paul is talking about the birds and the sky and stuff but I don't really listen to that because how am I supposed to hear the birds if I am listening to him talking? Duh! I like Mr. Paul but sometimes he talks too much.

I am walking beside Stacey's chair because I am still in love with Stacey. I like Ms. McIntosh too but she is way too old to be in love with. Stacey smiles at me and then Ms. Janice tells us all to gather around crisscross applesauce.

That means we have to sit on the ground with our legs bent up and listen to something Important.

Ms. Janice talks about the different kinds of feelings we all have like sadness and anger and happiness. Then she goes around the group asking everyone how they feel Right Now and then she talks about that for a minute. She is going to ask me how I feel and I am going to tell her that I feel great. It is a nice day and Stacey smiled at me and Ms. McIntosh came on the walk with us and Joseph said he is going to ask his mom if I can come visit him when we all go back home.

I want to go visit Joseph because he's a cool kid and he said he has a mom and a dad and a sister. I only have a mom but sometimes I don't have her. I used to go live with Grandpa when I didn't have a mom but when he died I had to get a caseworker. Her name is Mrs. Cortes and her job is to find me a Foster Family. That means they aren't really my family but they pretend to be for a while.

She found me one Foster Family and they were okay but they already have too many kids so I can't go back there. I don't know who I will go live with now. I have an uncle who lives a long way away and he would let me live with him but my aunt doesn't want me. Maybe I can live with Joseph except I don't think I want a sister.

Mrs. Cortes said not to worry and that she will find a place for me. She said, "Robby, you're a great kid and there will be plenty of people who want to make you a part of their family." I hope she is right but I think maybe she doesn't know I have Down Syndrome because if she did she would know that sometimes people don't want kids with Down Syndrome.

"Robby, what are you feeling right now, in this moment?" It is Ms. Janice and now it is my turn to answer the question but I'm not feeling great anymore. I don't want to tell her because if I do Mr. Paul will want to meet with me for a Breakthrough so I just look down at the ground and I don't say anything.

"Robby? Can you tell us what you're feeling?" But I'm not going to so I just keep looking down until she says, "Okay. Robby doesn't feel like sharing right now so we'll move on." For some reason that makes me want to cry.

Then I feel a hand on my head and I know it is Ms. McIntosh because it is exactly the way it felt when she put her hand on my head last night and I can smell her and she still smells good. I am still looking at the ground but my heart stops hurting as much but I want to cry even more and that's weird. She just stands there that way and she doesn't ask me questions or stare at me and I like that. Then it is time to stand up and walk some more but I don't feel like it so I don't get up.

"Robby, it's time to walk some more." That is Mr. Paul but I don't care because I don't want to walk and talk about stupid feelings so I don't get up and he can't make me. Ha!

"It's okay," Ms. McIntosh says. "I'll stay with him." So Mr. Paul and Ms. Janice and everybody else all leave down the trail and it is just me and Ms. McIntosh and I think oh great now she's going to try to make me have a Breakthrough but she doesn't. She just sits down on the ground next to me and doesn't say anything for a long time so I look at her and she smiles at me and then she winks like Grandpa used to do and for some reason that makes me smile at her.

Then she asks me, "Are you ready to meet up with the others?" But I don't know if I am or not.

"I don't want to talk about stupid feelings," I tell her and I think she will tell me it's good to talk about feelings but she doesn't. She nods at me and says, "Yeah, I don't want to talk about stupid feelings, either." I did not think she would say that because that is not what Grownups are supposed to say. Grownups are supposed to tell you feelings are not stupid.

Maybe she doesn't know what she is supposed to say so I tell her what Mr. Paul always tells me. "You have to talk about feelings. If you don't they build up and make you unhappy."

She looks at me and she is surprised. "But I thought feelings were stupid," she says and I can't believe a Grownup is talking this way so I tell her what else Mr. Paul always says.

"Mr. Paul says talking about feelings is good for you."

She looks at me for a minute and then she says, "Why do you think it might be good for you?"

I think about that. "Mr. Paul says keeping feelings inside makes you lonely. He says when you share feelings then you don't feel all alone."

"Ahh," she says. I don't know what ahh means. Then she says, "Do you feel alone?"

"Well, duh!" I tell her, and I am starting to think maybe she is Lower Functioning than I am because I am having to explain it all to her. "I *am* alone. My Grandpa died and I don't have a place to live." Sheesh!

Then she says, "Hmmm." I don't know what hmmm means either. She is a very confusing lady. She is nice but she is confusing. "That must be scary," she says. "Being all alone like that, I mean."

"I am not scared!" I don't mean to yell but I do because I am not scared and that is the truth. I am not a scaredy baby. "I am sad that I don't have a family and I miss my Grandpa."

"Oh," she says. She doesn't look mad at me for yelling. "That makes sense. I'm sad sometimes because I don't have a family, either."

That is weird to me because she does have a family so I wonder what she means but then she says, "And sometimes, I'm even mad that I don't have a family."

Boy do I know what she means about that and I tell her, "Yeah, I'm mad, too! Sometimes I'm really, really mad because Grandpa died and my mom is gone and I'm just a kid. Sometimes I want to hit things I get so mad. I get *really* mad."

"Wow," she says. "You *sound* really mad. What do you hit?"

"Yeah I *am* really mad!" I am happy that she doesn't tell me not to get mad. Grownups always tell me not to get mad but I do it anyway. "I hit my pillow when I get really, really mad."

"A pillow, huh? That sounds like a good plan. That way you can get the mad out but not hurt anything. What do you do when you're sad?"

"I cry or I just sit and be quiet."

"Hmmm," she says again and I still don't know what hmmm means but I think it must not be a bad thing. Then she says, "Yeah, crying can be good. It can get the sad out." I nod at her because she is right. She is right about being sad and about being mad and that makes me feel happy. Maybe she isn't *too* Low Functioning.

We stop talking for a while and then she stands up and says, "Well, if we're not going to talk about stupid feelings, let's stand up and walk. I'm too old to sit on the ground for such a long time." She rubs her back and makes a funny face at me and I laugh.

I get up because I don't feel sad or mad right now and I'm ready to finish the walk with everybody else and I'm happy that maybe I taught Ms. McIntosh some things today. She is very nice and I really like her but I can't believe she didn't know that feelings are good for you. Geesh. Grownups.

Chapter 15

Robby and I caught up to the group just as the walk was nearly over. I sent him on ahead and signaled to Paul, who stepped aside so I could fill him in on my conversation with Robby.

He whistled softly. "Nice job, Jessie. If you ever want a career change...."

I snorted. "Sure, Paul. Physician heal thyself right here in the flesh."

He laughed before jogging to catch up to the group. I took my time, enjoying the trail for the second time that day. It never failed to amaze me, the way the mountain changed depending on the time of day. The early morning had been cold and misty, but the fog had burned off leaving a clear blue sky, and the brilliant reds and yellows of the changing leaves were breathtaking. So enamored was I with the tree tops that I nearly ran over Corinne. Had she not laughed that tinkling laugh of hers, I surely would have.

"Corinne! What on earth are you doing here?" I caught my balance against a tree.

"Craftin', of course. It's Wednesday." She reached out a hand to steady me.

"You've lost me."

That tinkling laugh again. "I come on Wednesdays to run a craft group with the kids. I came early today hopin' we could share some lunch. Nora said I'd find you on the trail."

"I had no idea you volunteered here! When did you start and what made you decide to do it?" I took her arm as we exited the trail.

Melinda Clayton

"I started as soon as it opened. I got my background check done right away and asked Nora about volunteerin'. She was happy to have me." Corinne smiled, her blue eyes dancing, and lightly squeezed my arm. "It keeps me young. And you would have known about it if you kept in better touch. I took Wednesdays and Valerie took Thursdays."

"Valerie? Poindexter?"

"The very one. She does story hour with the children Thursday evenin's."

Valerie Burnett Poindexter had been the librarian in Cedar Hollow since I was a girl. Having originally come to Cedar Hollow for an internship to satisfy requirements for her degree program at Marshall University, she'd fallen in love with the village and never left. Her husband was the town's dentist, the first and only dentist Cedar Hollow had ever had.

"Hurry, now. Goodness, honey, you'd think with those long legs you could walk a little faster. We have to go back to the car to get the food and the boys. They can't come on campus, you know, because they haven't been cleared."

I stopped in my tracks. "What boys?"

Corinne pulled at my arm impatiently. "John and Michael, of course. Come on, honey, craftin' starts in less than an hour. We can eat out in the gazebo by the drive. The boys are settin' the food out for us." She tugged me forward again.

"John is here?"

"He sure is. I was so glad to see him! And that Michael seems like a nice fellow, too."

"Michael is here." I could hardly believe my ears. I didn't know whether to laugh or be angry, the entire situation was so preposterous. "Corinne, what have you done?"

"I'll have you know I didn't do a thing." She shot me a reproachful look. "My son called me yesterday after you left and told me he and his friend was comin' to town, and here

82

they are. There's nothin' wrong with that and I, for one, am mighty glad to see them. I thought it would be nice if we all had us a little picnic up here on the mountain before I go to work with the children. Isn't that a nice idea?"

Sure enough, there they were, standing in the gazebo. They were both dressed casually in jeans and hiking boots, resembling nothing so much as middle-aged choir boys ready to camp out and sing Kumbaya. They looked up as we approached, and John came forward and enveloped me in a hug.

"Nice boots," I managed to say. "Growlers?" I asked, knowing John's taste for expensive footwear.

He released me and shook his head. "Danners."

Of course. Nothing but the best for John. "You went shoe shopping without me," I accused.

"You ran off without me," John retorted. Touché.

I turned to face Michael, who seemed afraid to approach me. "Fancy seeing you here," was all I managed to come up with. As lame as it was, it was fitting. In my wildest dreams I'd never expected to see Michael Bell outside Billy May's cabin on Crutcher Mountain. The dissonance was jarring.

He stepped towards me cautiously. "I wanted to make sure you were okay," he said. "When you wouldn't take my calls, I called John. He was worried about you, too. So, we decided...."

"You decided to crash my party," I finished for him. "I'm not sure exactly what either of you think you can do here," I said. "And you certainly can't stay here."

"They're stayin' with me, of course," Corinne answered for them. "And I don't think they plan on *doin'* anythin', honey. They just wanted to check on you and make sure you're all right. They're flyin' back out Friday evenin'."

She took a Tupperware container of what looked like fried chicken out of a cooler. "Now sit down here and eat and quit bein' stubborn. It's a beautiful day and we're goin' to enjoy it. Tell me what you've found out about the goin's on up here."

At the age of forty-seven I had no more idea how to argue with Corinne than I had at the age of thirteen, so I sat down and did as I was told. Besides, the food was delicious and as Corinne had pointed out, it was a beautiful day. Surprisingly, I found myself happy to see them, Michael included. I filled them in on my conversation with Nora earlier that morning, leaving out the part about Virgil's accusations. I needed to talk to Corinne in private about that.

Michael listened intently, saying little. I imagined the whole scenario was overwhelming for him. In the space of thirty minutes he learned more about my history than he had the entire six months we'd known each other. John, on the other hand, interrupted every couple of minutes with a question or a comment, particularly when I voiced my suspicions regarding the Huffmans.

"I see why you're suspicious, Jessie, but how could they be involved? Weren't they fingerprinted before being offered their positions?"

I nodded, swallowing a bite of Corinne's fabulous potato salad. "They were, but criminal history doesn't always follow a person across state lines. Most agencies—this one included—do a state check but not a federal one. Federal checks are expensive, and as you know, with the ongoing budget cuts, agencies just don't have the resources. If a potential employee has a clean state record reaching back seven or more years, that's often accepted. Some state checks include a national check for sexual offenses or terrorist actions, but that leaves out a lot."

John reached for the thermos of sweet tea. "So you're saying it's possible the Huffmans have some sort of old criminal record in another state. If they've kept their noses clean here for the last several years, they could pass a background check with flying colors and no one would be the wiser."

"Exactly."

"Then the obvious question," he said, filling Corinne's glass as well, "is how long have they lived in West Virginia?"

"I don't know. That's what I'd been on my way to ask Nora when she hit me with everything else."

"Speakin' of everythin' else," Corinne broke in, "I heard about Virgil runnin' his mouth off down at the diner. Kay told me about it."

I handed her the platter of biscuits. "Do you know him? Nora said he knew Roy." I glanced over at Michael. Unless John had been telling tales out of school, and I didn't believe he would, Michael didn't know that part of my past. I had no intention of telling him.

"They worked in the mine together." Corinne waved away the biscuits. "He was a good bit younger than Roy. Must've been somewhere in his twenties back when Roy disappeared." She looked hard at me, a silent communication. "There was that group of 'em, you know. Played poker together and caused trouble for everyone else. Could be you saw him back then but wouldn't know him now, it's been so long, and Lord knows he hasn't aged well. Corn whiskey'll do that to you."

So Virgil may very well have been one of the drunken, nasty men I waited on during Roy's poker nights, pouring shots and emptying ashtrays when I should have been tucked into bed, visions of sugar plums dancing in my head. Isn't that how the rhyme goes? Not in my childhood. I shivered in the shade of the gazebo.

"Well," Corinne pushed back her plate and stood, "I've got to get to work with these children. Boys, I believe you can handle the clean up. Jessie, why don't you help me carry my craftin' supplies in."

I followed Corinne to her car where she handed me several bags of multi-colored yarn, construction paper, and other assorted art supplies. As we left the men packing leftovers at the gazebo, Corinne gripped my arm.

"I also heard what else he's been tellin' people," she said. "About that night." She searched my face for a reaction. Apparently satisfied that I could handle whatever she had to say, she continued. "He don't know nothin', Jessie. There ain't nothin' to know. He's just spewin' out hate, that's all. Besides, ain't nobody left but me and Darryl and Eugene, and what're they goin' to do to us? Throw us in jail? Chances are we'd die of old age before it ever got that far." She held up her hand to stop me from speaking.

"The mine shaft is filled in and we're just a bunch of old people, one foot already on the other side. Virgil's just causin' trouble, tryin' to get the attention off himself. I don't know if he's the one behind all this, but it wouldn't surprise me one bit."

We'd reached the Lodge. I handed Corinne her bags, and she reached out to pat my cheek. "Don't worry yourself about him, honey. He don't know nothin'", she repeated. "There ain't nothin' to know."

As she entered the Lodge, I turned back towards the gazebo, where John and Michael sat engrossed in conversation. They were two very handsome men, one my best friend in the world, the other undefined, which was exactly the way I wanted it. As I approached, John waved me over, patting the seat beside him.

"Sorry for the ambush, love." John smiled, his expression decidedly un-sorry. "But you left us no choice. Are you terribly mad at me?"

I sat next to him, bumping him playfully with my shoulder. "I want to be," I admitted. "But you make it difficult, showing up here in your $500.00 hiking boots." John's grin broadened.

"Speaking of hiking boots, I'm going to stretch my legs," he said. "It'll give you two a little time to get reacquainted. You haven't said two words to each other the entire time we've been here." He stood and strolled casually down the driveway, away from the Lodge, and I was left alone with Michael.

Chapter 16

For a moment we simply looked at each other across the table. I knew he had things he wanted to get off his chest, so I waited him out. Finally, Michael cleared his throat.

"Look, Jessie," he began, "I know you don't like people butting into your business. You're private. I get that. I even like it. But....," he stopped, playing with the food on his plate before continuing. "We've got some decisions to make. At least I do. I'm hoping we have some sort of a future together. I care about you, and I enjoy my time with you. I miss you when you're gone. But relationships are generally a two-way affair."

I felt my blood beginning to boil. "No, *you* look, Michael," I shot back, and I sounded a lot snippier than I'd intended. I forged ahead, anyway. "You're the one putting the relationship label on this. Not me. We enjoy each other's company. We have a lot in common. We hang out together, and yes, you spend the night. But I never called this a relationship. I never claimed to want a relationship; I made that clear from the beginning. So for you to come here to criticize my lack of investment in our *relationship* is completely out of line."

Michael dropped his fork and sat back against the railing of the gazebo, his expression inscrutable. "Well that certainly explains a great deal," he said, crossing his arms over his chest. "That clears things up nicely. Thank you for that."

I felt awful, but I didn't know how to fix it. I *hadn't* wanted a relationship, and I *had* made that clear from the beginning. And that's the problem with dating. You make things perfectly clear up front, yet people think if they hang around long enough, you'll change your mind. It infuriated me.

We sat in uncomfortable silence before Michael sighed and sat forward, elbows on the table. "You're right," he said. "You did make it clear. I suppose I just forgot somewhere along the way. I never expected, after I lost Angela and Noah..." His voice broke and he stopped.

Michael had lost his wife and son in a car accident several years previously. I didn't know the details, other than that they'd been struck by a truck driver on I-10. In spite of our argument, I longed to comfort him. I reached out to touch his arm.

He gave his head a quick shake. "I don't understand you, Jessie. We act as if we're in a relationship—*you* act as if we're in a relationship. What am I supposed to think?"

He stood and leaned against the rail, his back to me. "Look, Jessie," he said again, a nervous verbal tic, I realized, "it's obvious you've been through some sort of trauma. You don't want to talk about it, and that's fine. It's also obvious that it still affects you. I'm willing to help you through it in any way I can, if help is what you want."

He turned to face me. "But one thing you need to understand is that while I'm a patient man, I'm not a martyr. I'd love for us to move forward, but if moving forward isn't something you're ever going to want, I will eventually need to move on, for my own sake. You're right, you *have* made it clear from the beginning that you don't want a relationship, but if you'll remember, I've made it clear that I *do*. If we aren't going to be exclusive, we need to be very clear about that so that there are no misunderstandings and hurt feelings along the way."

I certainly had no right to expect anything else. I *did* enjoy Michael. I cared for him, more than I liked to admit. I was also very aware of his eligible bachelor status; he'd certainly have no problem finding dates. His goal was to find an exclusive, long term relationship and there were hundreds, if not thousands, of women in L.A. with the same goal. I wasn't thrilled at that thought, but I was not willing to commit to a relationship.

It wasn't that I wanted to see other people; I didn't. It was that I was too old, and too tired of the whole scene, to go through it again, much less to put anyone else through it. It hadn't been fair to my first husband and it wouldn't be fair to Michael. Michael was a good man; he deserved better. I was carrying around enough baggage to crush a man, and I didn't want to do that to him.

"Fair enough," I responded. "We'll see each other and remain free to see anyone else we choose as well. No misunderstandings, no hurt feelings. And this isn't awkward at all."

Michael laughed at my sarcasm, clearing the air. "Well, we need to move past the awkward phase quickly, because John is headed this way." He nodded towards John, who was slowly plodding his way back to us.

"It's safe," He called out when John hesitated. "She put me in my place nicely, and our non-relationship will continue as previously scheduled."

I couldn't help but smile, partly at Michael's humor, and partly because I was relieved that for now at least, it appeared we would be able to continue seeing each other in spite of my hang-ups. It wouldn't last forever; I knew that. Eventually Michael would find someone wonderful, someone without my history who would be thrilled to commit to a relationship. But until then, I'd enjoy him while it lasted.

"Ah, then," John said, joining us and sitting down next to me. "It's good to see Jessie remains the same emotionally stunted yet fantastically beautiful woman we've all grown to know and love." I smacked him in the chest and we all looked up at the sound of the Lodge door opening. Corinne stood chatting with staff before making her way carefully down the steps, art supply bags swinging on her arm.

"Hello there, children," she called out. "Have you had a nice visit?"

"Magnificent," John answered. "We've witnessed the rise and fall and rise again of the non-relationship of Jessie McIntosh and Michael Bell."

Corinne made a face. "John, you grew into such a silly man, but I love you. You stay out of Jessie's business. She's a grown woman. I'm sure she'll come to her senses soon enough." She gripped the railing and pulled herself up the gazebo step. "Jessie, when are you flyin' out?"

"Friday afternoon, after the children are all discharged."

"Stop by for a bite to eat before you go, won't you? You kids can visit before you leave."

I smiled. We kids all lived in the same city and would undoubtedly reconnect shortly upon landing, but what Corinne wanted, of course, was for us to visit with her. I realized for the first time how lonely she must get, and I made a mental note to call and visit more often. It pained me to think of Corinne being lonely.

"It's a date," I agreed. "In fact, if one of you guys will forward me your flight information, I'll see if I can get on the same flight."

"Will do." John bent down to hug me. I kissed Corinne on the cheek, and then Michael, too, bent down for a quick hug.

"Be careful up here, Jessie," he said. "I'm still uneasy about you."

"I'll be fine." I reassured him. I was touched at his handling of the whole situation. It couldn't have been pleasant for him, but he handled it gracefully. "How about we plan on one o'clock Friday? Does that sound about right?"

"Our flight is at seven p.m., so one o'clock will be great. We'll see you then." Michael gave my shoulders a final squeeze before they piled into the car. I waved at them as Corinne ever-so-slowly maneuvered the driveway. I couldn't imagine a life without Corinne in it, but then again, I also hadn't been able to imagine a life without Billy May, and here I was.

Chapter 17

My second night on the mountain I was even more exhausted than I had been the first, though I hadn't thought that possible. I was physically exhausted from clambering around the mountain, that's true, but even more, I was emotionally exhausted. For a woman who did her best to avoid emotions, I'd certainly been confronted with a plethora of them within a very short amount of time.

I retired early to my room to shower and change, looking forward to a quiet night of reading in bed. I'd brought a couple of books along and was looking forward to *Hidden Passages: Tales to Honor the Crones*. I wasn't familiar with Vila SpiderHawk, but a friend had recommended the book to me, describing it as a celebration of middle-aged women. I certainly thought the description fit me, and I was hoping for some words of wisdom to assist me in my journey. After the day I'd had, I needed a celebration.

Fresh from the shower, finally comfortable in my sweats, I rooted around in my suitcase in search of the book when I once again came across Billy May's trinket bag. Giving in, I picked it up. Obviously, it wasn't going to leave me alone. Switching off the overhead light I climbed into bed, clutching the pouch, and turned on the bedside lamp.

For a moment I simply held it, caressing the worn leather. When Billy May was alive, she'd kept it in an old steamer trunk at the foot of her bed. As far as I knew, the trunk was still in our old apartment above the store. I wondered who had removed the trinket pouch from it. It must have been Corinne; she was the only other person who would have known its significance.

Tilting the lampshade to better illuminate my lap, I placed a pillow across my thighs before working the stiff leather string loose and emptying the contents. Sure enough, the age-old quartz sparkled in the soft light of the lamp. The coquina shells had lost much of their vivid color, looking more than anything like the soft pastel petals from a spring bouquet of flowers. I sifted them through my fingers before realizing the bag was not empty. It crinkled in my hand.

Curious, I held it under the lamp, reaching inside to withdraw a folded piece of notebook paper, the left edge fringed from being ripped out of a composition book. Billy May's inventory book, I knew, the kind she'd used for years. *I don't trust them computers*, she'd always said. *But I do trust my own writin'*. I smiled at the memory.

Carefully, I unfolded the paper, smoothing it against the pillow in my lap. Billy May's looped handwriting greeted me, the same handwriting that had greeted me in the many long letters she had written to me during the years I'd been away. The letter in front of me was dated 8/12/09.

Dear Jessie,

It is a hot sunny day as I write this to you. The sky is blue and the flowers are blooming and everything seems right with the world. But little girl I have just come back from Dr. Hayden's office and the news is not good. I know that I am dying. The new doctor, the young one who took over when Graham passed on, is a kind man. He broke it to me as gentle as he could.

I am not hurting yet though he says I will before the end. Right now I am just going to enjoy every last minute I can starting with finally getting on that airplane to come and see you. In my heart I plan on talking to you about some things when I get there but in my mind I am afraid I might not be able to do it. I have wanted to talk to you about these things many times but I never seem to know where to start. After all these years of not talking it is near about impossible to begin. I am writing it down for you in case I cannot bring myself to speak the words.

You know that your stepdaddy was hurting people long before you came along and you know that I was one of them people. Him and his friends attacked me that night when I was a girl. You know these things.

What you do not know is what made them come after me in the first place. I never told you that part. Corinne and me, we been friends for our whole lives. You know that too. But Jessie what I have felt for Corinne is different from the love you feel for a sister or a friend. Now days, people on the TV talk about it all the time, but back in them days feeling a love like that for another woman was just not done.

Them boys that attacked me seen me hugging Corinne. That was all I done, but they could tell how we was feeling. That is why they come after me the way they did.

I stayed away from Corinne after that. That night when she showed up at the cabin was the first time I had visited with her in thirty years. We both felt the same old things that night but we put it away. We did not want anybody to be hurt by us.

Time went on and you all grew up. John Paul passed on. After a while there was nobody left for us to hurt with our feelings. That is what I am trying to tell you. Corinne and me, we can feel these things without hurting anybody now. I have wanted you to know about this part of my life but I have had a hard time finding the right words to tell you. I hope I can find the right words the next time I see you but if I can't at least you will have this letter.

Love for always and ever.

Billy May

I set the letter down and removed my glasses, wiping away tears. As insignificant as it may seem, I was hugely relieved that Billy May had wanted to share that part of her life with me. The gaping chasm I'd felt since John's revelation at the funeral finally closed. She had trusted me. She had wanted to tell me. Knowing her as I had, I now understood her inability to tell me.

I was also profoundly saddened to realize the deprivation Billy May had gone through the majority of her life. How lonely she must have been, not only during the years she lived on the mountain but afterwards as well. Surrounded by friends, taking on the role of mother to a damaged child, Billy May had nevertheless been alone in the most profound of ways. *You brought back the good years for her.* I remembered Mr. Lane's words from my first morning back in Cedar Hollow. I hoped with all my heart he was right.

I gently folded the letter and placed it back in the pouch, along with the stones and shells. As much as I wanted to curl into the soft linens of the bed, I knew sleep would elude me. I tucked the pouch back into my suitcase and changed into a fresh pair of jeans, retrieving my boots from under the bed. Maybe a walk in the cool night air would clear my head.

All was quiet in the Lodge and I wondered briefly where the children were. It was barely seven p.m., too early for them to have gone to bed for the night. Glancing across the common area and down the north wing I caught a glimpse of Sarah, one of the night staff, sitting in the open staff office at the end of the hall. She was bent over an open chart, pen busily flying. I thought of asking her where everyone had gone but I didn't want to interrupt her work. Instead, I quietly withdrew and headed back through the common area towards the front door. I patted the pocket of my jeans to assure myself I had the key and let myself quietly outside, locking the door behind me. As I had hoped, the night was cold and clear, and I inhaled deeply, grateful for the fresh air.

The night world was calm, the leaves rustling in the gentle breeze the only sound as I stepped into the courtyard.

I had no particular destination in mind, though having grown up in those mountains I knew better than to walk the forest trail alone at night. Instead, I turned towards the gazebo, thinking a brisk walk down the driveway would do me some good.

No sooner had I made my decision than I heard soft voices floating on the wind. Following the sounds around to the back of the Lodge, I made out the shadowy figures of the children, gathered around Bryan, the other night staff. Moving closer, I saw that he'd set up a telescope.

Sensing my presence he stopped speaking and turned in my direction. "It's me," I called out, not wishing to startle the children. "I thought a nighttime walk would be the perfect way to end the day, but it looks like you guys had an even better idea."

"Come and join us," he called back, and the children echoed the invitation.

As I got closer I could see that Stacey was positioned for the next look through the scope. "What do you see?" I asked. My question was met with a volley of excited voices.

"The Big Dipper!"

"The Bear!"

"Orion's pants!"

"That's not his pants, silly, it's his belt!"

"Same thing!"

"It is not!"

"Stacey," Bryan cut through the voices. "Why don't you show Ms. McIntosh what you were looking at."

Stacey beamed, her glasses glinting in the moonlight, and I stepped over to kneel down at her side while Bryan adjusted the scope. "Perfect!" She called out when he had it just right.

"It's the moon," she said shyly, and sure enough it was, the craters and mountains clearly visible through the lens. "I never saw the moon like that before."

Melinda Clayton

"What do you think of it?" I pulled away from the scope to read her expression. She giggled.

"It's weird! It's got holes in it."

I moved aside as Bryan helped the rest of the children line up for a look. Feeling movement by my side, I looked down to see Robby, his hand outstretched. I was pleased to see him; something about the little boy touched me.

Because I'd always known I couldn't have children, I'd never allowed myself to think about how my life might be different if I had. But seeing Robby's trusting face looking up at me, knowing his circumstances, I couldn't fathom the choices his mother had made. I didn't want to judge her; I knew from my own experience that life sometimes knocks us in a direction we hadn't anticipated. But how could she have abandoned this little boy? She'd forfeited such a treasure, one I would have given anything to have.

"How are you tonight, Robby?"

"I'm good, but I found this," he said in a rush. I struggled to comprehend. It was vitally important to me that I understand his words, not because I worried what he would say, but because he deserved that, and so much more. "It's yours," he said. "I found it at dinner. I got it back for you."

I held out my hand and he placed a toothbrush into my outstretched fingers.

"It's green. I know it's yours because it looks like the one we got last night." He hesitated, and I knew he was working to form the sounds correctly. "It fell out of Mrs. Huffman's apron pocket when she bent down to pick up Marcus' food. I don't know why she had your toothbrush." He looked at me expectantly.

Startled, I closed my hand around the brush. "I don't know either, Robby, but thank you for bringing it back to me."

"You're welcome," he said, before stepping up to take his turn at the moon.

100

Chapter 18

I hated to leave the beautiful night and the excited children behind, but I wanted to get back to my room and have a look at the toothbrush Robby had handed me. I was certain it wasn't the one he'd helped me pick out. I had used that one just after my shower earlier in the evening, and Robby said Mrs. Huffman dropped this one from her pocket during dinner.

All of which meant either by some coincidence Mrs. Huffman was carrying around a toothbrush that looked like mine, or I hadn't forgotten mine at home after all. My open bedroom door of the previous night suddenly seemed more significant, the memory of my toiletry bag on the bathroom counter. I had assumed it was untouched simply because everything appeared to be in its place.

I waved goodnight to the children and walked quickly back to the Lodge, my head spinning. Sarah was still hard at work at the desk down the children's wing, and on impulse I turned left, towards her office, sorry to disturb her but needing to speak with her. She looked up as I approached.

"Good evening, Ms. McIntosh. You must have found the kids outside stargazing."

"I did. It's a beautiful night for it." I gestured towards the stack of file folders on her desk. "You're working hard."

"Always." She made a wry face. "The paperwork is never done. Can I help you with anything?"

"I'm not sure." I'd acted so quickly I hadn't had time to formulate exactly what it was I wanted to ask her. I remembered hearing Bryan speaking with Robby when I headed for my room the night before, but I hadn't heard Sarah. That seemed as good a place to start as any.

"Do you and Bryan always divide responsibilities?" I asked. "I know it's an odd question, but I'm asking because I wondered if while he was running group last night you might have noticed something."

"We do," she confirmed. "Bryan hates charting, so I do that while he runs evening group."

"So you were here last night, then, at about this time?"

"I was." She looked concerned. "Is anything wrong?"

I hurried to reassure her. "No, not at all. I just wondered if you happened to see Mr. Huffman enter my room sometime during evening group."

She shook her head. "I didn't notice anything, but I get pretty caught up in my work. It's certainly possible he went in without me seeing." She looked at me curiously. "Why do you ask?"

"It's nothing, really." I didn't want to raise any suspicions. "It's just that I was sure I'd locked my door before dinner, but it was open when I returned. I'm probably paranoid, having lived in L.A. for so many years."

Her expression cleared. "No need to worry here. We're still remote enough to be fairly safe. Besides, the Lodge stays locked from the outside. If Mr. Huffman did enter your room, I'm sure it was to leave towels or linens or something. The poor man never takes a break, he or his wife. I don't know what we'd do without them."

"I'm sure you're right. I'd forgotten how peaceful the mountain is." I turned to leave. "Sorry to have disturbed you."

"No problem." She bent back over her work. "Let me know if you need anything."

"Will do, thanks." As I walked down the hall on the way to my room I noticed Mr. and Mrs. Huffman's light was on, glowing softly under their door. I could hear voices, low and insistent, but I couldn't make out the words. I've always been an assertive person, and I was tempted to knock, but what could I say? "Excuse me, but did you break into my room and steal my toothbrush last night?" Instead, I unlocked my door and stepped inside, turning on the overhead and locking the door behind me.

It was mine, all right, complete with my dentist's name and phone number stamped into the handle. My travel toothbrush, a freebie I'd gotten at my last cleaning. But why in the world would the Huffmans have wanted it? As I stood pondering that question, my cell rang. I fished it from the pocket of my jeans. John.

"Hello, gorgeous. How's life on the range?" His voice was a welcome link to reality.

"In the words of Stacey, weird."

"I won't ask who Stacey is because you probably can't tell me anyway, but what's happening, sweetie? You sound stressed. More stressed than usual, I mean."

I filled him in on the latest strangeness and to his credit he let me finish before saying, "Honey, why in the world would somebody steal your toothbrush? I mean, I'll be the first to say you have lovely teeth and your dental hygiene is exceptional, but really, don't you think it's possible you lost it somewhere along the way and the sweet old lady picked it up with the intention of returning it to you?"

"I don't think so, John. I didn't realize it was gone until I showered last night. Up until then, I hadn't unpacked anything. There's no way it could have fallen out or been misplaced."

"I still think you're jumping to conclusions," he said. "I don't mean to ridicule you, honey, you know that, but there could be a perfectly innocent explanation. After all, what is she going to do? Stab you to death with your own toothbrush?"

I smiled. Typical John.

"Sweetie," he continued, "I think the fresh mountain air might be getting to you. After all, you've grown used to smog. Your brain probably needs it in order to function properly."

Leave it to John to ground me with humor. He was right; I was freaking out over a toothbrush. I laughed.

"You do have a way with words. And you're probably right. This whole situation is so surreal; I'm off balance with it." I changed the topic. "So what are you guys up to tonight?"

John chuckled. "Mom and Michael are playing board games. They've quickly become best friends, I fear. He even let her win at Scrabble. *Scrabble*, Jessie! You know how awful she is at Scrabble! Seriously, though, he's a good guy. Much better than your usual type. I like him."

"Sorry, John, but he's straight. And I think Steve might disapprove."

"Very funny, Jessie. You know what I mean. What's that old song? Maybe it's time to come down from your fences, honey. What would Billy May say?"

"That's unfair, John, and you know it." I was irritated with him for that. It was way below the belt, and he did know it.

"Of course I know it. But what would she say?"

I blew out a frustrated breath. "Point taken. But Billy May isn't here, is she?"

"Jessie." John's voice grew serious. "It's time to make some changes, honey. You have years and years ahead of you. Let's see if you can make them happy ones."

I gritted my teeth. I loved John but he was pushing it, and he knew that, too. "But enough about me," I said, exasperated. "Let's talk about you."

John laughed. "Okay, honey, I'll drop it for now. Oh, I almost forgot. We went to the diner tonight for some of that famous key lime pie. Kay was there. She mentioned that Virgil hasn't come in for the last couple of days, said that's very unusual for him. No one else seemed to know where he'd gone to, either, so you make sure everything is locked up tight tonight. Until we get to the bottom of this thing, you need to be careful."

"No worries, John. I hear the kids coming in now, which means we're locked up for the night. I'll give you a call tomorrow."

"You should come to town tomorrow. We'll have lunch, and we can visit with the Sheriff if that'll make you feel any better."

I liked that idea. "I'll call you in the morning and we'll make plans."

We signed off, and finally, at the end of a very long and exhausting day, I climbed into bed, covered my head with a pillow, and wept.

Chapter 19

Let's see if you can make them happy ones, John had said, as if it were that simple. I was angry with him for that. It wasn't as if I hadn't tried. I'd spent the better part of my twenties modeling myself after my old college roommate, one of the happiest people I'd ever met, but it hadn't worked. In spite of my best efforts, I'd never been able to banish the darkness that lurked at the edges of my vision, waiting for the chance to pull me under.

My roommate's name was Tiffany, a fitting name for such a lighthearted young woman. Prior to meeting her, I'd recognized I wasn't a bubbly sort of girl. I wasn't the type of girl who whispered and giggled over boys or pinup posters. I was a serious child and an even more serious adult.

After meeting Tiffany, I understood that it was more than seriousness that plagued me; there was a darkness within me that I couldn't define. It's difficult to recount accurately the moments in time that shape our futures. We don't necessarily know that the nuances of a certain moment can influence us forever, but that's how it was with Tiffany. She influences me to this day; I continue to envy her lightness.

Billy May was fifty years old when I enrolled at Marshall. Until that time, she had never visited Huntington. I know that sounds crazy now, but I'd be willing to bet there are still old-timers up in those mountains who have never set foot in a city. In some places, the world moves on. In some, it simply doesn't. Is that a good thing, or a bad thing? I don't know. I only know that it's true.

The day I moved in I was a bundle of nerves. I was a hillbilly from a town of less than two-hundred. I was book-smart, but I didn't know anything about the world. Upon reflection, I suppose that isn't entirely true. In some ways, I knew more than anyone about the world. After all, how many just-turned-thirteen year olds know what it is to lose a baby, particularly one sired by one's stepfather? I was wise, and yet I wasn't.

We didn't own a car; everything we'd needed was within walking distance. The day I moved into the dorm, Raymond O'Brien drove us in his rattling blue Ford pickup truck. More than once I doubted we'd make it there before the tired old truck called it quits, but we did, backfiring and sputtering our way towards the school in spite of the plumes of oily exhaust trailing behind us.

We were awed by the sights and sounds around us, Billy May and I, but not Raymond. He'd been to Marshall several times with his daughter Isabelle, helping her just as he was helping me. Most recently, he and June had visited Marshall to pack up Isabelle's things and haul them home for the last time. She had dropped out the semester before, disappearing alongside a history major with an insatiable appetite for weed. By the time I entered Marshall that fall of 1981, Isabelle and her history major had headed to New York City to break into modeling. At least this is what she told her heartbroken parents, and it may have been true at that time.

Isabelle was the most beautiful girl I'd ever seen, a stereotype of the sexy redhead, with brilliant red hair and porcelain skin, a tiny waist and endless legs. Boys from miles around had always come courting Isabelle. Maybe it was because of that, or maybe it was because she was the youngest of Raymond and June's children; whatever the reason, she was spoiled rotten and selfish to the core, as Billy May would have said.

Since she'd been old enough to date, with poor Raymond shooing away the endless line of boys lurking at the front door, Isabelle had made it known to anyone who'd listen that one day she'd leave West Virginia, and her family, without looking back. I don't think Raymond took her seriously back then, chalking it up to adolescent angst, but Isabelle had been quite serious, as we were all to learn later. I'm sure Robby knew that better than anyone.

It must have been difficult for Raymond to drive Billy May and me to Marshall that sunny fall morning, but if it was, he didn't show it. He busied himself carrying my boxes in, imparting advice, sharing any helpful information with me he could. *If you work in the cafeteria, you can get discounted meals. You don't need to be going hungry. Isabelle said your resident advisor is the one you can take any concerns to. She's at the end of the hall.* He even toured us around campus, pointing out the buildings with which he was familiar. I made mental notes as we walked, grateful for the information.

When I was safely settled in my room, busily decorating with what little I'd brought from home, he left Billy May alone with me for our goodbyes. Billy May was not a crier, but her eyes were moist that day. We didn't say much; there wasn't much we hadn't already said, but when she hugged me she held on longer and tighter than usual before patting my cheek and letting herself quietly out the door.

It was right after Billy May left that I first met Tiffany. I admired her at first sight; everyone did. It was impossible not to admire Tiffany. Unpretentious, charmingly *real*, Tiffany had a way of taking over a room.

Just as I was tacking my last poster to the wall, cursing at the cheap tacks that kept impaling my thumbs, she came bursting through the door, talking a mile a minute. "Oh *there* you are! I wondered when you'd show up. I hope you don't mind I took the bed by the window. Look at that adorable quilt! You have such cute things." She wrestled with a box full of paraphernalia, dragging it through the door and across the room as she spoke. I left the job of fluffing my pillows to help her maneuver the box to her side of the room.

"I'm Tiffany," she continued with barely a pause. "What's your name?"

"Jessie," I managed to interject, taking in her mussed blonde curls and Polo shirt before she was off again, breathless from fighting with the huge carton.

"I got in this morning. My mom *finally* left after taking me out for lunch. Thank goodness! I didn't think she'd ever leave. We're going to have so much fun this year, Jessie! Are you as excited as I am?"

I *was* excited, probably even as excited as Tiffany. Her exuberance caused me to wonder why I was so reluctant to show it. "I am," I said, and I truly meant it.

We were opposites in many ways. Tiffany was petite and blonde; I was tall and dark. She was chatty and vivacious; I was quiet and reserved. She loved meeting new people and making friends; I was uncomfortable in crowds. It could have been disastrous, two young girls with such opposite personalities rooming together, but it wasn't.

We were close during those years, and I'm sure we still would be, if it weren't for me. Nowadays, we send Christmas cards and wish each other happy birthday on Facebook, but that's the extent of our relationship. I feel guilty about that; I really do. It's just that eternal optimism can be hard to swallow after a while, especially as one gets older and more jaded. Especially if that one is me. But back then I loved her. I suppose I still would, but being around her reminds me too much of how much I don't love myself.

"You're so grown up," she would say. "I wish I could be more like you. People respect you, but no one takes me seriously." And, "You're so together. You know exactly what you want. I'm a mess; I can't make up my mind from one day to the next."

I found it hard to believe Tiffany would want to be anything like me. I, on the other hand, didn't just want to be *like* her in those days; I wanted to *be* her. If I could have remade myself into anyone, Tiffany would have been it.

I watched her sometimes, the way she interacted with people. Tiffany brought energy into a room, a charge of atmosphere that was palpable. She had a gift for finding common ground with everyone she met. I once heard Tiffany engage in a serious conversation about farm equipment with a shy country boy from the next dorm over. I listened, in disbelief, as she debated the merits of no-till farming. She made that boy feel important without even realizing it. That's how she was.

Tiffany was most comfortable in the center of the crowd, but I could most often be found lurking in a corner, watching everything and praying no one would try to strike up a conversation with me. I lacked the ability to engage in small talk, or much of any kind of talk, for that matter. Whereas Tiffany infused energy, I felt like a black hole, as if my very existence might drain the light from those around me.

I had not acknowledged these things about myself until Tiffany. Truthfully, I don't think I'd even recognized them. Her lightness emphasized my darkness, highlighting my inadequacies. It was only after meeting Tiffany that I realized just how damaged I really was.

Don't misunderstand. It wasn't as if I'd never felt joy, never laughed aloud, never relished the moment. I had. Of course I had. It's just that, even as I did, the darkness loomed over me. Not even so much over me as under me, biding its time, waiting to engulf me. It never went away, not even on the brightest of days.

I did attempt psychotherapy, not once but twice. The first therapist outlined a meticulous treatment plan designed to encourage me to be an active participant in my own healing. She explained this to me in excruciating detail and I listened, desperate for help. We discussed my shortcomings and spent weeks devising action steps to assist me in reaching my goals. In the end, when confronted with so much paper and ink proof of my own shortcomings, I did what any rational person would do when confronted with such insurmountable odds. I quit.

The second therapist took a different track. He assured me of my inherent worth. He validated my feelings, no matter how terrible, how frighteningly horrid they were. He accepted me unconditionally, regaled me with never ending positive regard, sat in nonjudgmental acceptance of me. I quit him, too. If he couldn't see the flaws so obviously apparent within me, I didn't trust his abilities as a therapist.

It's hard to find one's way out of a circle.

My ex-husband had called me Inanna. My ex-therapists called me a veritable alphabet soup of labels, from PTSD to GAD to BPD. Names didn't matter to me, because I knew what the issue really was: darkness, pure and simple.

Sobbing into my pillow, I wondered if there could be any hope for me. This was actually an improvement over previous thinking, since previously I'd given up. Events lately, however, had made me wonder. After all, even Inanna eventually underwent a spiritual transformation that rendered her whole. Of course, that was only after her rotting corpse had hung on a hook in Hades for a while. Nothing comes free, not even for a goddess.

Chapter 20
Robby

Hi it's me Robby and I just got to look at the moon! I mean I've seen it before but not up close like that through a scope! Wow! Grandpa always said the moon was made of cheese but I know he was teasing me. It is much too big to be made out of cheese and anyway how would they get it out there in space? Ha! I hate cheese anyway.

It was fun and a little bit scary to be outside up on a mountain when it was getting dark but then they made us come in when it got really dark. Ms. Janice made us hurry up to get inside. I think she is a big scaredy baby. That's because she's a girl and girls are big scaredy babies but I'm not.

We came inside and we didn't have to do another Group because Mr. Bryan said looking at the moon and talking about it was our Group. Cool. Then he said we could have thirty minutes of Free Time to play board games or watch TV. I asked Mr. Bryan if I could write my mom a letter and he said "That's a wonderful idea, Robby." I have wonderful ideas a lot.

I don't know where my mom is right now but Mrs. Cortes said if I write my mom she will make sure my mom gets it. I used to write Grandpa letters sometimes when I didn't live with him. At first I didn't want to write him because I can't spell good but he said, "Hell, Robby, I can't spell good, either. But I sure would love to get a letter from you."

I did not tell my Grandma that Grandpa said the H word to me. He would have gotten in trouble because he was not supposed to use such language in front of the boy. I am the boy. Ha! That is what Grandma always called me. "Raymond, you shouldn't use such language in front of the boy." I miss her too but when she died I still had Grandpa. Now he died and I don't have anybody.

I hope my mom doesn't mind if my spelling is bad. I want to tell my mom about the mountain and the Lodge and Anthony and Marcus and Joseph. Especially Joseph because I want to go visit him at his house when we leave here even though he has a sister. I do NOT want to tell my mom about Stacey because my mom does not like it when I am in love with girls.

I want to tell my mom about Ms. McIntosh too. What I really want to tell her is what I heard Mr. and Mrs. Huffman say about Ms. McIntosh the other night. I don't get what the whole big stinking deal is. Like why is it a big stinking secret? Mr. Huffman told Mrs. Huffman to keep quiet and not tell anybody anything. Mrs. Huffman said she didn't see why he wouldn't tell anyone but then he got mad and said, "Opal, I am asking you to just keep quiet about it all. Is that too much to ask?"

He did not ask me to keep quiet because he did not know I heard him. I think I will tell Ms. McIntosh about it. I know that she is sad because her mom died and I think she will be happy if I tell her.

It is almost time for bed and I am really tired. I am too tired to write my mom right now. Maybe Mr. Bryan could get me some crayons. I think I will draw Ms. McIntosh a picture of the big old cheese moon instead.

Chapter 21

Thursday

I awoke late the next morning, feeling hung over. I hate that feeling, the I-cried-myself-to-sleep feeling. It's a feeling that should be reserved for people aged three or below. Pushing fifty was much too old for that feeling, but there I was, and that probably said more about my emotional state than I cared to realize.

I stumbled into the shower, keeping my eyes closed the entire time. I was too tired to open them and they were so swollen they wouldn't have opened, anyway. I showered until the hot water ran out, then stood for a while in the cold spray, hoping beyond hope that the ice cold jets would relieve my swollen eyes.

My hope was in vain. The shower over, a towel wrapping my hair, I groaned at my reflection in the mirror. Only a few short days ago I'd stood in my L.A condo regarding my reflection in the bathroom mirror and bemoaning the fact that I looked like my mother. That morning at the Lodge I would have been, if not exactly happy, at least relieved by that comparison.

Unfortunately, the reflection that greeted me looked at least five years older than the one the day before. As much as I disliked it, there was nothing to be done about it, so I dressed and headed for the cafeteria, hoping I wouldn't run into anyone along the way. My plan was to grab some coffee and yogurt and find Nora for our morning catch-up session.

I almost made it unobserved, but just as I filled a Styrofoam cup with coffee, Mrs. Huffman came through,

Melinda Clayton

wiping down the tables. Until then, we'd nodded in passing several times but hadn't had the opportunity to converse. In spite of my swollen eyes, I didn't want to miss an opportunity to get a better feel for the woman. I snapped the lid onto my cup and walked over to sit at the table she was cleaning. I had no specific plan; I'd just go where the conversation took me.

"It's a beautiful morning, isn't it? Looks like I missed the kids. Are they already on the trail?"

She didn't pause in her cleaning. "Mmm-hmm. They left about fifteen minutes ago." She glanced over at me and I noted the fatigue in her face. I tried to guess her age, settling on early sixties. Her gray hair was cropped short. She wore no makeup, no jewelry, just a cotton dress with a bold flower print, an apron tied over the front, thick support hose and sneakers on her feet. She looked like anybody's grandmother, and I felt a stab of pity for her, working so hard at an age when she should have been enjoying her retirement.

"Can I get you something?" she asked, sensing my curiosity.

I hadn't been sure how to approach the topic, but decided that was about as good an opening as I was likely to get. "Actually, maybe you can. You haven't found a toothbrush lying around anywhere, have you? Green, with the address and phone number of a dentist's office stamped into the handle?"

Did I imagine it, or was there a slight hesitation? If so, she recovered quickly, wringing out her sponge and starting on the chair seats. "No ma'am. I haven't seen a toothbrush lying around, but we have extras. Do you need me to get you one?"

"No, thanks. Robby helped me out." She was lying; she had to be. Why would Robby make up such a story?

"Oh, that's good. He's a sweet boy." She glanced at me again, did a double take. "Miss, are you okay?"

116

Damn. I sniffed, made a show of wiping my nose. "Allergies. I'm not used to it up here; it's been a long time since I've hung out in the woods the way I have this week."

"You better stop by the nurse's office on your way out, get you some medicine. Fall is one of the worst times for allergies around here. She'll hook you right up." She sloshed the sponge in the bucket of soapy water.

"I'll do that. Thanks."

She moved on to the next table, effectively ending our conversation. She hadn't been friendly, exactly, but she hadn't avoided me, either, and it was obvious she had a lot to get done before the kids returned from their hike. I had to admit the woman worked hard, regardless of my suspicions.

"I'll leave you alone and let you work," I said, standing, and she nodded at me as I left.

Nora was on the phone when I knocked and let myself into her office. I started to step back outside until she finished, but she waved me in and gestured towards the chair, rolling her eyes as she pointed to the receiver.

"You can't be serious," she was saying. "So the fact that he has a developmental disability means that any emotion he has is attributable to that? Are you *kidding* me?" She paused and I heard the faint, tinny sound of the voice on the other end.

"Oh, I understand what you're saying," Nora argued. "I just think it's ridiculous. The child is *depressed*. It isn't a part of his developmental disability. It has nothing to *do* with his disability, but you're telling me he doesn't qualify to receive mental health services because he has a developmental disability? That's outrageous!"

Another pause. "Well, I'm not finished with this. These kids fall through the cracks enough without funding streams fighting over who should pay for services." Nora slammed down the phone, slapping the desk in frustration.

"You know what I hate?" She didn't wait for an answer. "I hate it when mental health funding streams try to fit everything about a kid under a developmental disability label so they won't have to pay for services. Disability funding streams do the same in reverse, of course, but who loses out in the end? The kids do, that's who."

She leaned back in her chair, crossing her arms over her chest before noticing my face, and then, "Good Lord, what happened to you?" She sat forward, peering at me over her glasses.

I sighed. "Allergies. Mrs. Huffman already sent me to the nurse's office. I'm sure I'll be better by this afternoon."

Nora sat watching me, chewing on the inside of her cheek, eyes squinted. "Right," she finally said. "Allergies."

I hate that about therapists. It's as if they can read minds or something. It's very disconcerting, not to mention just plain creepy.

"Right," I agreed, and then quickly switched gears. "So tell me more about the Huffmans."

Nora started. "The Huffmans! Why?"

"Because I think they stole my toothbrush."

Nora raised her brows in surprise, then laughed. "Your toothbrush. Jessie, if you need a toothbrush, we have some in the supply closet, but why in the world would you think the Huffmans took yours?"

I reminded Nora about finding my door open my first night at the Lodge and filled her in on the missing toothbrush. When I got to the part about Robby returning the original to me after having seen it fall out of Mrs. Huffman's pocket, she interrupted.

"But that explains it, don't you think? Your toothbrush probably fell out of your bag and the Huffmans found it. No doubt they meant to bring you a replacement but just forgot it in the midst of everything else they're responsible for doing."

I shook my head. "Not possible. I hadn't even unzipped my bags. I set them straight down and left to join the kids on a hike, remember? Besides, I just asked Mrs.

Huffman if she's seen a toothbrush matching the description and she denied it."

"Okay." Nora rested her elbows on the chair arms and steepled her fingers. "But I'm sure there's still a logical explanation. As I said before, why on earth would they take your toothbrush?"

I shrugged. "I don't know, but I'd like to find out. I'm going into town today for lunch. I'm hoping to catch Sheriff Moore while I'm there. I'd like to know what, if any, progress he's making in the investigation.

Nora looked surprised. "Do you think that's wise? The Sheriff is liable to resent someone poking around his investigation. And the Huffmans...Jessie, I don't want to lose them. They're too valuable to this place. Before you go offending them, you need to make very, very sure you have your information right."

"Of course. Look, Nora, my goal isn't to offend anyone; my goal is to get to the bottom of things. I flew out here as a result of a string of weird happenings accompanied by a mysterious note. I have to get back to L.A. soon, but I don't want to leave until I have some idea of what's going on. Apparently someone wanted me here; I'd like to know who, and why."

"Just be careful, Jessie. I doubt you've been out in L.A. honing your investigative skills all these years. Oh, before I forget," Nora opened the top drawer of her desk, "Robby asked me to give this to you. I think it's something he drew for you last night. He's such a cute kid. He's meeting with his caseworker this morning, but he'll be back this afternoon. Ms. Cortes is having a heck of a time finding a placement for him."

"Placement? Don't tell me his mother has disappeared again." I reached out and took the folded paper from her, tucking it into the back pocket of my jeans. I'd look at it later, when I got to Corinne's. As it was, I'd slept much later than I'd intended and was in a hurry to get on the road.

119

"No, not at all. She's actually doing quite well, but it's a ninety day program. Robby will need to be in foster care until she's finished and the court approves of him going home. There's just such a shortage of good homes, especially for kids that have special needs, it's hard to find a placement."

"Poor kid. Any family would be lucky to have him. Tell him thank you for me, and I'll see him sometime this evening." Just as I stood, pulling my keys out of my pocket, the door opened and we both turned to see who it was.

I didn't know the man. He was older, heavyset—for some reason the word portly comes to mind—and tall, over six feet, filling the doorframe. He was dressed in tan work overalls, the kind mechanics often wear, the thighs stained with what looked like engine grease, and a ball cap, pulled low over long, gray hair. And he was clearly very angry.

"If you won't return my phone calls I reckon I'll just have to keep visitin' you in person. You owe me money, doc, and I'm here to get it."

Across from me, Nora sighed. "Good morning, Virgil. How nice to see you."

"Don't try any of that psychobabble shit on me." Virgil shut the door behind him and crossed over to Nora's desk, standing beside me. "Jessie Russell," he said, looking down at me. "You done got old, but I'd recognize you anywhere. Glad to see you're here, too, seein' as how you started up this place. This woman," he pointed at Nora, "is tryin' to cheat me out of my pay."

"Virgil, why don't you have a seat so we can talk about this in a civilized manner?" Nora motioned towards a chair.

"I don't need to sit; I ain't plannin' on stayin'. I just come to get my pay."

"Virgil." Nora's voice was deliberately calm; I admired her composure. "I gave you your final check on the day I let you go. It contained everything you were owed. You were only owed one week's pay at that time, remember? And that's what you received."

"I want to see them books." Virgil jabbed his forefinger towards Nora's face. "I'm gonna get me an attorney and I want to see them books. You owe me more; I know you do, and I *will* get it."

"Tell you what." Nora leaned her hands on the desk in front of her, ignoring his finger. "Let's schedule a meeting. How about Friday afternoon, after the kids are gone. Does one o'clock work for you? Bring your attorney with you, if you'd like, and I'll have Betty from finance come and go over your pay with you. Will that work?"

"Damn straight," Virgil responded. "I'll be here and y'all better be here, too." He turned and looked at me where I'd been standing speechless throughout the exchange.

"You got a crooked operation goin' on here," he said, and this time it was my face at which he pointed. "You better watch yourself. You don't want nobody diggin' around too hard in your background, do you little lady? Your stepdaddy was my friend, and he didn't just disappear; I know that much. I don't know what happened, but I know you and that Injun bitch had somethin' to do with it. You don't want to mess with me, girl; you'd better believe that." He turned and stomped out of the office, slamming the door behind him.

I stared after him, stunned by the whole incident. "And this is the man the Sheriff doesn't think is involved?" I finally managed to ask.

Nora sat down heavily in the desk chair. "He's loud and he's obnoxious, but he doesn't have a history of violence. At least, he hasn't had. But now I'm beginning to wonder. Whew!" She exhaled, whistling through her teeth. "What a morning. If you do see the Sheriff today, would you ask him to do a drive-by of the Lodge around one o'clock Friday afternoon? I don't know that I want to be isolated up here with that man."

I nodded my agreement. "I think that's a very good idea. I also think I should be involved, don't you? Since I started up this crooked operation you're running."

Nora laughed. "Absolutely, Jessie. I'd appreciate that, if it doesn't interfere with your flight."

"My flight isn't until the evening. I'll let Corinne know when I see her today that we'll have to have either a late lunch or an early dinner before I leave."

I waited until I heard the sound of Virgil's truck receding in the distance before I left Nora's office for my car.

Chapter 22

Michael was standing outside Corinne's house when I pulled into the driveway and I was surprised by how glad I was to see him. He looked more relaxed than I'd ever seen him, dressed casually in jeans and a denim jacket, his hair disheveled by the breeze. As I put the car in park, he strolled towards me, hands in his pockets. I turned off the ignition and he reached to open my door.

I stepped towards him, expecting a hug. Michael always hugged me by way of greeting, but not that day. Fallout from our discussion the day before, I assumed, and it hurt a bit, I had to admit. I had wanted to maintain some distance, had demanded it, really, and he was giving it to me, but I wasn't sure I liked it. *A woman composed solely of opposites*. Good Lord, I exhausted myself.

Michael closed the car door behind me and stepped aside, inviting me to take the lead as we strolled to a picnic table under the large elm in Corinne's backyard, our feet crunching through the leaves. "You look tired," he said, concern etched across his face. "Did something else happen?"

I shook my head. "No. Just allergies. I've gotten used to smog. All this plant life is killing me." I changed the subject. "I see you survived the night okay."

Michael laughed. "It was great, actually. I haven't played board games in years. And it was so quiet! I slept like a baby. Corinne is fantastic, isn't she?"

"She is," I agreed. "She's the closest thing to family I've got, she and John."

"That would be tough, I think." Michael squeezed my hand briefly before letting it go. "As you know, my parents are in Oklahoma. I don't see them often, but it's nice to know they're there. I suppose I take it for granted. And of course there's my sister and her children. I don't think I could have made it through that year without them." I knew he meant the year he'd lost his wife and son.

We sat across from each other and I realized this had been planned, Michael meeting me alone. Never before had I pulled into Corinne's driveway without her bustling down the steps to meet me. I didn't know the reason for it, so I waited.

"I was at work when I got the call," he said. This surprised me. Michael had never spoken in detail about his loss. "Angela had just picked Noah up at preschool. They were on I-10, headed home. There wasn't anything special about that day. Once they got home Angela would have gotten Noah a snack. She might have read him a story, and then they would have settled down together for a quick nap. A 'refresher' Angela used to call it. She would have called to ask what I wanted for dinner. I would have promised to be home on time, but I wouldn't have made it, because I never did. I meant to, but I never did."

"Michael," I started, but he held up his hand to stop me.

"It's okay. I'm not blaming myself, if that's what you're thinking. What I'm trying to say is that we had our routines, you know? We knew each other so well. I knew she'd forget to pick up Noah's milk at the corner grocery, and she knew I'd be home late. These weren't bad things. I mean, sure we'd gripe about it the way people do, but it's what we *did*. There was comfort in that fact. Does that make sense?"

I thought I understood. We take comfort from the familiar. I remembered one of my training classes when I was preparing to volunteer at the Lodge. That particular block was on behavior management. It wasn't required, but I took it anyway because it sounded interesting, and as it turned out, it was. We discussed applied behavior analysis and the ways in which behaviors are shaped.

One thing the instructor said had stayed with me. "People crave predictability. Some children will actually engage in challenging behaviors in order to receive the expected reprimand." It's reassuring, the instructor explained. It's predictable. I thought that sort of explained what Michael meant.

"You knew she'd forget to pick up the milk, and she knew you'd be annoyed. It's a part of what defined the life you created together. It's comforting to know someone so well you can predict their behaviors, even if the behaviors are annoying."

"Exactly!" Michael squeezed my hand again. "You're very wise."

I shook my head. "No wisdom here. I've just been therapized enough over the years to know the lingo."

Michael cocked his head, a quizzical expression flitting across his face before he plunged ahead. "She knew I'd never make it home on time, and I knew she'd roll her eyes when I showed up late. That's what I'm trying to explain about that day. There was nothing special about it, but *everything* was special about it because it's who we *were*.

"I loved all those little mundane pieces that made up our lives. And then it was gone. Some random truck driver decided to run a double route, amped himself up on speed, and wiped out my family, just like that."

He stopped, silent, rubbing at an imaginary spot on the grain of the picnic table. I reached out and placed my hand over his. "I'm so sorry, Michael. I can't even imagine what that must have been like for you."

He withdrew his hand, patting mine before sitting up and rubbing his jaw. "And I can't explain it, what it was like. It sounds crazy, but I don't even remember much of that first year. Thank God for my friends and family. Even now.....Jessie, that's why I'm telling you all this. I want you to know that I understand."

"What do you mean?" I wasn't sure I wanted to hear his answer.

"Yesterday, when we argued, I told you that it was obvious you'd been through some sort of trauma. I told you I'm willing to help as long as you want to move forward, but you know what, Jessie? I was a presumptuous ass. I haven't moved forward enough myself to help anyone else with the process. I'm not the same man I was before the wreck, not even close."

"You're a good man, Michael." I wanted to help him, but I had no idea what to do.

"Thank you, Jessie, I appreciate that. But after our conversation yesterday, I realized a couple of things about myself. The first thing I realized is that I hate being alone. I loved sharing my life with my little family. I loved the reality we created together. I've spent the last couple of years wanting more than anything to recreate that feeling. I'm lost without it."

"Go on," I prodded. I had a sinking feeling, fairly certain where the conversation was going.

Michael hesitated, clearly struggling to find the right words. "Since yesterday I've done a lot of thinking. I admire you, you know. Instead of diving into things, you hold yourself back. Something bad happened to you and you feel damaged. Because of that, you don't feel you can contribute to a relationship. Here I've been thinking if I could just recreate my family, I'd be whole again, but you've got it right. A relationship won't work if you aren't already whole when you enter into it."

I felt my cheeks burn at the truth of what he'd said. He knew more about me than I gave him credit for. That surprised me, but it shouldn't have. I remembered Therapist Number One telling me that depression is inherently narcissistic. I'd gotten angry at the time. I hated myself; how could I possibly be narcissistic?

"Because," she'd explained, "when you spend so much time wrapped up in your own misery, you don't notice anyone else." Maybe she'd been right after all. The thought shamed me. I hugged myself, suddenly chilly in the cool breeze.

Michael removed his jacket, handing it to me over the table. "It's a good thing, a healthy thing, holding off on a relationship until you're complete on your own. I think that's something I need to do, too. I still have some work to do. Jessie, I'm sorry for the pressure I've put on you. You were right."

"Where does this leave us, Michael?" I was suddenly terrified that he was saying goodbye for good. I'd pushed him away enough to deserve it, but my heart ached at the thought. I didn't want him to leave me; I just wanted him to not try to force me to do something I felt incapable of doing.

He must have sensed my thoughts because he reached across the table for my hand again. "You've said you want our status to remain undefined, but I'm suggesting a different definition than the one I've been pushing for. Let's take a couple of steps back and concentrate on our friendship. I'll remove my things from your condo when we get back—no more overnights—and we'll start at square one, a clearly defined friendship with no pressure. I don't think half-in and half-out has worked for either of us. It makes me expect too much and it makes you feel pressured. So let's focus on friendship. How does that sound?"

It sounded good. It sounded perfect, actually. Michael's friendship without the pressure. I liked the open-endedness of that; it gave me room to breathe. I smiled at him, and the relief must have shown on my face.

Just then, as if they'd known it was the perfect time—or, more likely, as if they'd been spying on us—Corinne and

Melinda Clayton

John made a loud show of rounding the house, arms laden with the makings of a picnic lunch.

Chapter 23
Robby

Hi. Well it's me Robby and I just had a stupid meeting with my stupid caseworker. Mrs. Jamison at church says we should not say stupid. She calls it the S word but it is not the real S word. I know that because Ernie says the real S word and it is s-h-i-t. I don't say that word but I know how to spell it because Ernie wrote it on the back of the bus seat with a black magic marker. Ernie is a big bully on the bus and he makes fun of me but I don't care because he is stupid. Ha! I said it again.

Mrs. Cortes has not found a place for me to go yet. She said for now she'll have to pick me up tomorrow and take me back to the family that has too many kids already but I can't live there for long. She said she'll keep looking for a family that I can stay with until my mom is ready to come home. I hate all this stupid moving around. I wish I could just live here at the Lodge forever. The people are nice and there are lots of things to do and I have friends here and nobody is a big stupid bully like big stupid Ernie on the big stupid school bus. Ha! I said a lot of stupids! Ha ha!

Mrs. Cortes took me back to the Lodge in time for lunch and then she went to see Dr. Wright. She said she had to check in with Dr. Wright but I know she went there to talk about me because that is what Grownups do. They tell you something stupid (ha!) but then they go and talk about you with other Grownups and try to Come Up With A Plan. I hope they Come Up With A Plan soon because I have to leave here tomorrow.

Stacey was glad to see me when I got back and so was Joseph and so was Anthony. Marcus looked glad to see me too but Marcus looks glad to see everybody. That is one good thing about Marcus. He always makes you happy because he always looks glad to see you.

Then Mr. Paul and Ms. Janice took us out to the horses and it was so cool! I love it here and I don't see why I can't live here instead of going to some stupid Foster Home where I can't even stay. That's just stupid.

Chapter 24

Over lunch we decided to visit with Kay, down at Peggy's diner. "Kay knows everythin' goin' on in this town," Corinne remarked as we helped clean up the kitchen. "And the Sheriff is there every day, too, round about two o'clock. That's the place to find him, if you're lookin'. He stops in for a cup of coffee before the end of his shift."

We agreed to walk, John, Michael and I, partly to exercise off the ham and cheese we'd had for lunch, partly because it was such a beautiful fall day.

"I believe I'll stay here," Corinne had said. "It's time for my nap. Jessie, will you be joinin' us for supper?"

"I can't today. I left word for Robby, Raymond's grandson, that I'd see him this evening, but that reminds me." I told them about the meeting scheduled with Virgil for Friday afternoon. "I won't be able to get here until sometime after two, probably more like two-thirty, so you'll have to have lunch without me."

"Well, now," Corinne said. "I'm glad you've taken an interest in Raymond's grandbaby. He's a cutie, ain't he? Poor little thing. Boys," she addressed John and Michael, "here's what we'll do. We'll have brunch around eleven and then I'll fix an early supper for all of us, around three, so I can feed y'all and let you get to the airport in time. Jessie, if you're goin' to be later than two-thirty give me a call and let me know. Now let me go get my rest before I get cranky."

I hugged Corinne goodbye and we left for town, walking along the side of the gravel road. I was tempted to reach for Michael's hand; we always held hands as we walked. But I didn't. I liked the idea of building our friendship; that was a new concept for me and I agreed with it completely. I'd never done that before. Since my divorce, I'd never stuck around long enough to care. It was the right way to go, and after that who knew what could happen? But I missed him, too. Instead of reaching for him I shoved my hands into my back pockets, and that's when I remembered Robby's drawing. I pulled it out for a look.

"What have you got there? Love notes from all the boys?" Michael teased me.

"I do, actually. From Robby. Nora gave it to me this morning and I forgot about it until now." I unfolded it, holding tight to the paper in the strong breeze, and held it out for all of us to see. I smiled at the huge yellow-white moon, resembling nothing so much as a big round slice of Swiss cheese, complete with holes. At the bottom of the page were three figures. I pushed my hair out of my face for a closer look.

"It's you, Jessie!" John laughed. "Look at that! It's your ponytail, and your plaid jacket." He was right. Robby's childish scrawl had captured me perfectly. But who was on either side of me, gazing at that huge moon?

Michael pulled the paper closer, squinting in the bright sun. "He drew your parents. See?"

On my right was the figure of a woman. Her short hair had been colored gray with crayon. She was dressed in a brightly flowered dress, an apron over the front, sneakers on her feet. The laces had been drawn in careful detail, neatly x-ing up the front and tied with a huge bow. Underneath, Robby had written the word *Mom*.

On my left, the tall figure of a man. His hair was also gray. Robby had colored the upper portion of his body red, as if he wore a red shirt or jacket. His bottom half was colored light brown. In the man's hand was what appeared to be a claw hammer, the claws disproportionately long. Underneath that figure, Robby had written the word *Dad*. At the very bottom of the picture, in all capital letters, Robby had written the words *YUR FAMLEY*. What was this?

"It's the Huffmans," I said.

"The Huffmans," John repeated. "You mean the groundskeeper and his wife? The ones with your toothbrush?"

I felt a chill. I had always had a feeling of discomfort around them, and now this. "It's them, John. I know you think I'm crazy, but that's them. That's exactly what they look like, down to the sneakers and the red jacket." I felt my voice rising, and I was comforted when Michael placed a hand on my shoulder.

"Robby knows my mother passed away. We talked about it, about how Billy May and his grandfather were such good friends. Why would he draw this? Why would he draw them as my parents?"

"Jessie, think about what you just said." John pulled me over to sit on the bench outside Peggy's Diner. "Billy May passed away, and Billy May was like a mother to you, but your birth mother may very well still be alive."

Michael sat on my other side. "John, are you thinking Robby knows something about the Huffmans that he's trying to tell Jessie? Do you think it's possible...?"

Michael didn't finish his question, but he didn't have to. I pictured Mrs. Huffman in my mind's eye. Fatigued, early sixties, short gray hair, trim build. *Was* it possible? Aside from the constant weariness, she looked nothing like the bleached blonde woman I remembered from my childhood, but so many years had passed. I couldn't fathom it; I didn't even want to consider it.

If it was her, what did she want from me? Money? I'd gladly give it all if it would keep her away from me. I wanted nothing to do with her, the woman who had left me to Roy. Surely she had known what he would do to me. She had to have known.

"I think it's possible, but I think we need to take a collective breath and calm down for a minute." John rubbed the back of my neck. "First of all, how would Robby know something like that?"

I shook my head. "I don't know. I have no idea. Maybe Raymond knew something?" I felt dizzy. "This is all too much."

Michael stood, pulling me to my feet. "Let's go inside. We'll get you something to drink and sort through this thing." I leaned against him gratefully as he led me through the door.

"Jessie! And John! Y'all come on over here and say hello!" I looked towards the voice and saw Darryl Lane and his son, Dennis, having a late lunch, accompanied by Eugene Cooper, another old friend of Billy May's. Eugene stood, grasping a walker for support. That was new. He hadn't needed the assistance of a walker the last time I'd seen him, at Billy May's funeral. That day he'd managed to climb all the way to the top of the bell tower unassisted.

Glad for the distraction, I followed John and Michael to their table. "Mr. Cooper, it's so good to see you. What in the world happened?" I pointed to his knee, which was enveloped by a cumbersome looking brace.

"Aw, I fell. Just getting' old, I reckon. Twisted it, is all. I'll be good as new in no time." He let go of the walker to give me a hug. "How've you been, little girl? I heard you was back in town. Got a little jealous when you stopped in to see Darryl but didn't come to see me."

"Now, Mr. Cooper, you know I love you both equally." I returned the hug, alarmed at the boniness of him.

"Pull up a chair and join us." Dennis stood to shake Michael's hand, reminding me of my manners.

"I'm sorry," I said. "This is Michael Bell, a friend of mine from L.A. Michael, these men are what pass for my family around here. Mr. Eugene Cooper, Mr. Darryl Lane, and his son, Dennis."

"A man friend, eh? We'll it's about time. You ain't gettin' any younger, you know." Darryl winked at Michael and to my embarrassment, I felt myself blush.

"I'm glad we ran into you, Jessie." Dennis helped Mr. Cooper back into the chair and set his walker aside. "Wanted to let you know that Virgil Young has been running his mouth off all over town."

"So I've heard." I waved at Kay, behind the counter. "He showed up at the Lodge this morning, demanding more money. Nora insists he's been paid, but he doesn't seem to think it's enough. He said he'd come back with his lawyer Friday afternoon to go over the books."

Darryl set his cup into the saucer, sloshing coffee over the side. "He ain't always been so mouthy. Trouble is, his wife took sick. Word is she got the cancer. He's stretched thin for money. Took on a fulltime job down at the garage, is what I hear, fixin' cars. But you know he's gettin' old for that kind of work. It's hard on the body, especially fulltime at his age. Don't see him in here no more. Reckon he's too busy."

Eugene nodded. "He wasn't never a particularly nice man, but he wasn't a mean one, neither. There was a lot worse." He peered at me from under bushy brows. "He was just one you knew you didn't want to get on the wrong side of. Reckon his wife takin' ill has brought out the worst in him."

"I'm sorry to hear about his wife," I said, and I was. "I'm not sure what to make of him, though. He definitely didn't show his good side this morning." I did feel bad for him, and I was glad the men had shared that information with me. It at least provided a possible explanation for his behavior.

Dennis removed his wallet from his back pocket and counted out money to pay their bill. "No, he hasn't been showing a good side recently, that's for sure," he said. "I've got my eye on him, Jessie, but I don't think he'll bother you. He's a lot of talk. Piss and vinegar, as they say, but I doubt

135

he's got the time or the energy right now to do much more than talk."

He replaced his wallet. "Ladies and gentlemen, I've got to get back to work. You take care, Jessie. Nice to meet you, Michael, and always good to see you, John. Give your mother my best."

We stood to tell them goodbye. I gave Dennis a quick hug. "Thanks for keeping an eye on him. You have my cell number if you need to reach me."

"I do," he assured me. "It's programmed in. And I'll call if I hear anything you need to worry about."

We settled ourselves back around the table as Kay came over with some menus. "John, Jessie, I wondered when you'd stop by. And who's the handsome young man?"

"Kay Langley, meet Michael Bell," I introduced them. "He's a friend of mine from L.A." Michael stood to shake Kay's hand.

"Nice to meet you, Michael. Any friend of Jessie's is a friend of ours. What can I get you folks?" Kay stood with pen poised over her order pad.

"What we'd really like is your time, if that's possible, Kay. Mom fed us enough lunch to last a week. If we promise to come back for dinner, can we borrow you for a minute?" John stood and pulled out a chair.

"I got a minute, sure. It'd be good to get off these poor old feet of mine for a bit. Riva!" She yelled over to the bar. "Bring all of us a coke, would you? Now," she settled herself in a chair with a grateful sigh and stretched her feet in front of her, "what can I do for you?"

"Kay," I began, "you're about the age my mother would be, aren't you?"

She looked at me curiously. "I don't reckon you mean Billy May, though she's the one I always thought of as your mother. You mean Lindy, of course." She smoothed her apron over her lap and we waited while Riva set our drinks in front of us.

When Riva left, Kay continued. "We were about the same age, but I didn't know her very well. Roy kept her up there on that mountain, you know. She wasn't never allowed to come in the diner or nothin' like that. Saw her in Mr. Smith's store every now and then. Pretty woman, but worn down lookin'. Unhappy, of course, but who wouldn't have been? Momma always felt sorry for her, said Roy was mean as a snake, which he was. Why do you ask, honey?"

Instead of answering her question right away, I asked another. "Do you know the Huffmans, Richard and Opal, working up at the Lodge? He's the groundskeeper and she does housekeeping."

"I do. Nice enough couple. Come in on the weekends, after the children have gone home. Kind of keep to themselves, sit back in the corner booth there. I always thought it was kind of sweet, like a date night for 'em, you know? Now I'll say it again; why do you ask?"

"I promise I'll explain it all in a minute, but one more question first." I glanced at John, seeking reassurance. He nodded for me to continue as Michael sat quietly. I wondered how much about my past Michael had figured out at this point. Probably most of it. I turned back to Kay. "Does Opal look like my mother to you? Does she look like Lindy might now, after all these years?"

That got Kay's attention. "Pshaw. Uh-uh. No. Not at all. Not even a tiny little bit. She's a whole lot shorter, for one thing. Totally different lookin' woman. What in the world would give you that idea?"

Michael handed me the picture Robby had drawn and I spread it on the table in front of Kay. "Robby O'Brien drew this for me. He drew the Huffmans and labeled them as my parents, see? I've had the feeling they've been watching me since I got to the Lodge, and I'm pretty sure they were in my room while I was out. They took my toothbrush. I know how crazy this all sounds. I can't make sense of it, either. Why would Robby have drawn this?"

Kay pulled the picture closer. "Robby drew this, huh? How is my little sweetheart? I wondered where he'd been. I miss him and Raymond comin' in. Used to come in every Wednesday. You tell him Ms. Kay said she misses him and he needs to come by and see me. I'll have a milkshake waitin'."

She adjusted her glasses and held the paper up to the light. "He did a good job, didn't he? That does look like 'em. But honey I don't know why he thinks they're your parents. Opal ain't the same woman as Lindy, I can promise you that, even after all these years."

"You're sure?"

"Without a doubt."

"Kay, do you know where my mother ended up? Where did she go?" I wasn't sure why I'd asked, other than that I hoped it was far away from anywhere I was likely to be.

"Honey, I don't know as any of us knew for sure where she left to, but you remember she run off with that railroad man. Rumor was they was goin' to Arizona, but I don't know if it was true. Far as I know, no one around here ever heard from her again." She hoisted herself to her feet with a groan.

"Now let me get back to work before Andrew comes lookin' for me," she said. "Give him the diner and all of a sudden he thinks he runs the place." She smiled fondly at the mention of her son.

"Is the Sheriff coming by today, Kay?" John asked.

"If he don't, it'll be the first time in a decade that he didn't. Should be here within the next ten minutes or so. You want me to send him over?"

"Please," John answered. "If you don't mind."

"I don't mind, honey." Kay straightened her apron and replaced the chair. "Y'all are a regular group of sleuths, ain't you? When y'all find out the answers to everythin', I'll be lookin' forward to hearin' 'em." She patted John on the head before returning to the kitchen.

She'd no sooner disappeared through the double doors than Sheriff Moore's cruiser pulled into the lot.

Chapter 25

I had never met Sheriff Moore before, and he looked nothing like I'd pictured him. Maybe I'd come to expect small town sheriffs to look like Officer Wimbley, the out of shape, befuddled deputy that had patrolled Cedar Hollow throughout my childhood. At any rate, Sheriff Moore looked anything but out of shape or befuddled.

The man was huge, well over six feet, and clearly a fan of the gym. His biceps strained at the hems in the sleeves of his uniform and the buttons of his shirt were clearly stressed against the bulk of his chest. His hair was buzzed short in a flattop, his face square. Even his jaw muscles were pronounced. As Kay directed him to our table, we slid our chairs closer together to give him more room. Vaguely, I wondered if his thigh muscles would fit under the table.

"Nice," John murmured, "very nice." I punched him on the leg while Michael stifled a chuckle beside me. "Behave, John. We have work to do." I shot him a warning glare.

Sheriff Moore crossed the room in three strides and pulled out a chair. "Kay says you folks wanted to see me. What can I do for you?"

His voice was deep and pleasant, also not what I'd expected, and his eyes were a piercing blue. I'd pegged him as a backwards sort, someone who blamed fires on little boys with an autistic disorder. Someone who couldn't be bothered with conducting a thorough investigation into the frightening incidents at a retreat for children with disabilities. I found his appearance at odds with my preconceived ideas, but appearances could be deceiving.

I held out my hand. "Sheriff Moore, I'm Jessica McIntosh."

His hand engulfed mine. "Pleased to meet you, Ms. McIntosh. How can I help you?"

I was a little surprised he didn't react to my name, but I continued. "I'm the owner of the mountain the Platte Lodge for Children is housed on. You're investigating the fire that occurred there."

Sheriff Moore remained expressionless. "And?" he prompted.

I was taken aback by his low keyed response. "And I'd like to know what progress you've made. Nora tells me you've pretty much written Virgil Young off as a suspect. I understand he has alibis for the day the office was trashed and the day the fire was set, but have you checked his alibi for the day the horses were let go? Or the day the chemicals were spilled? I'm assuming you've at least checked for fingerprints in all those places. He's a very angry man, Sheriff. Isn't it possible he had an accomplice?"

Sheriff Moore regarded me evenly. "Ms. McIntosh, with all due respect, I'm not at liberty to discuss the specifics with you. I'm sure you understand. We're in the middle of an investigation. Why don't you just tell me your concerns." His face remained impassive, his voice pleasant.

I felt my anger rise. "My *concern* is that all these things have happened in a matter of a few weeks. You've had ample time to check for fingerprints and follow up on leads, but you don't seem to have done those things. How dare you try to pin these things on an eleven year old boy with autism? Nora told me what you said. You should be ashamed." Beside me, Michael squeezed my leg, meaning, I'm sure, to calm me down, but I was on a roll.

"Is it because it's a program for children with disabilities? Is that why it's apparently been moved to the bottom of your list of things to do? What about the note that was addressed to me? Have you had it tested for fingerprints yet?" I fired the questions off without waiting for answers.

The man was immovable. "Ms. McIntosh, I can assure you nothing's been moved to the bottom of my list of things to do. We take all of our cases very seriously. I'm afraid that's all I can tell you. Now, if you'll excuse me...."

"Wait a minute! Can you at least do a drive by tomorrow afternoon around one o'clock?" I asked. "Mr. Young is coming to view the books. He feels he was shortchanged in his pay. I don't know what you know about him, or what you've discovered in your investigation, but don't you think it might be a good idea for you to at least be in the area when he comes tomorrow?"

"I'll make sure to do that," he said. "Now, I really need to go."

I couldn't believe it, but the man actually stood and tossed a business card on the table before walking away. He nodded at Kay and exited the diner, backing away in his patrol car and heading out of town while the three of us stared after him.

Chapter 26

I tried to use my drive up the mountain as a cooling off period. Unfortunately, it wasn't a long drive, and I'm known to have a hot temper. How dare he brush me off like that? Such an arrogant man. I parked outside Nora's office and barged in without knocking. She looked up from the pile of papers on her desk, surprised.

"Jessie?" She scooped the papers aside and motioned for me to sit down. "Are you okay?"

"I see what you mean about an impasse." I flopped into the chair and told her about my meeting with Sheriff Moore.

When I'd finished ranting, she gave me a wry smile. "So now you see what I'm up against. Not a lot of investment on his part, is there? I suppose all I can do is keep after him, but I don't have much hope he'll ever come up with anything."

"I'm leaving tomorrow," I reminded her. "You'll have to keep me posted on what he finds out, if anything. Looks like my trip here was wasted, doesn't it? Why would someone insist I come, and then not contact me once I'm here? It doesn't make any sense."

"I wish I knew the answers, Jessie. But I wouldn't say your time was wasted. You seem to have really enjoyed yourself up here with the kids."

"That's true." I thought about it. "I have enjoyed myself." And I really had. I almost dreaded leaving, but I had a life I had to get back to. Unfortunately, it was becoming more and more clear to me that I didn't especially like the life I needed to get back to.

After spending so much time in Cedar Hollow enjoying the mountains, seeing old friends, and most especially, working with the kids, I was more disgusted than ever with the artificial glitter and superficial drama of Hollywood. Here, kids were dealing with daily challenges, *real* challenges. There, forgetting to stock a dressing room with precisely chilled bottled water could trigger a self-important actress into a full-fledged tantrum. It was hard to imagine returning to that.

"Oh, by the way," I fished Robby's drawing out of my pocket, "the mystery of the Huffmans deepens."

She unfolded the picture and smoothed it on her desk.

"What do you make of it?" I asked.

"More importantly, what do *you* make of it?" She put on her glasses and peered at the drawing.

I sighed. I should have known that would be her response. Therapists never answer questions. "Well, I think it's odd that Robby apparently thinks the Huffmans are my parents, don't you? What could have given him that idea?"

She looked up at me. "That's certainly one interpretation of it. Another is that Robby is projecting his desires onto you."

"What do you mean?"

She folded the paper and handed it back to me. "Think about it, Jessie. He's a lonely little boy. His home life has always been unstable. His father left the picture years ago and his mother has been, at best, inconsistent. He lost his grandmother a few months ago and his grandfather shortly after. What do you think Robby wants more than anything right now?"

That was one of the easiest therapist's questions I'd ever had to answer. "A family, of course."

"And he knows you want one, too."

"Now wait a minute...."

Nora interrupted. "Just hear me out, Jessie. You're in mourning, too. You recently lost your own mother figure and your biological relatives, as far as you know, are nonexistent. Robby assumes you feel the same way he does, so he drew you a family. The Huffmans are about the right age, so he probably unconsciously used them as a model."

I had to admit in some convoluted Freudian way that probably made some sense, but it didn't feel right to me. "I understand what you're saying, Nora, but I don't know that I'm buying it."

Nora smiled. "I'd be surprised if you did. That would be totally out of character for you. By the way, speaking of Robby, he's back from his visit with his caseworker. Still no success with a placement. For now, he's going to have to go back to the temporary placement he was in before coming here."

My heart ached for the poor kid. "How's he doing?"

"Quiet. You know Robby. Refuses to talk about it. He did participate in equine therapy, so that's good. They're with Valerie now, from the library. He seemed to be enjoying story time when I glanced in. How could anyone not enjoy story time with Valerie? She's a hoot."

I smiled. "She's great, isn't she? When I was a kid she seemed positively bohemian, with her peasant blouses and broomstick skirts. She's done a lot for the town, that's for sure. Did you know she was only supposed to be here for a semester, while she was in college? She liked it so much she talked her fiancé into staying. Hard to imagine someone working to stay *in* Cedar Hollow. Most people try to get *out*."

"Oh, now, Jessie, it's a nice little town," said Nora. "Admit it. It pulls at you."

"It does," I admitted. "It's home, whether I like it or not. But right now what's pulling at me is a bunch of phone calls I need to return. I'll see you at dinner?"

"You will. I'll be here late, as always." Nora pulled the stack of papers back in front of her.

"It's a date, then. Leave your work at the office."

"Will do."

I let myself out and went to touch base with my assistant, whose calls I'd ignored for far too long.

Chapter 27
Robby

Hi it's me Robby. Well we are listening to Mrs. Poindexter from the library read us a story except she isn't just reading it she is acting it out with puppets. It's really cool. She has this one puppet that is supposed to be Greg Heffley like in *Diary of a Wimpy Kid* and it looks just like him with his hair sticking up and everything.

Mrs. Poindexter is reading from Tuesday in the book when Greg starts middle school and she is making the puppets act it out and it is really funny. And then we have to stop every now and then and talk about bullying and stuff because that is what Greg is talking about in the book. I raised my hand a minute ago and talked about big stupid Ernie on the school bus.

I can't believe it but Mr. Paul was right because it was nice to talk about it and tell people about Ernie and it did make me stop feeling lonely about it. And Mrs. Poindexter and everyone really listened to me and they gave me good ideas about what to do.

I will ask Mrs. Cortes to tell the bus driver to save me a seat behind him so I don't have to go to the back of the bus where Ernie is. I will tell Mr. Paul he had a wonderful idea because he always tells me when I have wonderful ideas. I have them a lot. Mr. Paul only has them sometimes.

Now Mrs. Poindexter is finished and telling all of us goodbye. I like her because she is really nice and funny but she is even older than Ms. McIntosh. There are a lot of old people around here but I guess that's okay because they are nice.

She is opening the door to leave and there is Ms. McIntosh! Mrs. Poindexter hugs Ms. McIntosh so I guess they know each other because you are NOT supposed to hug people you do not know. Mrs. Cortes says that is Stranger Danger and you are not ever ever ever supposed to let strangers hug you or touch you in Private Places. I learned all about it in a class she took me to.

One time a man I did not know put his arm around me at church and I said, "STOP! DO NOT TOUCH ME! THAT IS STRANGER DANGER!" And it really worked because the man jumped very far away from me and then Grandpa came really fast and he said, "It's okay, Robby. This is just Dennis Lane, Mr. Darryl's son. He came back to town to run the store for a while. But you did a good thing, yelling like that. You did exactly what you were taught to do in that class. Good job, Robby."

And I felt very proud because Grandpa said I did a good job. Then Mr. Darryl and Mr. Dennis and some other people came to Grandma and Grandpa's house for lunch and then he wasn't a stranger anymore. But he did not try to put his arm around me again. I don't know why not.

Ms. McIntosh is coming in now and I hope she sees me! I wonder if she got the picture I drew for her. I hope she did because I know it will make her happy because she will have a family.

"Robby!" she says, and I like the way she says my name because it sounds glad to see me. "Thank you so much for the beautiful picture!"

I say, "You're welcome," because that is Good Manners. Grandma taught me to have Good Manners.

Ms. McIntosh comes over and sits beside me and she smells like flowers. I wonder how she always smells good. Sometimes I smell good but only for a little while. It doesn't last like her good smell does. She pulls the picture out of her back pocket and puts it between us on the table. "Do you have time to tell me about it?"

I do have time because Mr. Paul hasn't told us to do anything yet. He and Ms. Janice are talking. We like it when they talk because then we can talk too. Right now Stacey and Joseph are talking and Marcus is listening to them. Anthony is not talking. He is just rocking back and forth and I hope he isn't Over Stimulated. Everyone is leaving him alone because sometimes if everyone leaves him alone he gets okay.

I nod at Ms. McIntosh so she knows I do have time to talk and then I point at the moon. "That is the big moon we looked at with the scope. I put the holes in it like it really does have."

"I know, and I love it." Ms. McIntosh is happy about that. "You drew it exactly like the real moon." She points at the bottom. "And is this me? Because it sure does look like me."

"Uh-huh. I put your ponytail in it."

"And my jacket. You did such a good job of making it look like me. And here, you drew someone and put *Mom*. Did you mean for that to be *my* mom?"

"Uh-huh but not your real mom. Your stepmom. You know, like Stacey has." Stacey has a real mom and a stepmom. Stacey lives with her real mom and Stacey's stepmom lives with Stacey's dad.

I don't think Ms. McIntosh knows she has a stepmom because she frowns but it isn't a mad frown. It's the frown I have sometimes when I am trying to read something that is too hard. For a minute she just looks at the picture and doesn't say anything.

Then she says, "It looks like Mrs. Huffman. It's her dress, and her apron. Even her shoes, and I like the way you drew the laces. Is it Mrs. Huffman? Or did you just imagine I had a stepmom that looks like her?"

I am glad she can tell who it is because those laces took a really long time to draw. I am quite talented at drawing. That's what Mrs. Pruitt says at school. She is the art teacher and she says, "Robby, you are quite talented at drawing." So I know I am.

I nod again at Ms. McIntosh. "It's Mrs. Huffman," I tell her.

"Hmmm," she says. She likes to say that word but I still don't know what she means when she says it. She is biting on her lips. My mom tells me not to do that because it will make your lips chapped. I guess Ms. McIntosh doesn't know that.

"But Robby," she says, and her voice is slow and quiet, "what makes you think Mrs. Huffman is my stepmom?" She turns her head sort of sideways and looks at me.

And now here comes the big secret and I can tell for sure she doesn't know about it and I can't wait to tell her because I know it will make her so happy.

So I tell her, "Because Mr. Huffman is your dad."

Chapter 28

I had no idea how to wrap my head around what Robby had just told me. He said he had overheard Mr. and Mrs. Huffman discussing me one night while he was in bed. Apparently Mrs. Huffman had encouraged Mr. Huffman to approach me and tell me who he was.

According to Robby, Mr. Huffman's response was something along the lines of, "You think after all these years she's really interested in knowing who I am?"

"But you're her father," Mrs. Huffman had said. "You have to let her know. You can't do this. It's not right."

"I'm doing this for me," Mr. Huffman had answered. "Not for her. She doesn't need it. I do."

"They argued loud," Robby told me. "Then Mr. Huffman made Mrs. Huffman promise to be quiet. But he didn't make me promise to be quiet because he didn't know I heard him. See? You do have a family."

I had barely managed to thank Robby again for the wonderful picture before excusing myself and escaping to my room, locking the door behind me. Once there, I had no idea what to do. Could it possibly be true? It seemed so farfetched, but it would certainly explain the creepiness factor I'd experienced since meeting them. If he was my father, it wasn't a coincidence he'd shown up to work at the Lodge. Had he been stalking me? What did they want?

As it had when I'd thought Mrs. Huffman might be Lindy, my mind immediately went to money. I had a lot of it; that was no secret. Is that what they wanted? Blackmail, maybe? But for what?

My adult life was an open book. I hadn't done anything that hadn't already been covered in one tabloid or another. Some of the worst things printed about me in those magazines weren't things I'd ever even considered doing, but they made for good print. Such is life in the Hollywood scene. There was nothing, no hidden secret, no shameful deed, for them to use to blackmail me. If blackmail was the aim, it wouldn't be my adult life that interested them.

It would be my childhood. I paced frantically around the small room, knowing I needed to calm down but not knowing how to do it. Was there a connection to Virgil Young? He'd been spouting off about Roy Campbell all around town for the last week. Now a man claiming to be my father was also here. Both had been hired to work at a facility that I started, on land that I own. Surely that wasn't coincidence.

What in the world was going on?

I pulled out my cell and dialed up John. After four rings I hung up before I could be directed to voicemail. I called Corinne's house next, but there was no answer. They'd obviously gone out, maybe to the diner again. I wouldn't call Michael. How could he help me? He didn't know the things we knew.

A part of me wanted to find Nora. I needed to talk it over with someone, and Nora did have a way of helping me put things in perspective. But she was so protective of the Huffmans. I understood her position; human service jobs, though among the hardest, are notorious for paying poverty level wages. She had a perfect setup with the Huffmans and they'd be very difficult, if not impossible, to replace if they left. I would fill Nora in, but not yet. Not until I knew a little bit more.

Sheriff Moore, then. As much as I didn't want to interact with that man, I wondered if I should call him. Too many odd things were happening, coming together in a way that made me nervous. I pulled his card out of my jacket pocket and looked at it. It was nearly 5:00, half an hour before dinner, plenty of time to call. Should I? I didn't know what to do; if only John had answered his phone.

I was afraid. It wasn't a feeling I was used to, not in my adult years, although I'd certainly felt it often enough as a young child. Re-experiencing those feelings brought on a profound loneliness. I wanted Billy May. I wanted to connect with someone who knew me and loved me. I did not want to be alone.

I had nightmares back then, nearly every night, in the years I lived with Billy May. I'd wake up screaming, fighting off an imaginary attacker who had been only too real before Billy May saved me. He could no longer hurt me during my waking hours, but he came back often to hurt me in my sleep.

Billy May, hearing my screams, would come and pull me into her strong arms. She would rub my back and talk to me. She always smelled of soap, a clean, safe smell. Sometimes she read books to me. Other times she whispered to me, over and over again, almost like a chant, while she rocked me. *Jessie girl, it's okay. You're okay. You're with me. You're surrounded by people who love you. We'll take care of you. No one can hurt you, now. You're surrounded by people who love you.* She would hold me as I fell back to sleep, and I knew nobody could hurt me as long as she was with me, not even in my dreams. She wouldn't let them. She wouldn't. How I missed her.

On impulse, before I even realized what I was doing, I scrolled to Michael's number and hit the button to connect. He answered immediately.

"Jessie! Is everything okay?"

I heard commotion in the background, laughter, conversation, Kay's voice yelling out someone's order. They'd gone back to the diner as they'd promised Kay. All of a sudden I longed more than anything to be back there with them. I could picture it, Kay in her pink dress and white apron, order pad in her hand.

Corinne and John would be drinking sweet tea, Michael iced water with lemon. They would be laughing and talking, Corinne probably filling them in on the gossip of the other patrons. John would order the pot roast, Corinne the chef salad. Michael would ask them for recommendations, always willing to try anything. *You're surrounded by people who love you.* My throat closed up and I couldn't speak.

"Jessie? Are you there?"

I swallowed. "I'm here, Michael. I just....I wanted to call." My voice trailed off and I fought against the urge to cry.

"Jessie, come back to town." Michael's voice was soft and insistent. "We miss you. We were just saying you should be here with us. We'll tell Kay to hold our order until you get here. Come now."

"I'm on my way," I said, and I ended the call. I'd tell Nora I needed to eat dinner with Corinne and John. She would understand. I did need to eat dinner with Corinne and John. And with Michael. I needed to eat dinner with Michael.

Chapter 29

Michael was waiting for me outside the diner, leaning against the wall to the right of the door, hands in his pockets. He didn't say a word as I stepped out of the car, just wrapped his arms around me in a bear hug. I hugged him back.

"Are you okay?"

"Right now I am," I answered. He took my arm and led me inside, and I had to laugh. It was exactly as I'd known it would be. Corinne and John were drinking sweet tea, and Michael had saved me a seat beside his, where his glass of water with lemon sweated on the table.

From behind the counter, Kay waved at me. "Good to see you. It's been a while." I had to laugh.

"Let me guess," I said as John and Corinne looked up at the sound of my voice. "John, you're having pot roast, and Corinne, it's the chef salad for you."

Corinne's face wrinkled in a smile. "And I took the liberty of orderin' you the veggie plate. Kay is bringin' it with the cornbread, of course." Of course. It's what I had always ordered for dinner at the diner. It had been my favorite since I was a little girl. Who in the world would know that about me but the people of Cedar Hollow?

"Come on and sit down, honey," Corinne ordered. "I'm glad you're here."

I took my seat beside Michael and John gave me a sardonic look over the top of the dessert menu. "You couldn't stay away from me, could you? It's the boots, isn't it? You're in love with my hiking boots. Admit it."

155

That feeling came over me again, the one I'd had my first morning back in town, when I'd sat with Corinne in her sunny kitchen. I felt like a normal person, doing what normal people did. I was having dinner with friends and family, in a place that felt like home. I was being teased by my best friend in the world. I knew all the people around me, if not by name at least by face or association, and they knew me, as well.

There was no need to explain anything, no agonizing decisions about what, if anything, to share with them. I wanted to bottle that feeling and keep it with me. I felt so happy for a moment I couldn't come up with a single smart-aleck remark for John. I just sat there with a goofy grin on my face.

"Whoa," he said, straightening up and setting down the menu. "What is this? Who are you, and what have you done with our lovely little sourpuss?"

"Now you hush, John." Corinne reached over and patted me on the hand. "What's got you smilin' so, honey?"

I shrugged, the grin still plastered across my face. "I'm just happy to see you guys." That was the best I could come up with, and it was true.

"Well, we're happy to see you, too, honey." She squinted at me. "I'm glad you're here, but did somethin' happen to bring you down here again today? I thought we weren't goin' to get to see you again until tomorrow."

I filled them in on my conversation with Robby.

"Jessie, have you spoken to Nora about this? Assuming Robby is right, I wonder if she knew the connection when she hired them." John's expression was serious now, all humor set aside.

I shook my head. "I haven't yet. But you know, John, you have a good point. Every time I've tried to discuss the Huffmans with Nora she's gotten defensive. I understand how hard they'd be to replace; they really do keep the place going. But if she knew about them, that adds a whole other

156

layer, doesn't it? What would her purpose be? It doesn't make sense."

We waited for Riva to set our plates in front of us and then ate in silence, mulling over John's question, before Michael spoke up. "Let's look at this thing from all sides." He set down his fork. "You were summoned here by somebody. Right now we have two suspects, right? Virgil Young, who was fired, obviously has anger towards you and had a connection to your stepfather, who disappeared under mysterious circumstances years ago. Virgil thinks you hold some blame for that."

Corinne and I exchanged a look, which Michael caught. "What?" He looked from one to the other of us. "I'm not stupid, you know. I don't care how the man disappeared. Given what I've picked up from the three of you, he deserved whatever happened to him. If you didn't have a part in it, you should have."

Corinne and I stared, while across from me, John chuckled. "I told you I like this guy, Jessie. He's much smarter than the bozos you usually bring around."

"Anyway," Michael continued, "the other suspect, or suspects, are the Huffmans. You haven't felt comfortable around them since you got here, and now you find out Mr. Huffman might be the biological father you've never met. Right?" I nodded agreement, spellbound.

"There are several questions here." Michael ticked them off on his fingers. "First, did Nora know, when she hired the Huffmans, that he was your biological father? Second, are the Huffmans and Virgil Young affiliated in some way, and if they are, did Nora know that, too? Finally, who summoned you, and why?" He sat back against the seat. "Did I cover them all?"

"You did." I was still absorbing Michael's apparent understanding of events. Once again, he knew more than I had given him credit for. "But where does that leave me?" I asked. "I don't know where to go from here. Do I confront

157

the Huffmans directly? Ask Nora? Call the Sheriff? What's my next step? Whatever it is, it needs to happen fast because we're leaving tomorrow." I was at a loss.

"You have the Sheriff's card, right?" John asked. "I think you should give him a call this evening to let him know what you've found out. It certainly makes the Huffmans look more suspicious and it's information the Sheriff needs to have. Then I think a conversation with Nora is in order. I have a feeling she knows more than she's let on."

"I think so too, John." Corinne spoke up. "Let the Sheriff know what's going on first. And don't you dare take it on yourself to go question the Huffmans, you understand? You leave the Sheriff to do the investigatin' with those people."

"What do you think, Michael?" I realized I really wanted his opinion on the topic.

"For the most part I agree, but I want you to be very careful," he said. "Don't forget about the things that brought you here—the horses, the chemicals, the trashed office, the fire, and finally, the note. Someone, possibly Mr. Huffman, went to great lengths to get you here. Maybe he doesn't intend any harm; maybe he just wanted to see you, but a man willing to go to those lengths to meet a daughter he's never known is unstable whether he means to harm you or not. I'm not really comfortable with you sleeping up there tonight."

"I'll be careful, Michael," I assured him. "Besides, nothing is any different than it has been all week. The only difference is that now I know about Mr. Huffman and I didn't before. That makes me safer, if anything. I'll be fine. I'll lock the door as I always do. And I'll call Sheriff Moore on my way back up the mountain."

"And you'll call us before you go to bed to tell us goodnight and let us know you're okay." Corinne pointed a finger at me.

"I will," I said. "You can tuck me in by phone."

We paid for our meal and stood outside in the cool, late afternoon for a moment before leaving. This had always been my favorite time of year in Cedar Hollow. The mountains were stunning, the air fresh. I could smell the sharp scent of the fallen leaves as they crunched under our feet. John helped Corinne into her car and I glanced over to catch Michael smiling at me.

"You actually look peaceful," he said. "I don't think I've ever seen you look that way before."

"I feel peaceful," I told him, surprised myself. "Crazy, isn't it? I'm surrounded by weirdness, someone may be trying to hurt me, and I feel peaceful. I never have been good at matching my feelings up properly with my circumstances."

He laughed. "Yes, I've noticed that about you. It's a part of your charm."

It was my turn to laugh. "I'm a messed up woman, Michael."

"No, Jessie." His expression turned serious. "You're a survivor. That's what you have to remember. Quit seeing the scars as disfiguring and start seeing them as a badge of honor. All warriors have battle scars, and you won the battle. You're still here. That's what counts."

I turned to look at him. "You sound like Nora."

"But I'm much more handsome," he said, waggling his eyebrows at me, and I had to agree that he was. "Not to mention, I'm smarter than the bozos you usually bring around. Oh, before I forget, what would I need to do to be able to volunteer at the Lodge?"

The question surprised me. "First, you'd have to undergo a background check, and then you'd have to go through some training. Why do you ask?"

"Corinne has given me an open invitation to visit and John said I can come back with him anytime," he said. "I'd like to take them up on that. I like it here, Jessie. It's a wonderful little town, and Corinne and John are fantastic. If

I do visit, I'd love to volunteer with the kids at the Lodge. Would you be okay with that?"

I thought about it before answering. To be honest, I wasn't sure I wanted Michael to be involved in situations so close to my own life. Cedar Hollow was mine, as was the Lodge. As were Corinne and John.

But I knew that was unhealthy thinking on my part. I didn't own John and Corinne; if they'd decided to befriend Michael, I had no right to come between that. I certainly wouldn't want him dictating my friendships; I could hardly do that to him. Besides, John and Corinne were family. No one could take that away from me.

As for volunteering at the Lodge, I knew he'd be wonderful with the kids and we needed all the volunteers we could get. After an initial hesitation, I agreed. "That would be fine with me, Michael, but why the sudden interest in working with kids at the Lodge? There are plenty of places in California that need volunteers, you know."

"As a matter of fact, I do know that," he said, "and I'm on the Board of Directors at one of those places, and I volunteer on Saturdays working with the kids."

I was stunned. "I had no idea." I felt a wave of shame. *When you spend so much time wrapped up in your own misery, you don't notice anyone else.* I really hadn't liked Therapist Number One, but I was beginning to think she had something there. It boggled my mind that I could despise myself the way I often did and be narcissistic at the same time, but it was becoming difficult to deny that my world had been completely wrapped up in...well, me.

"You couldn't have known," Michael put a hand on my shoulder. "I never mentioned it. I did it for Noah."

"What do you mean?" I searched his face.

"Noah had autism," he said. "He'd been diagnosed a few months before the accident. I started volunteering shortly after we received the diagnosis. I continued after I lost him, partly in honor of him and partly because it helped fill the void, working with other kids."

"Michael," I started, then stopped. Once again, I didn't know what to say to him. What a dear man he was, and how little I really knew about him. I found myself wanting to know more. Maybe I'd beat this narcissism thing after all.

I stood on my toes and kissed his cheek. "I'll give you the paperwork tomorrow, and we'll make sure you're ready by the next time you visit. And Michael...." I wasn't sure how to ask. "Someday, if you're up for it, I'd really like to hear more about Angela and Noah. I know you loved them very much. I'd also like to hear more about you. It seems I'm missing some pieces."

"Yes, I did love them very much" he said, "and someday, I'd like to tell you about them. And about me."

After a quick hug, I got in my car for the drive up Crutcher Mountain, keying in Sheriff Moore's number before setting out.

Chapter 30
Robby

Hi it is me Robby again and I am very tired today but I do not want to go to bed. If I go to bed then I will wake up and it will be tomorrow and then I will have to leave here. I wonder if I don't go to bed if it will ever be tomorrow. Maybe it will just be night forever. I would like to try and see but I don't think Mr. Bryan will let me. Grownups don't like it when you don't go to sleep because they are tired.

We are having a party in a few minutes with cake and ice cream and everything but it can only last half an hour so we don't get Over Stimulated before bed. That is what Dr. Wright told Mr. Bryan. "We'll give it about half an hour so they don't get over stimulated. Then give them an hour for bedtime routine and T.V. so they can wind down." I don't know what she means by wind down. We are not toys. Ha!

Everyone is going to be here. Dr. Wright will be here and Mr. Paul and Ms. Janice and Mr. Bryan and Ms. Sarah and everybody. Even Mrs. Cortes is coming. I hope Ms. McIntosh will be here too.

Mrs. Huffman tied balloons all over the place and somebody put all of our drawings and stuff all over the walls and it is very beautiful. We are all quite talented at drawing. Well maybe not Marcus but he can't help it and we like his drawings anyway. That is one great thing about this place. Everyone likes your drawings even if they aren't very good.

If I have to go to sleep and tomorrow comes I am going back to the Sloan Foster Family. They are nice people but they have too many kids. I don't know how long I can stay there and I don't know what happens if Mrs. Cortes doesn't find anyone I can stay with. I guess I just won't have a house. Maybe I will have to live in the woods.

Grandpa took me hunting sometimes and taught me a lot about the woods. I know what poison oak and poison ivy look like and I know not to eat mushrooms unless you buy them at the store. I don't know why they are poisonous in the woods and not in the store but Grandpa said never ever eat them in the woods because they have poison. There is a lot of poison in the woods.

There are poisonous snakes in the woods too and you have to be careful where you step. There are bears in the woods too. They are not poisonous but they will eat you. One time Grandpa and I went camping in a tent and it was fun and not scary at all because there were other people camping around us so there weren't any bears. I am a little bit afraid of bears but that does not make me a scaredy baby. Grandpa said everyone should be a little bit afraid of bears.

If I have to live in the woods where the bears are I could build a house out of branches and trees and stuff so they can't get in. I saw Cody do that one time on *Dual Survival* and it looked very easy to me. He just cut down logs and stuck them all together and covered them with branches and I know it cannot be hard.

On *Dual Survival* Dave always hunts for food and I could hunt for food except I don't think I could kill animals because I like animals. And I don't have a gun or a knife. I guess I will have to be like Cody and eat plants and bugs and stuff. Dave says he does not like plants and bugs and stuff because he needs some MEAT.

He says it big like that, "Cody, I do not like bugs I need some MEAT!" I think Dave should have said thank you when Cody gave him a bug because that is Good Manners but I guess his Grandma didn't teach him Good Manners like mine did. If I have to live in the woods I will be like Cody on *Dual Survival* and take what I can get.

I hope I can find water. Cody and Dave are always looking for water. One time Cody had to drink water out of his sock and I don't want to drink water out of a stinky old sock. One time on *Man vs. Wild* the guy drank his PEE! Can you believe that? Yuck! I will NOT drink my pee ever ever no matter what!

I will go with Mrs. Cortes back to the Sloan Foster Family tomorrow but then I really really hope she finds me a Foster Family that doesn't have too many kids. I could live in the woods but I would rather live with a Foster Family. I don't think I would like to eat bugs and drink pee even if I have to take what I can get.

We did not have bugs for dinner today that is for sure. We had lasagna and I love lasagna. It is my very favorite. After dinner we came back to the common area and talked about all the things we learned this week. It was Closure Group.

I raised my hand and I told them all the things I learned. I learned that it is good to talk about feelings. And I learned what to do about big stupid Ernie on the bus. And I learned that when someone is Over Stimulated I should let them Take Space. And I learned that Mr. Huffman is Ms. McIntosh's dad. Then Mr. Paul said, "Uh...okay. Thanks, Robby. And Joseph, what have you learned this week?"

Now we are getting ready for the party and I can't wait because the cake is chocolate and we have vanilla ice cream to go with it. Everyone is here except Mrs. Cortes and Ms. McIntosh but now I see them coming in the door together and it is almost time for the party! Yay!

Chapter 31

Sheriff Moore was actually quite pleasant on the phone. I told him my concerns about the Huffmans and he assured me he would look into them. Before ending the call, he thanked me and said, "Ms. McIntosh, please know that we are taking all of this very seriously. We'll patrol the area closely tonight, and I'll touch base with you tomorrow. If you have any concerns before then call me, regardless of the hour." I must admit that surprised me, particularly after his lukewarm response earlier in the day.

I ended the call just as I pulled into the lot by the office of the Lodge. Another car pulled up right behind me and an older, heavyset woman climbed out, shoving what looked like mountains of file folders and boxes across the car seat before slamming shut the door. She called out to me as I stepped from the Subaru.

"Ms. McIntosh? I'm Amelia Cortes. It's so nice to finally meet you."

I approached her and shook her outstretched hand. Robby's caseworker. I was glad to meet her, as well. "It's nice to meet you, too. Any news on a placement for Robby?"

She shook her head. "Unfortunately, no. We have some wonderful specialized foster families in the area that do great work with kids who have special needs, but there are never enough. With the economic crisis, the number of kids in the system has skyrocketed, and many of them need specialized care for either physical or mental health challenges. The foster families we have are stretched thin."

"And it's definite that the temporary placement can't keep Robby longer?" I asked.

She sighed. "Technically, Robby could stay with the Sloans. They don't have more children than our policy will allow. But it's too big of a burden on the family. They have two very young foster children with severe medical complications. Shaken baby, you know. It's a horrible situation. People get frustrated; they don't understand the damage they can do." She paused. She was a seasoned worker, and I shuddered at the thought of the things she must have seen.

"Anyway," she said finally, "Mrs. Sloan spends her week taking the younger children for multiple medical and psychological appointments. Robby's a high functioning kid; he doesn't have many outside services, but even so, for Robby to remain there would overburden the family."

"What happens if you can't find a home?" I'd never considered that there might literally be no place for Robby to go.

"Then we look outside the area, maybe to a residential facility, although those are usually reserved for kids having behavioral issues and are notoriously difficult to get into. They often won't take children with developmental disabilities. Even if we could get Robby in, I'd worry about his safety there.

"Or," she continued, "we look into transferring the case to an out of area agency in the hopes that another agency might have more available foster homes. He'd be away from everything he's ever known. Neither situation is ideal."

I knew Isabelle had an older brother. "What about placement with a relative?"

"We tried," she said, "and in most cases, that would be the perfect solution. Robby does have an out of state uncle who is willing, but the wife isn't. It isn't easy being a foster parent, and the wife has some health concerns. She doesn't want the added stress."

I thought about Robby, his freckled face screwed up in concentration as he tried to get the words just right. I thought about the tears in his eyes when I had mentioned his grandfather. His grandfather had been so kind to Billy May and me. *That is the way of the universe; it is all connected.* Billy May had always believed that. I felt as if she were with me, whispering in my ear.

I thought about Robby moving to a place where he knew no one. He was so young and vulnerable; it pained me to imagine it. That little boy needed someone in his corner. I hadn't planned to say what I said next; it just sort of popped out.

"I happen to be closely affiliated with a respite facility." I watched Mrs. Cortes' expression change as she realized the implication of what I'd just said.

"Oh, my God," she said. "It hadn't even dawned on me that that could be an option. But you're respite, not residential. You only operate during the week. How would that work?"

Obviously, I didn't know all the ins and outs of the system, but given my career choice I was pretty good at thinking outside the box. I was operating out of excitement, spouting things off the top of my head without thinking them through. I was used to giving orders and making things work, but I had to remember that although I owned the physical structure, the parent company had final say in programmatic issues.

"I'll have to speak with our parent company about this of course," I said, "and with Nora, since she runs the place, but you've said the temporary placement you've found would be overburdened if Robby stayed there indefinitely. What if he was only there on weekends? It sounds like the foster mother is run pretty ragged during the week, going to appointments for the other children. If Robby had somewhere else to stay during the week, would that ease the burden?"

Mrs. Cortes tilted her head, looking at me curiously. "What exactly are you suggesting?"

I turned to her, the idea taking shape in my mind. "What if the foster home could be his official placement, but he could receive respite services from us during the week? I'm sure there's red tape to go through, but I wonder if we can be creative enough to make it work."

She hesitated. "One huge issue would be funding. We can't pay the foster family to house Robby while also paying respite care to house Robby. And what about school? We were able to work this week into his IEP, his Individualized Education Program, but he has to return to school."

"Let's look at one issue at a time," I said. "As for school, we have a van we use when we take the children on trips to town. I can see if we could arrange for the driver to transport Robby back and forth to school."

"Okay," Mrs. Cortes said, "but even if he can, that doesn't take care of the funding problem. We can't double dip into funds."

I was almost afraid to say what I said next, but I did it anyway. "What if Robby remained in the foster care placement, but a private benefactor paid for him to receive respite services at the Lodge during the week?"

She stared at me. "Respite care is expensive. We're talking tens of thousands of dollars for the amount of time he would need."

"I have money," I said, "and I can't think of a better way to spend it." I really couldn't; that was the truth. I thought again of the Hollywood elite who surrounded me, with their multiple mansions and expensive toys. No, I really couldn't think of a better way to spend it.

Mrs. Cortes was practically dancing with excitement. "There are a lot of bugs we'll have to work out, but that just might work."

170

"I'll do my best to work things out on this end," I said, "if your department can work things out on your end. We close down during January and February due to weather, but by that time Isabelle should be done with treatment and hopefully ready for Robby to return home."

"I probably won't have any sort of answer from my supervisor until tomorrow, if even then," Mrs. Cortes said. "Will you be here for the brunch tomorrow morning?"

"I will," I answered. "I'll call our parent company first thing in the morning. That will at least take care of the short term problem, but what about the long term? What if his mother hasn't met all the criteria for reunification? Then what happens to Robby?"

"Then," Mrs. Cortes sighed, "we have to look at termination. Robby has been in the system for a long time. He used to have his grandparents, absolutely wonderful people, but with them gone we can't keep stringing this little boy along, hoping his mom can get herself together. He needs stability. The court will terminate parental rights and he'll be available for adoption."

"Could he be placed with me? In California?"

Mrs. Cortes' mouth dropped open. "Are you serious?"

"I am." Until then I hadn't known it, but I was.

"Well." She looked flustered. "Let's go sit over here." She led me to the rocking chairs on the front porch of the Lodge. Inside, I could hear the kids gearing up for their party, and I was glad I'd soon be with them. We settled ourselves before she continued.

"The issue for you would be time," she said. "It takes anywhere from four to nine months to become approved as a foster home in West Virginia, even longer if we're transferring outside the area. You'd have to undergo a home study, background checks, reference checks...we'd have to pull in your local agency. His mother is in a ninety day program for alcohol and drug abuse. She's got about six weeks to go and then the goal is reunification if she's met all

171

the criteria. I just don't think there's time to get you certified."

Although until our conversation I hadn't known I was joining the fight, once in it, I couldn't give up easily. "What about this. You start the ball rolling here for me to become a foster parent. I'll work with my local agency in California and you guys collaborate however it is you do it. Then, if she doesn't meet criteria for reunification, I can be considered an option for Robby."

"Ms. McIntosh," her tone was pensive, "I'm more than happy to start the ball rolling, believe me. But I have to warn you, it isn't easy to place a child out of state. It also isn't easy to be a foster parent. It's a huge commitment. Are you sure you want to open yourself up to this? It may all be for nothing, if Robby is placed back with his mother. And if he isn't," she placed a hand on my arm, "it will most certainly be a life changer for you."

"I'm sure," I said. I didn't know how I knew I was sure, but I did. "For Robby's sake I hope Isabelle gets her life in order. But if she doesn't, I want to be considered an option for Robby."

"Well, then." She leaned away from me, smiling. "I'll contact my supervisor right after the party and discuss all this with her."

As we stood to enter the Lodge, I wondered what I'd just gotten myself into. Even more than that, I wondered why. I didn't have the answers. The sorcery of Appalachia, maybe. I never could be as guarded inside those mountains as I was outside; they were my Achilles heel. I just hoped they didn't lead to my downfall; no poison arrows in the foot for me.

I thought of the strange gypsy woman on the plane. *Turn your colors back on. The universe is talking to you, and you must listen.* If this was what it felt like to turn my colors back on, I rather liked it.

Chapter 32

Half an hour later, stuffed with chocolate cake I hadn't been able to resist, I said goodnight to the children, promising I'd see them in the morning, and went in search of Nora. I wanted to get to the bottom of things regarding the Huffmans and I agreed with John that Nora must know more than she'd been willing to share. I also needed to fill her in on my conversation with Mrs. Cortes. I felt sure Nora would back up my plan, and I was hoping we could call the parent company together first thing in the morning.

I found her in the common area in conversation with Bryan, the night staff. When she saw me she motioned for me to join them. "We were just discussing Robby," she said. "Still no word on a placement."

I hadn't planned on discussing things in front of the other staff but given the perfect opening, I decided to go ahead and let Nora know about the discussion I'd had with Mrs. Cortes earlier in the evening. They both grew visibly more excited as I outlined the possible plan. "That's the perfect solution, if it can work," Bryan said. He turned to Nora. "Can it work?"

She rubbed her chin thoughtfully. "It just might," she said. "We have to be so careful about funding streams, but this might actually be workable. They'd have to renegotiate a fee for the Sloan family, of course. If Robby isn't there during the week their fee will go down, but I don't think that will be an issue for them. They're not in it for the money. They know by now the money often doesn't even cover the expenses."

"Can we call the executive director first thing in the morning and run it by him?" I was eager to have some sort of answer before leaving town. I needed to know that Robby was taken care of.

"Of course," she answered. "Meet me in my office at eight and we'll see if we can reach him. Hopefully we'll get him just as he arrives, before anyone else has a chance to grab him. What a great idea, Jessie. He's a good kid. I've been worried about what's going to happen to him."

"Me, too," I agreed. I thought back to how excited Robby had been to see Mrs. Cortes and me at the party. He had saved us a seat, and I'd barely sat down before he asked me if I'd met my dad yet. I told him I hadn't, that I had to think about it some more before approaching Mr. Huffman.

"I guess you're being shy," he'd said, making me smile. "I'm never shy," he stated with conviction. I had to agree that he certainly wasn't.

I wanted to speak with Nora alone but I didn't want to be rude to Bryan. I needn't have worried because just then Bryan checked his watch. "I've got to get going," he said. "It's time to get the kids started on evening routine. I'll see you guys in the morning; I'm planning on staying a little later on my own time to see the kids off, if that's all right."

"I'm sure they'd love that, Bryan," Nora answered. "Here's hoping you have a quiet night. How's Anthony doing? He looked a little anxious earlier."

"I think it was just the buzz around the party that got to him," Bryan answered. "He doesn't like changes in routine, but he's fine now."

"That's good," Nora said. "If they need a little extra time tonight to relax before bed, it's fine to give them half an hour extra."

"Thanks, that's good to know. I think we're okay, but they might enjoy a little extra time together, since it's their last night." He gave a little wave before turning to leave.

"I know you're ready to get out of here, but can I have a few minutes before you go?" I asked Nora, as we watched Bryan rejoin Sarah and the children in the group area.

"Why don't you walk me back to my office," she suggested, "and we can talk in private."

I waited until we were settled in Nora's office before broaching the subject. I hadn't been sure how to approach her; I didn't want to accuse her, but I needed to ask her some pretty pointed questions. As I usually did, I settled on a direct approach.

"Nora, Robby overheard the Huffmans talking a few nights ago while he was in bed. He shared the conversation with me, and I must admit it's a little worrisome."

Nora lowered herself into her desk chair, her expression concerned. "What was it about?"

"Apparently they were discussing me. Mr. Huffman seems to be under the impression that he's my father. My biological father, whom I've never met." I told her what Robby had said.

Either Nora was an excellent actress, or my words caught her completely by surprise. As I spoke, her eyes grew wide and she put a hand to her throat. "Oh, my God. Why would he think that? I mean, is there a possibility?"

I laughed aloud at the question. "Sure, there's a possibility. I mean, *someone* is my biological father. It could be him as well as anybody; I certainly wouldn't know. Technically I guess anyone over the age of sixty could be in the running." This hadn't gone the way I'd expected it to.

"I suppose I was hoping you could shed some light on the topic," I said, but I was losing hope that she would be able to do that. "Did you know this information before you hired them?"

"Absolutely not," she shook her head emphatically. "Not that it would have stopped me hiring them, because they had excellent credentials and there were no warning signs about questionable behaviors. But if I'd known he

175

claimed to be your father, I would have run it by you first, out of respect. Goodness," she shook her head again. "Give me a minute to get my bearings; I wasn't expecting this news."

I believed her. She looked as shocked to hear it as I had been. "You really didn't know, did you? I had convinced myself you did."

"I really didn't know," she confirmed. "Why would you think I did?" She looked at me quizzically.

"Because whenever I mentioned being suspicious of them, you jumped to their defense." I felt guilty even saying it.

"I suppose I did," she conceded, "but not for the reasons you thought. Before the Huffmans came along we had gone through three groundskeepers and two housekeepers. At the rate we were going, I was thinking I'd have to hire new ones at the beginning of every week. The Huffmans have truly been a blessing to this place, and they came with excellent recommendations and credentials. I checked them out myself.

"The way it all came together seemed almost like providence, me needing them and them needing a place to go. It just couldn't have worked out any better than that. What a lesson, huh? If it sounds too good to be true...." She didn't need to finish the thought. "In hindsight, I guess they made themselves fit what we needed in order to get hired on. Unbelievable."

We sat in silence for a minute. "Have you contacted the Sheriff?" she asked finally. "This puts a whole new spin on things. All this time, I had suspected Virgil. Now we have to accept that the Huffmans may be responsible for the things that have happened here."

"I talked to Sheriff Moore this afternoon, so he's aware," I told her. "He said he'll check into it. As for whether or not they're responsible, my friend Michael seems to think it's possible they did all those things to be able to meet me without having to reveal who they are. If they meant to harm the children—or me, for that matter—they could have certainly done it by now. But as Michael says, even if their intent isn't to cause me harm, they'd have to be pretty unbalanced to go to such lengths to get me here."

"Good point," Nora agreed, "and I have to tell you, I'm more than a little embarrassed by this. You haven't felt comfortable with them since you got here, apparently with good reason. But I completely missed it. I didn't pick up on a single red flag. What kind of therapist misses something like that?"

"Cut yourself some slack," I advised. "They weren't acting weird around you, just around me. I always felt like he was watching me, and then that whole business with the toothbrush. Which, by the way, still doesn't make sense. Why would they want my toothbrush? As some sort of a keepsake? That's even creepier."

Nora sat forward. "DNA?" she suggested. "What else could it be? Think about it. Maybe he wanted a sample of DNA to prove paternity."

I thought about that. "That makes sense, but for what purpose? I mean, it isn't as if my mother is going to go after child support at this late date."

"Maybe he's just curious." She shrugged. "It's possible he just wants to be sure. We could always ask him."

Now it was my turn to look shocked. "Seriously? Just call him in here and ask him why he took my toothbrush?"

Nora shrugged again. "Why not? I run the place, and that's a concerning behavior. It concerned you, didn't it? Yes? Well, now it concerns me. I have every right to ask why he did it. But let's catch them off guard. Instead of asking them to come in here and possibly putting them on alert, let's go to them. They should be finished cleaning up after the party by now. Let's see if they're in their rooms."

I couldn't believe what Nora was suggesting. "Don't you think that could be dangerous?"

"I think it would be worse to leave you here tonight without knowing what's going on, don't you? At least now there are people around, more people than usual because of the party. Look, Jessie, they have no history of criminal behavior, at least not within the past seven years, which is as far as we can check. They may be acting strangely, even illegally, but it's highly unlikely they'll show violence towards us. As you pointed out earlier, they've had ample opportunity to hurt any of us, but they haven't. Let's just nip this in the bud right now."

Nora had a point. "Okay," I agreed, standing up, wondering vaguely if this might be the worst decision of my life. I hoped it wasn't like in the horror movies, when everyone in the audience knows the heroine is making a terrible decision but she doesn't see it. Not until she's dying, anyway, with a knife protruding from her chest. "Let's go," I said, before I could change my mind.

We exited Nora's office and walked briskly across the courtyard to the Lodge. The lights were all on, the children relaxing and watching a video in the common area before bed. We waved at them before we turned down the hallway toward my room.

I caught a glimpse of Robby's face as he waved and I could tell he was troubled. I wanted so much to tell him we were working on a solution for him, but I didn't want to give him false hope in case it didn't work out. I hoped I'd get a chance to visit with him before bed. I gave him a wink and turned down the passageway.

I must admit, I was not expecting what we saw next.

Chapter 33

"From what I understand, you need a strand with the follicle attached."

It was comical, the way they jumped so high at the sound of my voice. Clearly, they hadn't expected me. Mrs. Huffman dropped the hairbrush she'd been holding—*my hairbrush*—and to my surprise, burst into tears. "Richard, I told you this was a bad idea," she said, covering her face with her hands.

Mr. Huffman patted her on the back, his eyes on me. "So you did, honey. I should have listened to you." He moved away from my toiletry bag, which was now sitting on my bed instead of on the sink where I'd left it.

"Richard? I think we need an explanation." Nora entered the room behind me. "What in the world are you two doing? This is inexcusable, you know, completely unacceptable." She laced her arms across her chest and stared at him. I moved to stand beside her.

Mr. Huffman dropped his gaze and sighed, his shoulders slumped. "You're right, of course. It is unacceptable, and I'm sorry. I'd like to explain, not that that will make it any better. Actually, I've wanted to explain since the beginning, but I just wasn't sure how to go about it."

Nora nodded towards the bed. "I think you'd better find a way to go about it now. Your choices at the moment are to either tell us what's going on, and God knows there better be a fantastic explanation, or pack your bags to go while I put in a call to Sheriff Moore. This is serious business,

Richard. You, too, Opal. Have a seat, both of you. We're listening, whenever you're ready to talk."

Mr. and Mrs. Huffman sat tentatively on the foot of the bed facing Nora, the look on their faces a mixture of embarrassment and regret. Mrs. Huffman sat with her knees pressed together and her head bowed, hands clasped in her lap. Mr. Huffman leaned forward, staring at the floor, elbows propped on his thighs and hands dangling between his legs. We waited in silence until he looked up.

"This is hard to talk about, because I don't know where to start." He pinched the bridge of his nose between thumb and forefinger, closing his eyes, seemingly exhausted. "The truth of the matter is, Ms. McIntosh, and please forgive me if this is too shocking to you, but I believe I may be your father."

So there it was. What Robby had said was true. I hadn't doubted Robby, but neither had I expected to hear it straight from the horse's mouth, so to speak. I didn't respond to him right away. What does one say after hearing such a revelation? The only father figure I'd ever had was Roy, and what a sorry excuse he had been.

I suppose I could have felt angry at Richard Huffman for having left me to be raised by such a man as Roy Campbell. Or I could have felt thankful that a biological relative of mine had come to light after all these years. Watching Mr. Huffman, taking in his haggard expression, I might even have felt sorry for him, and certainly for her, as she sat quietly weeping beside him.

But instead of those things, what I mostly felt was apathy. I'd had enough therapy to understand that my lack of feeling was likely a defense mechanism, and I was grateful for it.

I glanced at Nora and she held a hand towards the Huffmans, palm up, indicating that the next move was up to me. I took advantage of it. "You'll understand my skepticism,

Mr. Huffman, but what exactly would make you think that?" I asked.

"Lindy," he answered. "You're Lindy Russell's daughter, ain't you?" He leaned his head back, peering into my face.

"In genes only," I told him. "I haven't seen her since I was a little girl."

He grunted and looked away. "That's what I'd heard. It's terrible it turned out that way, but it ain't too surprising for me to hear. Lindy did the best she could. You should know that."

"Mr. Huffman...."

He interrupted me. "She was my first love I guess you could say, though I don't know how much about love a sixteen year old boy really knows. Not much, I expect. Least not enough to have good sense.

"We was raised up right next to each other. Played together when we was little 'uns. I reckon I fancied myself in love with her by the time I was ten. She was a beautiful girl." He looked back at me. "You favor her, you know."

I was getting impatient with the whole conversation. "Nora, do we really have to listen to this?"

Beside me, Nora looked transfixed. "Let's hear what he has to say, Jessie, okay? It might help you in the long run, hearing more about your past."

"I'd 'preciate it if I could finish telling you," said Mr. Huffman. Reluctantly, I nodded for him to go on.

"Thing was, all the boys was in love with Lindy. Time she was thirteen, fourteen, she already looked...." He hesitated, casting about for the right word. "Mature. She looked like a much older girl, if you know what I mean. It got her a lot of attention. When she started coming of age and boys began taking notice of her, she ate it up."

"So she was the town slut," I said. "Is that what you're getting at? Because I really wouldn't expect any...."

He interrupted me again, raising his hand in protest. "No. No, that's not what I'm telling you. That's the thing. Everybody thought that about Lindy, I reckon because of how she looked and all the attention it brought her. Even I thought that about her, at first. And she did love to tease the boys. But I found out later that's all it was. She just teased; she didn't do nothing with them, just made them think she might."

Beside him, Mrs. Huffman blew her nose loudly, stuffing the soiled Kleenex back into her apron pocket. He reached over to pat her on the knee. "It's all right, honey. I should have listened to you, but it'll be all right."

He addressed Nora. "Opal here didn't do nothing. I shouldn't have drug her into this. She tried to tell me there was a better way, but I'm a stubborn old fool. I just want you to know none of this is her fault. It's all mine."

"We'll get all that sorted out later," Nora told him. "For now, why don't you finish explaining things." It wasn't a question, the way Nora said it, and Mr. Huffman knew it.

"All right," he said. "Where was I at? Oh, right. Lindy teasing the boys. That kept them coming around, you see, and she needed them around. Needed to feel like she was loved, you know. They didn't love her, of course, but I imagine to her at that young age it felt like they did. I know it did, 'cause she used to tell me so. It was the closest thing she had to love, anyway. Other than me, but I'll talk more about that in a minute."

This was turning out to be pretty interesting after all. I leaned against the dresser, waiting for the next revelation. It didn't take long.

"Things was always rough for her at home," Mr. Huffman said. "Her momma was a tough woman, hard on Lindy, and her daddy was a mean son of a bitch. I don't mean to be disrespectful but there ain't no other way to say it. Didn't nobody want to tangle with him. Folks used to say he'd kill you soon as look at you, and I reckon that was true.

Wasn't nobody wanted to find out for themselves. Many was the time Lindy come knocking on our door, crying about something they had said or done to her. More often than not she had a bruise or two to show for it. Momma always took her in, felt sorry for her."

I slid up on the dresser beside Nora. This explanation was obviously going to take some time.

"Lindy was the youngest," he said. "All the older ones had done run off. Didn't nobody even know where they went to. I couldn't blame them. Wouldn't nobody have wanted to hang around that house any longer than they had to."

As much as I didn't want to, I was starting to feel a little bit sorry for Lindy. I'd never thought of her as a child, only as the neglectful mother I'd known. It sounds awful, I know, but I'd never considered her life before me, what it might have been like or what might have caused her to make the choices she'd made. I'd been too wrapped up in how she, as a mother, had failed *me*.

In my defense, I hadn't known anything about her childhood; I didn't remember her ever talking about it. I never even knew she had older siblings, and all I remembered her ever saying about her parents was that she didn't have any, to speak of. That was exactly how she'd said it, with a little snort, "I ain't got no parents to speak of."

What Mr. Huffman was telling me didn't excuse what Lindy had done, but it did put it in some perspective. I saw her in a different light, as a little girl in need of love. The image was powerful.

Mr. Huffman coughed. "Dr. Wright, Ms. McIntosh, this is going to take more than a little bit of time to tell. Would it be okay if we all go over to our place for the rest of it? I need some water for my throat and you all might as well settle in and get comfortable while you listen. I think Opal's got some coffee cake or something over there, don't you honey?"

Next to him, Opal nodded. "Zucchini bread," she corrected in a muffled voice. "And Dr. Wright, I'm so sorry. I didn't—*we* didn't—mean to do things wrong. Ms. McIntosh," she looked at me, "I don't even know how to make it up to you. We didn't mean any harm. I hope you'll believe that. Maybe you'll understand once you've heard the whole thing."

Nora looked at me, her eyebrows raised. "Do you mind going to their rooms?"

I shrugged. It made no difference to me where we heard the rest of the story. I still didn't know what their purpose was, but I was fairly certain Mrs. Huffman was telling the truth. They hadn't meant me harm.

With the matter decided I followed them out, almost locking the door behind me before concluding there was no point, since I was visiting with the perpetrators. Besides, when the guy who breaks into your room holds a master key, what good is a lock?

Chapter 34

As I walked through the door I saw with surprise that their rooms were cozy and bright. Instead of a room with a bath, as I had, their suite consisted of a combination kitchenette and living area with a door, presumably leading to the bedroom and bathroom, off to my right. The apartment was small but spotless, with everything in its place. Nora and I seated ourselves on a red plaid couch and Mr. Huffman sat in a worn leather chair, a roughhewn oak coffee table separating him from us.

"Can I offer you something to eat? That zucchini bread we talked about? Or maybe some coffee or water?" Mrs. Huffman stood wringing her hands in the tiny kitchenette. It was all rather surreal; in the space of twenty minutes I'd gone from thinking the Huffmans might be undercover ax murderers to being offered zucchini bread and coffee in their cheerful apartment. I felt like a child settling in for a bedtime story, but I already knew this one didn't have a happy ending.

Nora asked for bottled water and I declined, still full from the chocolate cake I'd had earlier. Mrs. Huffman retrieved a couple of bottles from the refrigerator and handed one to Nora, another to Mr. Huffman, before taking a seat in the rocking chair beside him. Mr. Huffman took a long drink and set it aside, wiping his mouth with the back of his hand.

"Lindy and me was close," he resumed his story, "but she wasn't in love with me the way I was her. I was smitten, that's for sure. Daydreamed about that girl all the time, just waiting for the day she'd realize I was her knight in shining armor." He chuckled quietly. "Course, I guess that was hard for her to recognize since what I looked like was a skinny, pimple faced boy with big feet.

"That last summer, when I was sixteen, I was about to be sent up to Morgantown to stay with my grandparents. My mother's family. They was getting on up in years and needed some work done on their place. The plan was for me to stay on with them for a couple months over the summer, repair the roof, replace the fences, that sort of thing. I was excited about it because I hadn't ever been away from home like that. It made me feel grown up, like I was becoming a man.

"So I was excited, but I was heartbroken too, because I couldn't imagine being away from Lindy for that long. On top of all that, I was worried about her safety. Seemed like her momma and daddy had been fighting more that spring, and for whatever reason they always tended to take their frustration out on Lindy. Wasn't a day to go by that spring that she wasn't at our house, crying and bruised up.

"Wasn't like it is now. Back then, you didn't get up in other people's business. Wasn't nobody to call for help, least not so far as we knew, and probably wouldn't have called, anyway. The thinking was that a man's family wasn't nobody else's business. About all we could do was to give her a place to run to, so we did."

Nora and I both sat quietly while he took another long drink of water. Next to him, Mrs. Huffman also remained silent, picking at a loose thread on her apron. He set the bottle back on the coaster and sat back in his chair.

"The day before I was to leave was a hard one for Lindy," he said. "'Round about seven o'clock that evening I heard her knocking at the door. She had her own way of knocking to let us know it was her, a little pattern she liked to tap out against the wood. Anyway, I was by myself that evening. Everyone else had gone to a supper at the church, but I'd stayed home to pack my stuff for the trip the next morning.

"I'll tell you what, I was glad she had come over. I really was. I recognized she didn't feel the way about me that I felt about her, but it was just about enough for me that she would even consider me her friend. I wanted to be around her any way I could. It pained me sometimes to see her running off with all them boys that come around her house, and I don't need to tell you what my sixteen year old imagination pictured them doing, but it was me she run to when she wanted a friend, and that almost made up for it.

"All them things was running through my mind when I went to open the door for her that last evening. When I got it open, I seen right away that she was having a rough time of it. That wasn't no surprise. I was used to seeing her cry; she cried almost every time she come to hide out at our house, but that evening it was worse than usual, and I could see the red outline of a handprint against her cheek where her momma had slapped her.

"She come right in and leaned against my chest. That was something different. Lindy didn't never touch me, not since we was little kids. She didn't say nothing, just laid her head against me and cried. Lord, I was so taken by surprise it took me a minute to put my arms around her, but when I did, we just stood there for a bit. I didn't know what to think. On the one hand I wanted to protect her from anybody ever hurting her again. I could just see myself marching up to her house and telling them not to ever lay another finger on her. I'd done it often enough in my daydreams.

"On the other hand, her stepping into my arms that way was a scene right out of another one of my fantasies. I reckon I was plumb full of fantasies about that girl in one way or another." He chuckled again. "I was such an inexperienced boy. Hadn't never had a girlfriend, though God knows I'd tried enough. Anyway, what I ended up doing in the end was standing there waiting on her to tell me what to do."

He was quiet for a minute, reaching over to clasp Mrs. Huffman's hand before turning back to Nora and me. "After a little while, Lindy pulled away from me and said, 'You're leaving me tomorrow, and then there won't be nobody to care about me.' She looked so sad when she said it. I tried to tell her I'd only be gone a little while, but she shook her head and told me to hush.

"Well, you can see where this is going. She was in a vulnerable state and I was a teenage boy. I wouldn't never have started anything with her on my own, and I swear to God that is the truth. For one thing, I'd have been too scared to. For another, I wasn't sure I'd know how, and I didn't want to look any more foolish than I already did. But it didn't take much encouragement from her for me to jump right on board.

"She was wild, I'll tell you that. Angry and rough with me. Hurtful even. I didn't know what to make of it; I really didn't. I didn't know girls ever acted that way. My experience had been that boys was always supposed to try to get to first base, and girls was always supposed to make them stop.

"Here I was in a situation where the girl was insisting on doing things I'd only ever dreamed about, and I reckoned it must be from all them nights she'd snuck out of her house to run off with all them boys. I figured she had more experience with it all than I did and maybe that's just how it was done.

"I feel awful about that now, have for the last forty-eight years." To my surprise, I saw tears in his eyes. "Just plain awful. It didn't take long for me to figure out she hadn't never done any of them things before, either. For the life of me, I couldn't understand why she had come on that way, why she had insisted with me the way she had.

"Now I can look back and understand it for what it was, a desperate young girl needing somebody to love her and not knowing any other way to ask for it. She just needed to feel like somebody cared, that's all. And I did; I truly did. It was a terrible mistake, doing what we did. That wasn't the right way to give her what she'd needed from me; I only wish I'd had the maturity to know it at the time. I like to think if I'd known I was her first, I would have made us stop. I like to think that, but I don't know.

"When it was all over I asked her, 'Why didn't you tell me?'" She touched me here on the cheek," he rubbed his cheek with a forefinger, "and said, 'Because you wouldn't have done it if you'd known.'

"I told her I loved her, and she laughed a little bit and kissed me on the cheek. Then she said, 'I know you do,' and she stood up to put her clothes back on. She was crying while she did it. Truthfully, I don't know as she'd ever stopped crying. I told her I'd write her while I was gone, and she told me that would be nice, and then she left, just like that.

"I did write her while I was gone, sometimes every day, but she didn't never write me back. A couple of times I asked Momma about her, but Momma said she hadn't come around since I'd left. I had only planned on being gone through the summer, but my grandparents was a lot more poorly than they'd let on. I ended up being gone much longer. I enrolled in the school in Morgantown and finished my junior year there.

"After six or seven months of not ever hearing back from Lindy, I finally quit writing. By the time I was to return home, I'd almost convinced myself it had all been a dream. When I did arrive home, Momma told me Lindy had up and disappeared. Rumor was she'd met a man from over in Huntington and gotten pregnant, running off with him.

"I couldn't hardly believe that, knowing as I did at that time that Lindy wasn't all them things folks said she was. I started counting up the months, and that's when it hit me. If she was pregnant, if she had run off because of that, that baby must surely be mine."

189

Chapter 35

I needed a break from Mr. Huffman's story. The tiny apartment had gone from cozy and quaint to suffocating and oppressive. I was overly warm and longed for a breath of fresh air. I excused myself and stepped out into the hallway, grateful for the momentary escape. The Lodge was quiet and I was disappointed I had missed telling Robby goodnight. I walked briskly through the darkened common area and stepped out onto the porch, drawing in a lungful of the cold night air.

I wasn't sure how to feel about the things I'd heard that evening; the whole scenario was overwhelming to me. As far as I was concerned, for all intents and purposes my life had begun at the age of thirteen, when I went to live with Billy May. The years before that were largely a blur. I remembered fighting and screaming, I remembered loneliness and fear, and I remembered my mother leaving me. I had done a fairly decent job of blocking out memories of my last summer with Roy, but I knew they were right under the surface.

Hearing about a history that included me but wasn't incorporated into my own frame of reference was unsettling. Mr. Huffman had used the word *fantasies* when talking about his relationship with my mother. I had had fantasies too, as a young girl, none more prominent than the one in which my nonexistent father suddenly appeared, charging up the mountain, rescuing me from Roy and sweeping me off into a better world.

In that particular fantasy he was bigger than life, a man strong enough to knock Roy into next week, as Corinne used to say. As it had turned out, that father never appeared no matter how hard I summoned him. Instead, I'd been saved by a tiny woman barely five feet tall who'd not only rescued me, but who had knocked Roy past next week and right out of my life.

I had once wondered aloud if my father might have loved me better than my mother had, had he stayed around. I could still remember Billy May's answer. *Well, honey, it's his loss that he never met you, and her loss that she left you behind. You seem lovable enough to me.* I had liked that, the idea that maybe they hadn't abandoned me because something was wrong with *me*; maybe they had abandoned me because something was wrong with *them*. The idea had never really stuck, my insecurities too great, but it had comforted me nonetheless.

Now that nonexistent father was sitting a few feet away from me on Billy May's mountain. The cowardly Ares on the land of Athena. The warrior god known for his egotistical cowardice, and the warrior goddess known for her strength and compassion.

The numbness I'd previously felt was quickly giving way to anger. How dare he? How *dare* he? He wasn't worthy of setting foot on Billy May's land. The knowledge of him there turned my stomach. Billy May had cleaned up the mess he'd left behind. He, my own flesh and blood, had chosen to leave me, while she, a stranger, had chosen to save me.

Had he had a good life? Had he known peace and happiness? While Roy had been raping me, where had he been? Enjoying the sun, maybe, or a beer with friends? Maybe he'd been hiking in the mountains, or fishing with buddies. While that humid West Virginia sun beat down on my battered body, mosquitoes sucking the blood from my secret parts, had he been holding up a trout, proud of his catch? Was it captured forever in some Kodachrome photo a friend of his had taken in the excitement of the moment? Much like Roy's pockmarked face was forever immortalized in my own memory?

Where had he been? Oh, damn him. Damn him to hell. I was overcome with rage, my hands gripping the railing so tightly they began to tingle, the circulation cut off.

Smaoinigh sula gniomhu tu, Billy May whispered in the breeze against my cheek, speaking her father's ancient language. Think before you act. And then I knew she was with me. Billy May had always been with me. *Bí comforted, beag amháin.* Be comforted, little one, she said to me, and I strained to hear more, desperate for her voice. *The signs are all around you, little girl. Listen to what the universe has to say.*

I loosened my grip on the railing and tilted my head back to look at the sky. The night was clear, and as I always had, I marveled at the stars. No place on earth is better for star gazing than Crutcher Mountain on a clear night. *Listen to the universe*, she had said, and so I did. I took a deep breath and let the presence of Billy May's voice clear my head, felt the embrace of her in the wind against my shoulders, and at last I was comforted.

Chapter 36

I heard Nora's voice as I approached the Huffmans' door. "I can't guarantee anything until we hear the rest of what you have to say," she was saying. "Richard, Opal, I believe you when you say you meant Jessie no harm, but we still need to understand what it was you were doing in her room, going through her things."

I knocked once and pushed open the door. "Yes," I said, "we do need to understand that."

Nora turned to me, "Oh good, Jessie. You're back. Are you okay?"

I nodded. "Just needed some air. Sorry to have left so abruptly. Mr. Huffman, you have more to tell us?" I took my seat on the couch.

"I do," he said. "I know how this must seem to you, but I want you to know I did look for you."

"That's certainly something I'd love to hear about," I replied, "so let's hear it. How did you try to look for me?"

"Mrs. McIntosh," Mrs. Huffman broke in before he could answer my question. "This must be awful for you. I can't imagine what you must be feeling right now, but please know that Richard never stopped searching for you. Our whole marriage, nearly forty-three years, he's been trying to keep up with you."

"I have," Mr. Huffman agreed. "When I got back home and starting putting together the pieces I questioned everybody I come across. All anybody could say for sure was that Lindy had run off with a man dressed like a coal miner. Said she'd gotten herself in trouble with him and then run off

195

with him to Huntington. Didn't nobody even have a name for the man, but I tried to track Lindy down by her maiden name, Lindy Russell.

"I spent near about the whole summer before my senior year taking the bus back and forth to Huntington. I reckon it was a senseless thing to do, but what else could I have done? Wasn't no internet back then, no technology like there is now. I walked all over town hoping to catch sight of her. I asked everybody I run into if they'd met a girl by that name.

"I finished out my senior year and joined the service. Traveled all over the place for the next few years, but I didn't never stop thinking about Lindy and that baby. I met Opal here when I was stationed in Millington, Tennessee back in '67. She come from a little town name of Covington, was teaching up in the high school there. What was the name of it, Opal? Byars Hall, that's right. Anyway, I told her all about Lindy soon as we got serious.

"It was Opal suggested I write letters. We wrote them together, must have written near about everybody in Cabell and Wayne Counties. Wrote the hospitals, the sheriff's departments, the police department...everybody we could think of to write. We figured if Lindy or the baby had had any sort of trouble, one of those places must know about them. Nothing, though. Didn't hear nothing back.

"I got out in '71 and we moved back to this area. I saw more new places than I can remember during my time in the service, but West Virginia was always home to me and that baby kept pulling at me. I guess I thought my chances of finding Lindy was better if I come back to Logan, where we was both raised. I went to work as a mechanic and we started thinking about having a family of our own, but that wasn't meant to be."

"I wasn't able to," Mrs. Huffman spoke up. "After a couple years of trying, I found out from the doctor I had some cysts in the way. They thought maybe they could save the ovaries, but they couldn't."

Mr. Huffman patted her knee. "That was a rough time for us, but we did okay, didn't we, Opal? Somewhere along the line we decided if we couldn't have our own, we'd work helping other kids, ones that needed us. We spent a lot of years doing that, and I reckon we might have helped one or two along the way. I hope we did, anyway.

"Without no kids of our own, and with both of us working, we was able to save up a little bit of money. Opal seen I was still eaten up with wanting to know about that baby. When we had saved up enough, she suggested I hire someone to help me, a private investigator. What year was that, Opal? Around '74?"

Mrs. Huffman shook her head. "It was in '73, right after my surgery, remember?"

"That's right," he nodded. "I remember now. Hired a guy from Charleston to go find Lindy. Smart, that man was. Sharp. Man by the name of Rogers. Samuel Rogers, a sheriff's deputy who did investigating on the side. Took him a few months to get a lead, because as it turned out Lindy hadn't gone to Huntington after all.

"Rogers went back to the beginning. When I'd gotten home that summer before my senior year, rumor was that the man Lindy was with looked like a coal miner, but he wasn't anyone folks in our town recognized. Rogers figured he must have been a temporary hire from somewhere close by.

"He went to the mines all around Logan County looking for information about mine workers. Found out one mine, Rock Creek, had hired temporary diggers from Cedar Hollow for a week that summer when they hit a big vein. Rogers got a list of all the names and started going through it, one by one. Eventually tracked down Roy Campbell, here in Cedar Hollow."

I flinched at Roy's name. It was odd, hearing it spoken by Mr. Huffman.

"Once he found Roy, he found Lindy. Said she had three kids, the oldest a girl the right age to have been mine. He watched the family for a couple days, used to joke he hoped I got things settled before a bear got him, hiding out on that mountain like he was. Said it was a sad situation, from what he could tell. Lot of fighting." Mr. Huffman glanced up at me. I nodded. Yes, it had certainly been a sad situation.

"The evening of the second day, right when Rogers was about to call it quits and head home, he saw Roy Campbell get in his truck and drive away. Rogers waited a few minutes to be sure, then went up to the shack they was living in and knocked on the door. Took a few minutes, but Lindy finally opened it a crack.

"Rogers said he just come straight out and told Lindy I wanted to see her. Told her why, too. Said she looked plumb scared to death, refused at first to have anything to do with him. He finally told her he wasn't leaving until she agreed to meet with me and answer my questions. She agreed of course. He didn't leave her much choice. Rogers told her he'd come pick her up the same time the next day, while Roy was at work.

"I couldn't believe we'd finally found her. I halfway didn't expect her to be there the next day when he drove out to get her, but she was. Rogers said he could hear kids inside the house and she called back to someone," Mr. Huffman paused, "you, I reckon, told you to take care of the little 'uns, she'd be back after a while. Then she climbed up in the truck with him. Said she didn't say a word all the way to our place, over in Logan. Just sat there with her hands in her lap, looking out the window."

I thought back to that time period and realized it wouldn't have been strange to see Lindy climb into a truck with a man. That was right about the time she left me. For a period of time spanning several weeks she had snuck out while Roy was at work, going to meet the train conductor she eventually ran away with. I'd gotten used to watching over my half-siblings while she was gone. I wouldn't have thought anything of it.

"Rogers brought her right to our house," Mr. Huffman was saying. "I tell you, I was shocked at how she looked. The girl I remembered had been pretty, but Lindy wasn't pretty no more. Looked old. Old, and tired. I reckon she had really had a rough go of it. I felt so bad for her; she was pitiful. But at the same time I felt a little bit angry at her, too. If she'd just told me instead of running off...." He didn't complete the thought.

"She come in and sat down at the kitchen table with us. Opal got her something to eat. At first she wouldn't say much, just sat there looking scared to death. Wouldn't answer none of my questions for the longest time. Then she put her hands over her face and started crying, asked me what I wanted. I told her I wanted to know about the baby. Was it mine? But she wouldn't tell me. 'Richard,' she said to me, 'look at the life you have here. Such a good life. I've made a mess of things. I never do seem to make the right decisions.'

"We told her we could help her. Me and Opal both told her that. If the little girl Rogers had seen was mine, I wanted to help raise her. I'd give them money or whatever else they needed. Me and Opal had already discussed taking her in, if Lindy would let us. We would have done anything. But Lindy just kept saying she couldn't mess up our lives. I couldn't make her understand I *wanted* to be a part of that child's life. Of your life." Mr. Huffman reached in his back pocket, pulled out a handkerchief and blew his nose. Mrs. Huffman put a hand on his shoulder.

"Before too long," he continued, "she said she needed to get home, told Rogers to take her there. She stood up and walked to the door, but right before she walked out she

Melinda Clayton

turned back to me, her face all splotchy from the crying, and said, 'If you're serious, you need to come tomorrow. I'm leaving him. I'm taking the kids with me, but if you're serious about what you're telling me, I'll leave Jessie there for you. She'll have a better life with you than I could ever give her.'

"Well let me tell you, that was music to my ears. Me and Opal looked at each other and right away we both said yes. We didn't even need to discuss it. It was a dream come true to hear them words. She hadn't even told me for sure the baby was mine, but I didn't care."

I was trying to make sense of the things he was telling me. "So, Lindy offered to leave me for you," I said. "She had planned on taking me with her when she left?"

"Oh, yeah," he answered. "She was taking all of y'all with her. She was plumb desperate to escape that man. When I showed up and she come to meet me and Opal, she saw I could give you a better life than she was able to do. I reckon compared to the life y'all were living in that shack, we must have looked pretty rich."

"Then what happened?" I asked. "You chickened out? Because clearly you never came for me."

"But I did," he said. "I did come for you. Me and Opal both did. Come for you that next day just like I said I would. Pulled up to that little shack and seen right away something was wrong because Roy's truck was there. He wasn't supposed to be there, you see. Was supposed to be at work. Lindy was going to tell you about me and explain why she wasn't taking you with her so you wouldn't be scared when me and Opal showed up. Then she was going to leave you there waiting for me.

"But something had happened. Something went wrong, because when we got there you was gone, too. Lindy had taken you with her. Roy come out on the porch and laughed at us. Called me a few choice words, told me I should have known better than to believe anything Lindy told me.

Said you was gone with them, gone to Arizona with the train man."

I couldn't breathe my throat had closed up so. Finally I managed to say, "But I wasn't. I was there. I was there with Roy."

Chapter 37

I remembered that day as if it were only yesterday. How could I forget the day my mother left me?

They had been fighting the night before, she and Roy. I remembered that, too. I didn't know what they were fighting about. They always fought; that was nothing new. He accused her of something, she accused him back. It was a tiny cabin, only one room sectioned off with sheets. It wasn't as if I could escape their yelling, but over the years I'd developed a pretty strong ability to block it out, like white noise in the background.

They argued behind their sheet while I fed my half-siblings dinner and got them settled in bed, climbing in with them. They continued fighting off and on throughout the night, waking the three of us with their shouts and cries. I pulled the babies closer and shushed them. The last thing we needed was for Roy's attention to be diverted from our mother to us, and I knew that's what would happen if Roy heard us.

I don't know when the fighting finally ceased. Sometime before dawn. When I awoke, the sun was shining through the window beside the door making a bright, white rectangle upon the floor across from our shared bed. My half-siblings were no longer next to me; I could hear my mother talking softly to them on the other side of the curtain. I climbed out of bed and parted the sheets.

"There you are, Jessie!" My mother grabbed my arm and pulled me to sit at the table across from her. She was dressed, her hair styled, and I noticed with surprise that she was wearing bright red lipstick. I couldn't remember the last time I'd seen my mother wearing lipstick, couldn't really remember if she ever had. "Listen up, now," she said, "because I got some things to talk to you about and I ain't got much time."

"Why are you dressed up?" I asked her, but she ignored the question.

"The little 'uns and me is goin' to be leavin'," she said. "But you ain't comin' with us."

I wasn't sure I'd heard her right. "What do you mean?" I asked. Of course I was going with her. Where else would I go?

"You're stayin' here," she said, and I remember starting to feel afraid. She wasn't herself; her cheeks were flushed, her eyes overly bright. My gaze landed on a suitcase by the door.

"Where are you going?" I asked her, the initial prick of fear turning into panic.

Before she could answer me, I heard Roy's truck come barreling up the rutted drive, loose gravel spraying against the front wall of the house as he skidded to a stop, nearly shearing off the front steps. What was he doing home? He was supposed to be at work. Roy had never shown up in the middle of a work day; it was the only time I think all of us felt safe.

"Oh, my God," my mother said then, the blood draining from her face. "Oh, my God," she repeated, jumping up and grabbing Leroy from where he'd been crawling on the floor. "Jessie, there ain't no time for me to explain. There ain't no time; there ain't no time! Lenny Sue, grab that suitcase, baby, quick now. Quick!" She turned to me, frantic. "Jessie, we're leavin' but you cain't come. Oh, my baby doll, you have to stay here."

I grabbed at her arm. "No, Momma! You can't do this! You can't leave me here with him!" I clung to her, begging her to take me with her as Roy came bursting through the door.

Momma screamed and clutched Leroy tighter in her arms. Roy stood in the doorway, blocking the sunlight. Then he grinned.

"Figured today was the day," he said, "so I come to tell you goodbye. Wouldn't want you to leave without a proper goodbye, seein' as how you're my wife and all." Roy kicked the suitcase out onto the porch and turned back to Momma. He unbuckled his belt, pulling it through the loops with a *whish*.

The cabin was small enough that there was no way to escape hearing the noises they made some nights, but even so, all I knew were sounds. I didn't know, at that time, what he had in mind for Lindy, though I fully realized it as I allowed myself to remember that day. Back then I assumed he meant to beat her with the belt, as he often had me. And truthfully, he may have planned on doing that as well, in addition to raping her.

Dimly, I could hear another truck approaching and I recognized it as the one Momma had gotten into several times over the last few weeks. Roy heard it, too. He paused, his pants halfway down his hips.

"You lucky bitch," he said to Momma. "You lucky, stupid bitch. Get out of here. If I ever see your ugly face again I'll kill you." He yanked his pants up, slid the belt back through the loops.

"But leave her," he jerked his head towards me as he fastened the buckle. "She ain't goin' nowhere. You takin' what's mine, I'm takin' what's yours. That's fair, ain't it? It's the only way I'll let you go. Take them squallin' brats; I don't want no shitty diapers to be changin'. But leave her. Somebody got to look after me. She can do the cookin' and cleanin', and soon enough whatever else I need, too. I 'magine she'll be better at all of it than you ever was."

I gripped Momma's arm harder, terrified. She couldn't leave me with him. She wouldn't.

Momma clutched my chin and made me look at her. She was breathing hard, her eyes boring into mine. Had she been trying to tell me? I couldn't help but wonder now. "Baby doll," she said, "I got to take the younguns with me. They ain't old enough to fend for themselves and you know that asshole won't take care of 'em." She scrubbed for a second at the dirt on Leroy's face before reaching out to me again.

"But you got to stay behind," she had said. "I ain't got room to take you. You're big enough to care for yourself, and besides, Roy is goin' to need somebody to take care of him. You be good now, you hear me?"

She gripped my chin again, hard, and hesitated for just an instant before she grabbed Lenny Sue by the hand and ran past Roy, leaving her suitcase on the porch where it had landed.

A few seconds later I heard the truck drive away. I was afraid to move. Roy seemed to have forgotten about me for the moment and I didn't want to remind him that I was still there, right where Momma had left me. For a long time he stood staring down the mountain after the truck. Then he turned to me.

"Get the hell out of here," he muttered through gritted teeth. "Get out of my sight, but mind you get back in time to cook me some supper. I ain't supportin' your ass for free, you better believe that."

I hadn't even had time to dress; I still had on the flimsy nightgown I'd slept in, but I ran anyway, towards the creek where I'd always gone when Roy frightened me. I stayed there all day, curled up on the ground with nowhere else to go. Later, years later, I'd find a cave to hide in when Roy came after me, but that day I made do with the muddy banks of Rugged Creek.

While I had lain there in the mud, desperate and afraid, my father had finally come charging up the mountain to save me, but he was too late.

Chapter 38

On a bookshelf against the wall behind the Huffmans, a clock softly chimed the half-hour. It was only eight-thirty but it seemed much later. I could feel Nora scrutinizing me, gauging whether or not I was able to continue. Across from me, Mr. Huffman reached a hand towards me, then let it drop into his lap.

"I know that now," he said, "but I didn't know it then. I didn't find out until much later. I'd give anything...." His voice cracked and Mrs. Huffman put a hand on his arm. "I'd give plumb anything to be able to go back to that day and do it again." He exhaled a long breath and swiped the back of his hand across his eyes.

His sincerity was obvious, but I still didn't understand how, if he'd spent all those years searching for me, he could have given up so easily that one fateful day. "Why didn't you come back?" I asked. "You had tracked me down once before; why didn't you do it again?"

"I did," he said. "I did, but not quick enough and not in the right place. I thought she'd changed her mind about leaving you with me and Opal and taken you to Arizona, you see. It would have been like Lindy to do that; she always was a flighty girl. Like she'd told me just the day before, she couldn't never seem to make the right decisions, and it had taken some convincing from me and Opal to get her to agree to leave you with us in the first place.

"At that time, I had run out of money for the private investigator. I didn't have no way of sending him to Arizona after you, but me and Opal figured we'd save up some more and find you again. After meeting Roy Campbell I was relieved you was out of that situation. Lindy didn't always make good decisions, but I did believe she would do the best she could for you. I understood she didn't mean to let me have you, but I was bound and determined to find you again anyway because if you was mine, I wanted to provide for you. Rogers told us to give him a call when we was ready to hire him again, so we did.

"He went out there to Arizona...." He turned to Opal. "How many times, Opal? 'Bout five? Five times over the next four or five years, but Lindy and her man, name of Floyd Bowden, wouldn't stay put long enough for him to catch up to them. Could have found them easy if Bowden hadn't quit working the rails, but he quit soon as they got to Arizona. Found out later he'd filed a workman's comp claim for a foot injury he somehow got backing up to couple a wagon.

"Anyway, Rogers would track him down to one little town doing some odd job or another, mainly construction, and by the time he got out there, they'd have moved again, going where the jobs was at. 'Bout the time Rogers would start to feel like he was getting closer, me and Opal would have to save up some more money before he could get out there again.

"Finally, Rogers tracked Bowden down to Flagstaff. Flew out there again and sure enough, that's where he was at. SDB, that big construction company, was working out there and Bowden was contracting with them. But when Rogers got there...." Mr. Huffman glanced at his wife, and I caught the look of uncertainty on his face. "Opal?" he asked.

"Ms. McIntosh," Opal addressed me. "You've waited a long time to learn these things. I know all of them must be troubling to you, and some of them are just plain bad. Do you want Richard to go on?"

I thought carefully before answering. "Mrs. Huffman, it isn't so much that I want him to go on. I need him to go on. Now that I've learned this much, I need to know all of it." I turned to Mr. Huffman. "Whatever it is, I can handle it. Just tell me."

He nodded. "All right, then. Rogers caught up to Floyd Bowden. Followed him a couple days but something was off. Bowden was living in a rental. Had two kids with him, a girl around about eleven or twelve and a younger boy, looked to be seven or eight. You'd have been close to eighteen by that time, but there wasn't no sign of an eighteen year old girl. Wasn't no sign of Lindy, neither."

"She had left him?" I asked. It seemed the logical explanation. "But why would she have left the kids with him?"

Mr. Huffman shook his head. "She hadn't left him." He reached for the nearly empty water bottle and drained it. "That's what Rogers thought at first, too, but that wasn't it. There had been a house fire."

At first what he was telling me didn't sink in. "A house fire?"

"Bad one," he said. "Happened about six months before. Bowden told Rogers Lindy didn't make it out. Said she died trying to make sure the kids got out. From what they could tell, Lindy thought Lenny Sue had made it out first. When Lindy got out there, she didn't see Leroy so she ran back in to find him. She never made it out. Later, they found out Leroy was the one who got out first, ran over to a neighbor's to call for help."

I sat quietly, trying to take it all in. I didn't know what to feel. For nearly all of my life I'd believed my father had abandoned me at conception and my mother had abandoned me to a monster. In the space of two hours I'd found out that wasn't the case. Now my father was sitting across from me and my mother was dead. My head was spinning.

Beside me, Nora cleared her throat. "It's late, and I know we're all tired. This has to be emotionally draining for all of you. Richard, bring us to how you ended up here, at the Lodge, and then let's all call it a night. We have a busy day

211

tomorrow and I know all of you are going to need some time to process."

Mr. Huffman removed his glasses and rubbed his face. "Rogers found all that out from Bowden when he finally confronted him. He asked Bowden where you was at. Said the man looked surprised. Said Bowden asked him, 'Jessie? Lindy's older girl? Lindy didn't bring her. Left her there with her their daddy,' and he pointed at the two kids.

"Well, you can imagine how I felt when I heard that," Mr. Huffman said. "At first I didn't want to believe it. All them years, you'd been back here with that man, just a few miles from me and Opal. I tell you what, it was about more than I could stand to hear. My heart just plumb broke in two when I heard that.

"Rogers got back from Arizona and come straight here, to Cedar Hollow. Went right up to that old shack but could tell right away wasn't nobody there. The woods had done grown over it, looked like it'd set empty for a long time. He went down to the town, then, and stopped in at the diner. Said he asked the woman at the counter if she'd ever heard of you. I don't recall her name now, but I believe it was the momma of the woman there now."

"Peggy," I told him. "It was Peggy's diner."

"That's right, the name of the place. Should have remembered that," he said. "Anyway, Rogers said as soon as he spoke your name everybody in the place shut right up. Just stopped talking and stared at him. Said the temperature must have dropped thirty degrees. Peggy come from around the counter and pointed at the door. Told him she didn't know who the hell he was or what the hell he wanted, but he didn't have no business coming around her place asking nosy questions. They just about run him out of town, I tell you."

My family. I had to smile. Those people were my family, keeping me safe from what they perceived as a threat. Why would they have thought otherwise? As far as any of them had known—as far as *I* had known—I had no kin. There was no reason for anyone to be asking about me unless they had some sort of malicious intent.

"Rogers did some digging around," Mr. Huffman was saying, "and was able to piece together that Roy Campbell had taken off years back, when you'd have been twelve or thirteen, and the woman over at the grocery had raised you after that. We went over there, me and Rogers did, to that store."

That both shocked and frightened me, and I'm not sure why. The closeness of two worlds colliding, maybe, both to do with me but only one known by me.

"Met Billy May Platte, the owner. Nice woman. Very nice woman. It put my heart at ease a little bit, that this was the woman raised you. We made small talk with her, found out you was at Marshall by then. She was a sharp woman, too. After a couple minutes of talking to her, she squinted up at me and said, 'Who are you, and what is it you really want?'"

That would be my Billy Momma. Yes, indeed, she was smart. My heart swelled.

"I looked down at her then," Mr. Huffman said. "She was a tiny woman, but she was a tough one. I seen my search was over. She had took good care of you, that woman had. You was grown by then. You'd made it. I didn't reckon you'd have any need of me, and I heard by her words that y'all was close. I'd heard enough about Roy Campbell by then to know what them couple of years with him must have been like for you. She had saved you from that when I hadn't."

He watched me, but I gave nothing away. It was over. No point in bringing Roy up again. Besides, over the last week I'd begun to believe that there might be some sort of contentment out there for me. I was longing to break free from the past that had held me hostage for so many years.

Mr. Huffman continued to study me. "I reckon I know what he did, anyway," he said. "I reckon I do, the bastard." He pulled his handkerchief out and blew his nose again.

"Didn't figure you'd have any use for me. After all I'd found out, I couldn't blame you. I'd failed you. I reckoned if I was you, I wouldn't want nothing to do with me, either. Kept in touch with Rogers, though. Went to your graduation from Marshall. Went to all your premiers. Always kept up with you."

This absolutely shocked me. He'd kept up with my career?

"Heard about Ms. Platte's passing, too, and about you opening up this place," he said. "It was the perfect opportunity, you know. I couldn't pass it up. I needed to see you."

"Why?" I asked. "After all these years, why now?"

"I'm getting old," he said. "Haven't been well these last few years. Heart disease. It's genetic, from what I understand. Cholesterol is the problem. Always high, my whole life, no matter what I did. They tell me my children will likely have the same problem." He paused.

"So the toothbrush, the hairbrush you dropped, Mrs. Huffman, when I surprised you this evening. For DNA tests? Was that the idea?" I had to get to the bottom of that.

"It was," Mr. Huffman confirmed. "I always felt in my heart you was mine, but I didn't want to burden you with medical stuff if you wasn't. I had to make sure." He sighed. "The truth is I'm on borrowed time. Ain't going to be around too much longer. Now Opal," he said, when she stirred beside him, "you know it's true."

He looked back at me. "Ms. McIntosh, all them years I tried to find you to provide for you, I set that money aside. I been saving it up for you, just kept on saving it even after you was grown and didn't need it. A hundred a month is what I saved. It ain't much, but it's all I could do, and it rightfully belongs to you. Needed to make sure you got it before I'm gone."

I waved that away; the last thing I was concerned about was money. Suddenly, I felt as if I couldn't listen to anymore, not that night. "Mr. Huffman, and you too, Mrs. Huffman, I'm truly grateful to you both for explaining things to me, but as you can imagine, it's a lot to take in. I hope you won't think I'm rude if I excuse myself. I'm feeling a little overwhelmed. Nora, I appreciate you staying so long, but you must be exhausted. You should go home, and I really think it's time I head to my room."

I didn't mean to be rude, but it was just too much. I found myself unable to continue.

Chapter 39

"One more minute, Jessie," Nora held out a hand to stop me as I stood to leave. "We still don't have all the answers."

I doubted we would ever have all the answers, but I sank tiredly back onto the couch. "What do you mean? Nora, I really don't want to do this any longer tonight."

"The fire," she said. "The break in. The chemicals. What about those things? Jessie, that's what got you out here to begin with." I was reeling so much from all the revelations of the evening that I'd completely forgotten.

Nora looked at the Huffmans. "Am I to assume you're responsible for those things?"

"No ma'am," Mr. Huffman answered emphatically as Mrs. Huffman vehemently shook her head. "Absolutely not. We didn't have nothing to do with those things. We'd never do something that might hurt these kids. You've got to believe that."

"Don't you think it's a little too much of a coincidence that they happened right after you started working here?" Nora pressed him.

"Yes ma'am, I do," Mr. Huffman answered, "and that worries me. But we didn't have nothing to do with them things happening. It's true as soon as Rogers found out about this place we went and applied for a position. Didn't get hired on at first, so we reapplied when we saw the ads in the paper for a groundskeeper and a housekeeper.

"I didn't know how often Ms. McIntosh visited, but I figured before long we'd come in contact with her if we was

217

here. We'd have a chance to get to know her a little bit, have a chance to get some DNA. Up until then, we hadn't figured how to go about getting a sample. Thought about sending Rogers out to California to see if he could get one somehow, but he's older now, you know. Not working as much.

"When this come up, it was just perfect. If it turned out for sure you was mine, Ms. McIntosh, we'd be set to tell you the truth about things. Didn't know exactly how we'd do it, but that was the plan."

"Did you ever consider approaching me directly?" I asked. "Just explaining and asking me for a sample?" It seemed like such a simple solution.

"Would you have given it?" Mr. Huffman asked.

That was a good question. I didn't know the answer. More than likely I would have thought they were kooks. When you have a lot of money, people do unbelievable things to try to get their hands on it. What would I have done if a strange, elderly couple had approached me in L.A., told this fantastic story, and asked for a DNA sample? I probably would have thought they were pulling some sort of scam and called security. I wasn't sure what made it different hearing it up on Crutcher Mountain, but for some reason it was.

"Ms. McIntosh," he continued, "the way we went about planning things out might be wrong, but we didn't mean no harm to nobody, and we did not do them things y'all are asking me about. I swear to God we didn't have nothing to do with that." Mr. Huffman slapped his thighs for emphasis.

"I suppose it's really up to the Sheriff to figure all this out now," Nora told him. "Sheriff Moore is aware that Jessie suspected you might be her father. As for your jobs, I'm going to need to sit down and figure out the best way to handle all this and a great deal will depend on what we hear from Sheriff Moore tomorrow."

"Fair enough," Mr. Huffman replied. "Just know we want to stay if you want to have us."

We left them sitting side by side, both looking a little confused and even more worried. As Nora and I softly closed their door behind us, she grasped my shoulder. "Are you okay?"

I shrugged. "I'm numb," I said. "Information overload. It'll take some time to sort things out."

"Yes, it will," she replied. "And if they're telling the truth, we still don't know who's responsible for the vandalism. I'm not sure what to think about all this, but something still seems off to me." She yawned. "I don't suppose we're going to solve it tonight. I'll see you in the morning; give me a call tonight if you need to." She gave my shoulder a pat.

"Will do," I said, though of course I wouldn't. I waved goodbye as Nora turned to go, then let myself into my room. I was beat; what I really wanted was a long, hot bath, but I knew Corinne and crew would be getting worried by now. I had promised to call them. I flopped across the bed and dialed. It was Michael who answered.

"We were about to send out a posse," he joked. "Seriously, is everything okay?"

"It's been an interesting evening," I said. "It's too much to go into tonight, but we'll definitely have stimulating dinner conversation tomorrow."

"I can hardly wait. Can we have a hint?"

I smiled. "Sure," I told him. "Let's see. My father has been lurking around here trying to get a DNA sample, I've been stalked by a private investigator nearly my entire life, and my mother died in a house fire when I was eighteen. Is that enough?"

It was so quiet I thought the call had dropped. "Wow," he finally said. "Yes, that will definitely be an interesting dinner conversation. I'm speechless. So the Huffmans are the ones, after all, who set the fire and wrote the note?"

"They say they had nothing to do with any of that," I replied. "For some crazy reason, I tend to believe them."

219

"You need to keep your guard up," Michael said. "If they aren't the ones, then we still don't know who is. Are you okay tonight?"

"I'm fine," I said, "just really needing some space from it all right now. I'm going to take a hot bath and go in search of a cup of tea. This is all going to take a while to sink in; there's no need for me to dwell on it anymore tonight."

"Sounds like a good plan," he said. "We'll see you tomorrow at two-thirty. Call if you need anything."

"Will do," I said for the second time that night, and that time I actually meant it.

Twenty minutes later, bathed and in sweats, I let myself quietly out of my room and padded barefoot across the common area. My plan was to visit the kitchen in search of teabags. Hopefully, Mrs. Huffman kept a supply. I suppose I could have simply knocked on their door and asked, but I'd had enough of the Huffmans for the night.

From the office at the end of the children's wing Sarah looked up and waved. Bryan was apparently just wrapping up a fifteen minute check of the children, clipboard in hand. Just as he looked up to greet me, we both heard a muffled sound.

I knew that sound. As Bryan immediately started towards the darkened bedroom I stepped forward. "I'll take care of it, Bryan. I had wanted to visit with him tonight, anyway."

"Thanks, Jessie. Fill me in on what's going on, okay?" Bryan's expression was worried.

"I'll let you know."

Bryan headed to the office and I stepped into Robby's room. He was turned to the wall, facing away from me. I was surprised to see he was on the bottom bunk. All I could make out in the dim light was the vague shape of his little body, curled tight. I could hear Anthony snoring softly on the top bunk. I could hear Robby crying on the bottom.

I sat on the floor beside his bed and placed my hand gently on his back. I felt his shoulders shaking as he cried and I knew the loneliness of those tears; I had shed them often enough myself. What I wanted more than anything in that moment was to take his pain away. A little boy should not have to know such pain.

Somewhere within my memory I recalled a song sung to me by Billy May on a terrible night thirty-four years before. *Osda adenedi*, I sang quietly to Robby in the language of Billy May's Cherokee mother. *The good spirits will watch over you.* One way or another they would; I'd make sure of it. This was the promise I made.

Chapter 40
Robby

Hi. Well it is me Robby and I am not having a very good night. No I am not. I told Anthony he should sleep on the top bunk tonight because I thought he would rock and keep me awake and I don't want to go to sleep. But he did not rock. He went to sleep and now I don't know how to stay awake. I do not want to sleep because I do not want tomorrow to be here.

If I fall asleep and tomorrow gets here do you know what will happen? I do. Mrs. Cortes will come for the tour and brunch and stuff. I like Mrs. Cortes and she is a nice lady but she is not a mother or a father or a grandfather. Well maybe she is to somebody but not to me. Everybody else has a mother or a father or a grandfather or maybe even a grandmother coming. I have a caseworker and that is not the same thing. It is not the same thing at all.

I don't want to live in the woods like Cody and Dave on *Dual Survival*. I don't want to eat plants and bugs and drink my own pee. I want to live in a house with a mom or a dad or maybe even both. That would be awesome. I don't really want a sister but I will deal with one if that is the only family that will take me and I will be nice to her. I will eat spaghetti if that is what they give me to eat but I don't like spaghetti.

Mr. Paul says sometimes you have to compromise. At first I did not know what that means but Mr. Paul says that means people have to work together to make things work out right. I will compromise with a family if one will take me even though I don't like sisters and I don't like spaghetti and I have Down Syndrome.

I want my Grandpa but he is not here. He will never be here again. That is what Mrs. Jamison at church said. "Robby, he's gone. He's not here anymore." I kind of hated her when she said that but that was bad because you are not supposed to hate people. Grandpa is not here and nobody is here. That makes me so sad but I am not a crybaby. I am not. Even if I have tears I am not a crybaby.

Now somebody is here and I guess they heard me but I am not a crybaby. Then I smell her and she has done her Evening Routine and I know it is Ms. McIntosh because she washed her hair. That is her hair smell. I am glad she is here. I know she will not ask me stupid questions and try to make me have a Breakthrough and I am right and I am so glad she is here.

She sits down on the floor and puts her hand on my back and rubs it like Grandpa used to do. Then she sings me a song. I don't know what she is saying but it is a pretty song anyway. She rubs my back and sings to me and tells me people love me.

She says, "You're okay. You're with me. You're surrounded by people who love you. We'll take care of you." I don't know who the people are who love me and will take care of me but I believe her and then I know it is okay to go to sleep. That's a good thing because I am very tired.

Chapter 41
Friday

Surprisingly, I slept soundly. I hadn't expected to after the revelations of the previous night and I was grateful for it. Apparently, the human mind is only capable of processing overwhelming experiences in small quantities. At least, that seemed true for me, since I managed to block out all the troubling thoughts and memories quite successfully as soon as my head hit the pillow. When the alarm buzzed at six a.m., I arose without hitting the snooze button, feeling unexpectedly refreshed.

I was anxious to call the parent company with Nora to discuss the plan for Robby, and even more anxious to see Mrs. Cortes and learn what she'd found out about my proposition. The phone call would have to wait, since the main office wouldn't be open until eight, but I was hopeful Mrs. Cortes would arrive early for her breakfast with Robby.

I dressed quickly and stepped out into the hallway. I could already hear the children up and about, dressing, making their beds and readying for morning group. I made my way past the common area and headed for the kitchen in search of coffee. Mrs. Huffman was there, supervising the breakfast preparations. I greeted her on my way to the coffee pot.

"Good morning," she returned the greeting, coming to stand beside me. "Did you manage to sleep okay?" Her tone was apologetic.

"I did," I assured her. "You?"

"Not so much," she admitted, giving me a wry smile. "Ms. McIntosh...."

I interrupted her. "Why don't you just call me Jessie? It seems a little odd, under the circumstances, being referred to as Ms. McIntosh. Wouldn't you agree? And if it's okay with the two of you, I'll call you by your first names as well. It's a little late in the game for Mom and Dad, but Mr. and Mrs. Huffman doesn't feel right, either."

She broke into a genuine smile then, and I realized it was the first time I'd ever seen it. It made a world of difference. "Yes, that would be nice," she agreed, and then just as quickly the smile disappeared. "I need to let you know we really are sorry for dumping all this on you. Like Richard said last night, we never could figure out exactly how we should tell you, but last night probably wasn't the best way."

I shrugged. "Last night was a little overwhelming, I have to admit," I told her, "but I don't know that there would have ever been a right time or a right place. Obviously, we'll talk more at some point when things have quieted down. And there's still the sample you had wanted. I'll certainly cooperate with that. For now," I glanced out at the dining room, "let's just concentrate on making this a great day for the kids. What can I help you with?"

She looked relieved. "I'll take all the help I can get," she said. "We're going buffet style this morning, with all the company coming. Would you mind setting the plates and flatware out at the end of that counter?"

I was happy to help, not only because she needed it but also because it kept me occupied while waiting on Mrs. Cortes to show up. Opal had just set the last steaming bin of eggs on the buffet when I caught a glimpse of Mrs. Cortes through the doorway to the common area.

"Are you all set?" I asked Opal. "If you are, there's a caseworker out there I need to speak with."

"I believe we are," she answered, "and I thank you for your help."

"You're very welcome," I told her. "I'll be back in a couple of weeks and we'll talk more then and figure out how to go about getting tested."

"You have a safe trip," she replied. "We'll look forward to seeing you when you get back."

I hung up my apron and made my way to Mrs. Cortes, where she stood quietly observing morning group. She turned as I approached and I could tell by her expression the news was good. Before I could prepare myself, she grabbed me in a hug.

"It's a go!" she said, and I felt a weight lift from my shoulders.

"On our end, anyway," she continued. "Oh, Ms. McIntosh, this is just the best thing that could have happened. The Sloans are so happy they don't have to give him up, and the agency is thrilled with the whole idea. You're brilliant!" She let me go and stepped back, clasping her hands in front of her. "I can't wait to tell Robby."

I couldn't wait either, but we had to until we got clearance on our end. I checked my watch. It was just before seven. Parents were beginning to show up, sitting with their children, chatting with each other, talking with Mr. Paul and Ms. Janice.

"One more hour," I told her. "Nora and I are going to call the executive director as soon as the office opens. Keep your fingers crossed."

"Fingers and toes, both," she said. "We've got some paperwork to do, of course, and a contract you'll have to sign, but as soon as you give me the go ahead, we're set."

"In the meantime," I told her, "I've got to stay busy or I'll go nuts. Are you ready to join the group?"

"I am," she said. "I've got to meet Joseph's family. He's been begging me to let Robby come for an overnight. They've bonded over *Ninja Turtles*."

I laughed. "Then let's get to it." I followed her into the common area.

I spent the next fifty-five minutes meeting the parents of the children and answering questions. They were very gracious, thanking me for opening the Lodge and asking if their children could at some point return. Marcus' mother had brought all the staff a thank you card and a flower.

"It's such a wonderful thing you're doing," she said. "We love our children; you know that. But sometimes we desperately need a break, just to recharge, you know? This week has meant the world to Marcus and me. Thank you."

"It's meant the world to us, too," Ms. Janice told her. "We love the kids, all of them, and Marcus is such a sweetheart." We all glanced over to where Marcus sat laughing at Stacey's attempt to scoop eggs onto a piece of toast. As we watched, Robby reached over to help her.

It was true, what Janice had said. We did love all the kids. *I* did love all the kids. I looked forward to keeping up with them and hoped they would follow through and come back again at some point in the future. I was already thinking a yearly reunion might be a fun idea. I'd have to mention it to Nora.

And at some point, I needed to thank Robby. By alerting me to the true identity of the Huffmans, he'd unlocked the key to my past in such a monumental way I wasn't sure I'd ever wrap my head around all of it. It was quite a gift he'd given me, and I wanted him to know that.

I checked my watch: seven-fifty-five. Time for the call, thank goodness. I excused myself and rushed across the lot to Nora's office. She was waiting for me.

"Ready?" she asked, and I nodded.

Her instincts had proven correct, and she was able to catch the director before anyone else snagged him. Setting the phone on speaker, she explained my proposal. To my relief he was not only supportive, but quite enthusiastic about the idea.

"I don't see any problems with that at all," he said, "as long as the Department is okay with it. In fact, I think that's a nice, creative way to use the Lodge." After instructing Nora to draw up a contract for me to sign, he asked how the parent visits were going, wished us a good day, and ended the call.

I couldn't believe it had been so easy, and I was so giddy I could hardly stand myself.

Chapter 42
Robby

Hi. Well it is me Robby again and I fell asleep last night and now it is the next day but that's okay because right now it is awesome. Mrs. Cortes talked to Joseph's family and I am going to spend the night at his house next weekend. Yeah! And his sister is even really cute because she is just a baby so she isn't mean yet and I can tell she likes me because she laughs at me.

Oh! And then you won't believe this but Joseph's mom asked me if there were any foods I don't like and I said spaghetti and she said, "Then we'll make sure that's not what we have for dinner when you visit." Can you believe it? Then she smiled at me and she is so nice!

And then Mrs. Cortes talked to Stacey's mom and guess what! She said Stacey and I can call each other when we want to. That makes me so happy because I am in love with Stacey and she said she is in love with me too. But don't tell my mom.

Anthony's mom and Marcus' mom are nice too but they said Anthony and Marcus do not do overnights. I guess Marcus does not do overnights because he wears a diaper and maybe he is embarrassed. His mom said I can come visit him sometime and Mrs. Cortes said she will take me. Mrs. Cortes is doing a great job.

Anthony's mom said he does not do overnights because they make him anxious. I am not sure what anxious means but I think it probably means he gets Over Stimulated. She said we can meet and play together some afternoon at his house so that is cool and Mrs. Cortes said she will take me there too.

Anthony is not Over Stimulated now because he is wearing his weight jacket. He asked Mr. Bryan for it this morning. I think that was a very very smart thing for Anthony to do. He is a very smart kid he just has autism but nobody at this place minds.

Here comes Ms. McIntosh and she is smiling so big! It is that smile where you can see all of somebody's teeth and I can see all of her teeth. I guess she is really really happy today. She is coming over to see me and I am so glad. Mrs. Cortes is coming too and I can see all of her teeth too. Wow these people are happy!

Ms. McIntosh sits down next to me and just looks at me and smiles with her teeth and then she says, "Robby, I have some news I think you might like."

I wonder what that could be but then she says, "What would you think about spending more time at the Lodge?"

And I think she must be teasing me because she already knows I love the Lodge but I can't stay here because I have to go back to the Sloan Foster Family so I tell her that.

So then she says, "Yes, but what if you only stayed with the Sloans on the weekends and you stayed here during the week? The van driver could take you to and from school and during the time you're here, you could do activities with the other kids."

I hope she isn't teasing me because that is exactly what I want to do. I wanted to live at the Lodge. I don't think she would tease me in a bad way. I think she really means it.

She is still talking to me. "It won't be the same kids each week, you know. Every week will be different. And I won't be here all the time, either, but I will come back and visit every couple of weeks. How does this all sound to you?"

For some reason my voice won't even work. I am trying to tell her that is the coolest thing ever but the words are stuck somewhere in my mouth and won't come out so I just jump up and hug her instead so that she will know how happy I am and now my teeth are all showing too. We are some very happy people.

"And Robby," she is saying into my ear and she has her arms wrapped around me, "thank you for telling me about my dad. I didn't even know I had one until you told me."

Ms. McIntosh told me last night that people love me and will take care of me and I believed her and she was right. I think a whole bunch of people love me. I think a whole bunch of people love her too. It is nice to have people who love you. This has been the very best day of my life.

Chapter 43

By eleven-thirty the children and their parents were gone, including Robby and Mrs. Cortes. I hugged them all goodbye and reminded Robby that I'd see him again in a couple of weeks. He barely stood still long enough to hear me, he was so busy making plans with his friends. "Make sure to bring your Michelangelo!" was the last thing I heard as the door closed behind them.

I helped Opal with the cleanup before leaving to join Nora in her office for our meeting with Virgil Young. As I made my way across the lot, I saw Sheriff Moore's patrol car cruising slowly past the Lodge. He gave me a nod and I waved back, pleased to see that he'd remembered.

I didn't know what to expect from Virgil. In some ways I had come to feel sorry for the man. It did sound as if life had taken a hard turn against him recently, but on the other hand, his comments and actions towards both me and Nora were uncalled for and unjustified, and his threats regarding my past were more than a little concerning to me.

I found Nora accompanied by an older woman in a business suit, laptop computer perched precariously on her knees. "Jessie," Nora said, standing, "this is Betty Littles from finance. She's brought Virgil's pay history with her. We'll print it out for him as soon as he arrives."

We exchanged greetings as I took a seat and Betty tilted the lap top towards my view. "As you can see," she said, "he's been paid in full."

"I've no doubt he has," I told her. "From what I understand, he and his wife are experiencing some tough times right now. Nora, I think I forgot to mention it to you with everything else going on, but from what I hear Virgil's wife was recently diagnosed with cancer. People in town seem to think that's what's causing his current bad mood."

"Oh, that's too bad," Nora said, concerned. "I had no idea. I'm sure losing his job at this particular time added exponentially to the stress. Unfortunately, I had no choice. It's policy. But it does shed a new light on his behavior, doesn't it?"

"It does," I agreed. "At least he was able to find another job. He's working fulltime as a mechanic down in the village."

"Good, I'm glad he found work," Nora said, "but it makes me wonder if he'll show up today. I'm sure he doesn't have vacation time. He'd have to take unpaid leave." She drummed a pen on her desk and checked her watch. "He's nearly fifteen minutes late as it is."

"Should we call him?" Betty asked. "If he isn't going to show I need to get back to my office. Fridays are busy in the payroll department."

"I suppose we probably should. I'm sure we've all got things we need to be doing. Or planes we need to be catching," Nora said, smiling at me. "I've got his home number here." She opened the file on her desk and began to dial.

After four rings a machine picked up instructing callers to leave a message. Nora waited for the beep. "Virgil? If you're there, can you pick up the phone? We're all here waiting for you up at the Lodge and just wanted to make sure you're still coming." She paused, waiting. "Virgil, if you get this within the next few minutes give me a call."

She replaced the receiver. "Let's try him at the garage in town," she suggested. My guess is that he wasn't able to leave work."

Someone answered on the first ring. "Johnson's garage, can I help you?"

Nora set the phone on speaker. "You can," she answered. "I'm looking for Virgil Young. Is he able to take a call?"

"Well, he would be," answered the male voice, "Except he didn't show up to work today. He ain't here."

"Then it seems we have a similar problem," Nora answered, "because he isn't here, either. If you see him, could you have him call Dr. Nora Wright?"

"Sure thing," answered the voice. "And if you see him, tell him to call the garage."

Nora disconnected and exhaled loudly. "Well, there you have it. Let's give him fifteen more minutes. If he doesn't show, we'll just assume we've been stood up."

I felt slightly uneasy. Darryl Lane and Eugene Cooper had said Virgil had never been particularly nice, but wasn't known for violent outbursts. Clearly, the stress was affecting him in unpredictable ways.

What if Virgil was already at the Lodge somewhere waiting and biding his time? Everyone was gone. The Huffmans had gone on their date to the diner, the staff had gone home. Only Nora, Betty and I remained. I hated to be paranoid about the whole thing, but I thought I had a pretty valid argument that thus far, the events of my life supported a healthy dose of paranoia. I hoped Sheriff Moore was still patrolling.

"If he doesn't show, we could always send him copies of what we have," Nora was saying. "I'll document in his personnel file that he didn't show but we mailed the information. Betty, can you print those out for me?"

By the time Betty had printed out the needed documents and Nora had readied them for the mail, making the required notation in Virgil's file, twenty minutes had passed. Virgil was obviously not planning to attend, but my anxiety only heightened.

"Nora, do you think it's possible he's up here somewhere?" I hadn't wanted to ask, but I couldn't help myself.

Nora paused in the shuffle of papers and looked up at me. "Jessie? Are you okay?"

I wasn't, actually. My palms were sweaty and my heart rate accelerated. I hated to admit any of that to Nora, especially in front of Betty, but I couldn't ignore my intuition.

"Something feels wrong," I said. "Someone wanted me here. If they're going to contact me at all, it has to be now. What better time than when we're up here alone?" I was dismayed to hear the strained note in my voice.

"Maybe that's what they've been waiting for all along," I rushed ahead. "For everyone to leave. Think about it, Nora. Virgil made a scene and agreed to a meeting at this time, after he knew everyone would be gone." I paused. "Now, nobody seems to know where he is. Something just doesn't feel right."

Nora observed me for a minute before turning to Betty. "Betty, we're okay here if you need to go," she told her. "I know you have work waiting for you back at the main office. Thanks for coming; I'm sorry it was a waste of your time."

Betty jumped at the opportunity to leave, quickly packing her laptop away and gathering her purse. "I appreciate it, Nora," she said. "I really do have a lot to do. Ms. McIntosh, have a safe flight."

She paused in the doorway, looking back at me curiously. "I'll let you know if I see anyone lurking around outside, but I'm sure you ladies are fine. People no-show all the time, as you well know, Nora. No one seems to have any respect for anyone else's time these days."

"You're right," Nora agreed. "No-shows are common. I think I have about a seventy-five percent show rate. Have a great weekend, Betty."

"Okay," Nora turned to me when Betty was gone. "Let's get you packed and ready for your flight. I think we're safe, but I do understand your concerns. I'm a little nervous too, I have to admit. I always am when everyone leaves; it's quite isolated up here." She stood. "I think I'll leave things as they are today. I can come in early Sunday and finish my paperwork. Let's get out of here."

As Nora locked the office door behind us I glanced around for Sheriff Moore, but I saw no sign of him or of anyone else. I couldn't shake the feeling that something bad was coming. It was a feeling I'd known well as a child; I knew not to ignore it. I was on high alert as we crossed the lot to the Lodge.

We entered the darkened building, eerily quiet without the voices of the children, and went down the long hallway to my room. There was little packing for me to do; I'd never really unpacked to begin with. I threw a few things into my suitcase and Nora placed my hairdryer and brush into the hygiene bag.

"Is that it?" she asked, and I nodded. I grabbed the bags and turned to leave, Nora right behind me.

It was then that I thought I saw a shadow from somewhere out in the hall.

Chapter 44

"Nora," I began, but before I could say anything else she interrupted me.

"It was me, Jessie," she said. "I'm the one who wanted you out here."

"What?"

"Have a seat," she said, motioning towards the bed. "Let's chat. You have a few minutes before you have to leave, don't you? And we need to be alone for this chat."

I sat as instructed, too shocked to do anything else, and she hoisted herself up onto the dresser across from me. "What really happened to my father?" she asked.

At first I thought I must have missed something. "Your father? What do you mean?" I had no idea what she was talking about.

"Is Virgil right about his accusations?" she asked. "Did you kill him? Or did one of those old people you hang around with down in the village?" She crossed her arms over her chest and leaned against the mirror. "It wasn't until after I killed Floyd Bowden that I began to wonder," she said.

My mouth dropped open. What on earth?

Nora laughed. "Jessie, you've grown into such a beautiful woman, but that look really isn't very flattering. Close your mouth."

"Nora," I tried to recover, "What is going on here?"

"That would be Lenny Sue to you," she responded. "Lenora Suzette Campbell. Remember me? Granted, I've changed somewhat over the last thirty-seven years. What do you think? Didn't I clean up well?"

"Lenny Sue?" I was dumbstruck. "Why didn't you tell me? Oh, my God, why didn't you say something?" I was scrambling for words; so many thoughts were spinning through my brain I felt dizzy.

Across from me, Nora sighed. "I can see you need a moment to collect yourself. Really, Jessie, you have got to learn to breathe during panic attacks. It'll make them pass so much more quickly. In through the nose, out through the mouth. Why is that so difficult for you?"

From my seat on the bed I struggled desperately to do exactly what she was suggesting. I felt faint, as if my chest were being squeezed. In through the nose, out through the mouth.

"That's better," she said. "If you don't learn to breathe properly, one of these days you're going to faint from lack of oxygen. You really are a mess, aren't you?"

I didn't answer; how could I?

"Anyway," she said, kicking off her shoes and pulling her legs up to sit cross-legged on the dresser, "it isn't that I care so much about what happened to him, you know. It's just that—and I'm sure you can understand this—I need some closure. Truthfully, until Floyd died I never even thought about my father. It was a shame about Floyd. He was a good stepfather to me. I hated to have to kill him."

My chest was squeezed again; I tried to concentrate on my breathing. In through the nose, out through the mouth.

Across from me, Nora spread her arms, palms up. "But what else could I do?" she asked. She didn't wait for an answer. "When he began to put two and two together about our mother's death...well, you can see I really had no choice."

Dear God, what was she *talking* about? According to Richard Huffman, Nora—Lenny Sue—would have been twelve years old when our mother died.

"It's all really rather fascinating, isn't it?" She cocked her head quizzically to the side. "The whole nature versus

242

nurture debate, I mean. Take us for example. You," she pointed at me, "are obviously a wreck. Panic attacks, generalized anxiety, depression....A classic case of Post-traumatic Stress Disorder." She paused a few seconds to consider before adding, "In addition, I would certainly diagnose you with Borderline Personality Disorder on Axis II.

"But how can you help it?" she asked. "Look at what you've been through. It's all very understandable. Your issues are a direct result of the abuse you suffered. Me, on the other hand," she placed a hand on her chest, "even though I spent all of my formative years—those early years are so important, you know—in the same awful environment as you, I don't suffer from any of those problems."

"You're crazy," I finally managed to gasp through the spasms in my chest.

"Oh, undoubtedly," she nodded. "I never meant to imply otherwise, but that's exactly my point." She sat forward, eyes shining with excitement. "That's what's so fascinating. We share the same mother and our formative years were spent in the same environment. But I didn't develop any of the post-traumatic symptoms you have.

"I'm inclined to think there's a genetic factor involved, indicating that in our case, anyway, nature wins. What's different about us? Our fathers, of course. Yours, as we've just recently discovered, is sane. Mine, as we both know, was not.

"Roy was obviously sociopathic," she said. "No conscience whatsoever, no ability to empathize, no consideration for others. And here I am, a chip off the old block." She spread her arms wide again.

"Of course," she went on, "I'm a lot more polished than he was. Did you know that with the appropriate social skills, sociopaths can be amazingly successful in their chosen fields of study? Most likely due to our ability to manipulate the people around us, wouldn't you think? That, and our

243

total lack of regard for following the societal rules most people follow. Some experts speculate that many people in positions of power are probably sociopaths. Isn't that incredible?"

I'd figured out by now that Nora wasn't expecting any responses from me. I sat quietly, trying to regulate my breathing. I was mesmerized; I'd never witnessed anything like it. It was as if she were unraveling before my eyes.

"We would be a fabulous study, you and I," she said. "But of course there isn't much way we can do that, under the circumstances. That's a shame."

"Nora," I said, when she became quiet, "what do you want from me?"

"Nothing too sinister," she said. "Just the truth. As I was telling you a few minutes ago, I never thought about my father until after I killed Floyd. That's when I started to wonder about myself. Killing our mother made some sense, you see, because she'd never been very good at mothering. I had a great deal of anger towards her. I'm sure you can understand."

She rubbed at her chin, thoughtful again. "I suppose that's why that one was so brutal. But Floyd was different. I *liked* Floyd. He was a good guy. Still, it didn't bother me to kill him when I realized I needed to. I wasn't brutal with him; I just cut his brakes. All of our cars were always so junky; it wasn't suspicious when he wrecked due to mechanical failure.

"Anyway," she said, "it kind of bothered me that I could kill someone I liked and not worry about it. That's not normal, wouldn't you agree?" Again, she didn't wait for an answer.

"I didn't have many memories of my father," she said. "I'd been so young when we left, but I'd heard our mother talk about him enough to know he was evil. I started wondering if I was like him. Of course, I never got to talk with him about it because by the time I got back here, he was gone. Or dead. Whichever. It sparked my interest, though, so much so that I decided to study it. As you can see, I've done quite well at it."

I couldn't help but wonder what her plan was for me. There were already at least two people dead at her hands. Would I be the third? Surely she couldn't let me go, not after all she'd told me.

"Don't look so worried, Jessie." She laughed again. "Goodness, you're in no danger from me. We're *both* killers, aren't we? You know my story; now I want yours. Quid pro quo, as they say.

"Besides," she continued. "No one would believe you if you tried to tell them anything I've just shared. You've been paranoid all week. Do you think that's gone unnoticed?"

"What do you mean?" I asked. Of course I'd been paranoid; someone was after me, but I couldn't think of anything I'd done to undermine my credibility.

"What I *mean*," she said, "is that all those things you've been spouting off about never happened." She began to laugh. "Oh, Jessie, I'm sorry. Just let me catch my breath. It's all so amusing, and you couldn't have played into it any better than you did. Here I was trying to figure out how to get information from you without having to kill you for it, and you gave me the perfect method."

"I still don't understand," I said. I doubted I ever would.

"I panicked a little at first, when you decided to go to Sheriff Moore yourself, but then I realized that was perfect," she said. "He wouldn't have a clue what you were talking about. The vandalism, the chemicals, the horses," she began laughing again.

"The whole bogus investigation. It never happened," she finally managed to say. "None of it. I made it all up to get you out here. I never had any conversations with Sheriff Moore about any of it." She was positively gleeful.

"But what about the fire? And the letter? You didn't make those things up," I said.

"No," she said, "the fire was real enough. A problem with the wiring. We're actually in litigation with the contractors right now because of it. They endangered the children with their sloppy work.

"But the letter...." She grinned. "That was a nice touch, don't you think? There was no original given to anyone. Just the one I showed you. So when you went accusing Sheriff Moore...." She snorted, wiping at her eyes as she laughed.

I was so confused, trying to grasp the things she was telling me. "And the Huffmans? Are they in on it with you?" Through my fear and confusion, I felt a small pang of disappointment. I had so hoped things were as they had said.

"No," she said, turning serious. "No, I had no idea he was your father. How crazy was *that* whole thing? But once you became suspicious of them, it took any heat off of me if something did happen to you. Between them and Virgil Young, there was no way I'd ever be suspected of anything."

"But you always defended them." I didn't know what to believe.

"Mmm." She nodded. "A paradoxical approach. The more I defended the Huffmans, the more you suspected them. I'm brilliant at what I do, Jessie. I truly am. Just ask anybody in the field. Some would call it narcissism, I suppose, but in the end it doesn't matter. The fact remains: I'm brilliant at what I do.

"That's why you'll tell me what really happened to my father. That's also why you'll never repeat a word of what I've told you." She pushed her hair back from her face. "No one would believe you. I'm a well-respected psychotherapist, an expert in my field. And you," she pointed at me again. "You are a woman slowly losing her grip on reality.

"You dissociated your second morning here, right in my office, remember? And Mrs. Huffman can vouch for the fact that you'd obviously spent a night crying. Even Betty witnessed your paranoia this very afternoon.

"Add that to the conversation you had with the Sheriff," she said, "and Jessie, you look a little unbalanced. Heavens, you're not stable to begin with, but the conversation with the Huffmans last night would be enough to throw anyone off kilter.

"I'll have to have you hospitalized for your own safety if you start babbling about things. And if that fails, the idea of you committing suicide isn't farfetched at all." She winked at me.

In my pocket, my cell began to buzz. I glanced at my watch. Three o'clock. I'd told Corinne I'd be there by two-thirty at the latest. It would be one of them calling to check on me. Maybe, just maybe, they'd come looking for me. I could only hope.

"Ignore the phone," Nora said. "We have more important things to discuss."

"And so do we," came a deep voice from the open door. "Dr. Wright, you're under arrest for the murders of Lindy and Floyd Bowden." Sheriff Moore had his gun drawn. "Lower yourself slowly to the floor, hands behind your back."

As Nora had pointed out, I never did seem to get my breathing right during a panic attack. I passed out.

Chapter 45

The first person I saw was Michael, leaning over me as I lay...where was I? On one of the couches in the common area. I struggled to sit up.

"No, honey, lie back down." This was Corinne. "You don't want to sit up too fast or you might faint again." I craned my neck, trying to see her. Instead, I saw Richard and Opal Huffman, standing off to the side and looking terrified.

"Nora," I said. "Where is she?"

"On her way to Huntington to be booked." John's voice this time. "Good Lord, sweetie, you certainly do take the prize for dysfunctional families."

In spite of everything, something about that struck me as funny and I laughed. "It's nice to win at something," I said. "Might as well be dysfunction." I sat up again, this time more slowly. "Since I seem to have missed the end of the party, could someone please tell me what happened?"

"You passed out right as my deputies were handcuffing Dr. Wright." Sheriff Moore stepped into my line of vision and squatted in front of me. "You okay, Ms. McIntosh? We were just about to call an ambulance. I still think it might be a good idea."

I shook my head. "No need for an ambulance. It was just a panic attack. I'm used to them, although I can honestly say I've never passed out from one before. Then again, I've never found out that my half sister killed my mother before, either." Even saying it made me feel dizzy again. Michael gently eased me back down on the couch.

"If you don't mind, Sheriff," I said, "I'll listen from down here. And I'm sorry, by the way. I owe you one hell of an apology."

He smiled. "Accepted. And just so you know, we've been investigating Dr. Wright for some time, thanks to a tip from Mr. and Mrs. Huffman. Richard, you want to fill her in on that part?"

Richard Huffman pulled a chair up in front of me where the Sheriff had been squatting. I heard his knees crack when he sat down. "You remember I told you I kept up with you," he said, and I nodded. "And," he said, "you remember I told you I kept in touch with Sam Rogers, the investigator." I nodded again.

"Thing was," he said, "when Rogers was finding out about that fire, seemed like there was some suspicions around it. Some of the folks in town thought there was more to it than was being told. It was early in the morning, just after sunup. Lenny Sue made it out fine and so did Leroy, even though they'd have both been sleeping when it started. Floyd Bowden was at work, getting an early start before that Arizona heat come down.

"Couldn't nobody seem to understand how it come about that Lindy didn't make it out. It was only one section of the house that burned, over to where her and Floyd's bedroom was at. If she'd gone back in looking for Leroy like Lenny Sue had said, it didn't make no sense to some that she'd gone back to her own bedroom. What would have been the sense in that?

"When they dug her body out, some folks said she had a cracked skull. Didn't look like no furniture or nothing fell on her. Seemed odd to folks, but the police said it was accidental, said maybe she hit her head when she fell or something, and they closed the case. Lenny Sue had told them that Lindy run back in looking for Leroy, and I reckon that was enough for them. But them townfolks that had seen her body had some doubts.

"That stuck with Rogers. That's the kind of investigator he was, you see. He paid attention to them things. Then, 'bout the time you was getting started out there in Hollywood, Rogers heard that Floyd Bowden had died too, in an automobile accident. Seemed like a whole heap of tragedy on one family.

"By that time, Rogers had spent so blamed much time trying to track you down and keep up with you that he got involved in it. We was close friends by then, me and Opal and him, and he started caring for himself how you was doing and what you was up to. He'd like to meet you sometime, if you're ever feeling up to it.

"Anyway, we started thinking maybe he ought to keep an eye on them others, too, since they seemed to have such a hard time of it. I had been Lindy's friend at one time, probably the only one she ever had. Didn't seem right not to keep an eye on them kids. Somebody needed to do that for her, and she hadn't never had nobody else.

"By that time Lenny Sue was old enough to be on her own. Rogers learned she was going to University of Arizona, paid for with all that insurance money she had done collected. Townfolks was suspicious about that, too. Meantime, Rogers tracked Leroy down to a foster home.

"I reckon Leroy was about fourteen or fifteen by then. He was a quiet kid, kept to himself. He remembered Rogers from when he'd come looking for you. When Rogers went up to him outside the school one day, Leroy was ready to talk.

"Said he'd been trying to get the caseworkers to listen but wouldn't nobody pay attention to a kid. Said he thought his sister had murdered his mother and Floyd. Told Rogers that Lenny Sue was evil, always fighting with everybody, bad fights. That poor kid was scared to death. Thought he was next, or maybe even you."

It was strange to hear that all those years ago someone had worried about me, someone who shared my own genes. Not just someone—my brother. Over the years,

I'd often wondered what had become of that filthy little baby. I prayed Richard wasn't about to tell me Leroy was dead, too. I didn't want to hear that.

"Please," I said. "Just tell me he's not dead."

"Oh, no," Richard said. "He's living outside of Tucson, working in a factory there. Got a pretty little wife and a couple of kids. He hit a couple of rough spots along the way, as you might imagine, but he's made a right nice life for himself. He never did see Lenny Sue again; he never did want to and apparently she didn't neither. He asks about you sometimes, though.

"Anyway, after what all them townfolks had told Rogers, and then with Leroy saying the same thing, we—me and Opal and Rogers—knew we'd have to keep up with Lenny Sue in case she ever decided to come after you. She finished all her schooling out in Arizona 'round about ten years ago. She got married for a little while but it didn't last long. I don't reckon it would, would it? Then all of a sudden she ended up moving back out here.

"That raised our suspicions even more. We couldn't see no reason for her to move back to the place she was born after leaving it all them years ago. It wasn't like she had no kin out here. Leastways not except for you, when you come back visiting.

"Then Ms. Platte passed on and you opened up this here Lodge. Me and Opal read about it in the paper, when they did that big write up on it. Said in the paper that Dr. Nora Wright was to be the clinical director. That's when me and Opal, and Rogers too, knew we had to do something, because that was just too big of a coincidence.

"So Opal and me applied for them jobs. Rogers called Sheriff Moore and told him everything, all of them suspicions. The Sheriff here, he's a good man. Listened to everything we said and took it serious."

Sheriff Moore knelt back down in front of me. "Ms. McIntosh, with the help of the Huffmans and your parent company, we've been monitoring Dr. Wright since she was hired. In the beginning all we had to go on was speculation, but when you questioned me in the diner I knew she was setting you up for something.

"You spoke as if she and I had had ongoing contact, but we hadn't. I had never spoken to Dr. Wright. Clearly, she had deceived you. We didn't know what she had planned, but we decided to increase our surveillance. We knew that if in fact she did make some sort of move against you, today would most likely be the day to watch for it.

"We had just put our men in place when you entered the Lodge with her this afternoon. When she confessed to killing her mother and Mr. Bowden, we made our move. Ms. McIntosh, we fully believe she meant to do you harm. If it hadn't been for the Huffmans here, she may very well have succeeded."

I looked at Richard where he sat in front of me. Opal had moved to stand behind him. I had so much information to sort through; it would take a long time. But one thing I did know: Richard Huffman was a good man. I couldn't quite yet process the fact that he was my father, but I hoped to get there someday. I looked forward to it.

"Thank you," I said to him, and to her too. It was hard for me to fathom tracking someone for nearly fifty years, intervening when they needed it. It was mind boggling.

"I didn't save you the first time," Richard said, and a tear slid down his cheek. "But by God, come hell or high water, I was going to save you the second time."

That is the way of the universe, Billy May whispered in my mind. *It is all connected.* I finally understood what she meant.

Chapter 46
Saturday

"Jessie, you should write a book." Valerie Poindexter shook her head in amazement. "You have the most incredible family history." I laughed. As the town librarian, Valeria thought everyone should write a book.

We were having breakfast in the diner, Corinne, John, Michael and I. It seemed as if nearly all of Cedar Hollow was there, our tables all pushed together. As Darryl Lane had remarked not even a week before, news travels fast in a little town of two-hundred-sixteen residents.

John had called and cancelled our flight home the evening before, in light of all that had happened. We'd agreed we all needed a night to regroup. I'd spent the night at Corinne's house, but none of us had gotten much sleep, staying up most of the night to rehash the events of the past week.

I'd been right that the phone call Nora had instructed me not to answer had been from John. They knew something was wrong when they hadn't heard from me by two-thirty. They immediately called the Sheriff's office only to be told he was already at the Lodge. Upon hearing that, they'd all three piled into Corinne's car for the trip up the mountain.

"Where we found Nora being hustled out by two deputies and you sprawled across the bed, lights out. Always the drama queen," John had remarked.

"Pot," I said, punching him in the arm, "meet kettle."

Now, sitting in the diner surrounded by friends, I once again had that feeling of home, but this time it wasn't tinged

255

with sadness. I'd learned so much about myself over the past week, not just about my history, but about myself. *Turn your colors back on*, the gypsy woman had said, and I believed that was exactly what I was doing. Maybe it had taken a series of shocks to wake me up to my own life; I didn't know, but for whatever reason I felt more alive, and more hopeful, than I'd felt in a long time.

I also realized that life was bigger than just me, and as odd as it sounds, that was a relief to me. I was so tired of being stuck inside myself; it was wonderful to focus on other people. I thought maybe I'd give Therapist Number One a call to let her know I'd finally figured that out. I *didn't* think I'd make an appointment, however. Given my recent experiences regarding psychotherapists, I thought it might take some time before I was ready to sit in an office alone with one.

"When are you going back to California, Jessie?" Eugene Cooper's question pulled me out of my thoughts. I was glad to see the walker he'd been using a few days earlier was gone.

"I'm not sure," I answered him. "John and Michael are going back this evening, but I think I may stay awhile."

Kay refilled our coffee cups. "It'll be nice to have you around," she said. "I know Corinne will enjoy it."

"That I will," said Corinne. "I've missed the kids since they all left home. I told Jessie she was welcome to stay with me, but I believe she wants to stay up on Billy May's mountain. I don't blame her. It is a healin' place."

"It is," I agreed. "But there's also the practical matter of introducing a new clinical director to the staff tomorrow. Luckily, our parent company was prepared, since they'd been aware of the investigation into Nora. But I'd still like to be there to make sure everything runs smoothly. And to see Robby again. He won't be expecting me." I smiled at the thought of surprising him.

Michael had agreed to tie up a few loose ends in L. A. for me. He had a key to my condo and would look after it until I returned. I didn't know exactly when that would be. I had several projects lined up, but I wasn't looking forward to them. In the back of my mind, I was considering handing them off to Michael, if he was interested.

Looking over at him absorbed in conversation with Valerie, I wasn't sure he would be. He seemed to have fallen hard for Cedar Hollow. I couldn't imagine him stepping back from the Hollywood scene, particularly not for a little backwoods town in West Virginia, but Michael was full of surprises. If anyone could strike a balance, it would be him.

I caught his eye across the table and winked at him, making him laugh out loud. He had filled out all the paperwork to apply for a volunteer position at the Lodge, and I had promised to turn it in for him first thing Monday morning. It would take a couple of weeks for the background checks to be completed, but I was eagerly anticipating that time.

I had a lot of things I needed to figure out, none more pressing than what I wanted to do with the rest of my life. In the midst of all the confusion, one thing was certain: I wanted Michael to be a part of it, one way or another. What that would look like, I didn't know, but I was ready to find out.

I also looked forward to getting to know the Huffmans. Richard had insisted I take the money he'd saved up all those years, but I couldn't do that. I didn't need it. We'd finally reached a compromise. It would be saved for Robby, for whatever expenses he might have in the future, and I would oversee the account.

I looked up at the tinkling of the bell to see Dennis Lane holding the door open for his father, Darryl. They made their way to our table and Dennis pulled up a couple of chairs.

"They're goin' to keep her another night," said Darryl. "It was the chemo. Folks always say that's the worst part. They got her hooked up to fluids, tryin' to rehydrate her. Virgil is a mess. He don't hardly know what to do, with her so sick."

Darryl had been to Huntington to visit Virgil Young's wife. Virgil had rushed her to the hospital late Thursday night after she had become ill. Luckily, the garage understood the circumstances and was holding his job until he could get back.

I had ordered flowers to be sent to the hospital first thing that morning. I didn't know how Virgil Young felt about me aside from all the stress, but I was ready to make a fresh start. I also had a new understanding regarding some of his anger. Two of his three tickets had been related to his wife's illness. He'd gotten them on I-64, both times while rushing his wife to the hospital. I didn't know if our parent company could waive their policy in light of the special circumstances, but I planned on asking.

"How are you doing, Jessie? I hear you've had a heck of a week." Dennis Lane spoke quietly beside me.

I laughed. "It's funny, isn't it? On the surface, Cedar Hollow is just a sleepy little mining town. People would never guess the things that go on here."

"That's what makes it home," Dennis said. "Knowing the people, knowing their histories and caring about what happens to them. To outsiders it might not look like much, but we know how rich life here really is. It's never boring."

I smiled. "Dennis, we probably need to sit down and figure out that store."

"No rush," he said. "Like I said before, I'm not going anywhere. This is home."

Home. I tested the word on my tongue, looking around at all the familiar faces, people I'd known and loved since I was a girl. This diner, this town, Billy May's mountain—these were my roots.

Yes, I decided. It was home, and I was happy to be there.

Book Club Discussion Starters

1.   Jessie's ex-husband accused her of being a woman composed entirely of opposites. What did he mean by that?

2.   Robby has some interesting insights into Mrs. Jamison, the Christian woman from his church. How does he describe her role? Why might he feel this way?

3.   They gypsy woman on the plane tells Jessie, "You've turned your colors off." How had Jessie turned her colors off? What makes her agree with the gypsy woman?

4.   Robby states several times that "grownups ask silly questions." Given the examples he cites, is his assessment accurate?

5.   When Jessie was a teenager she once remarked to Billy May, "Maybe you should have just left me there." Billy May responded, "Ain't nobody got the power to destroy you but you." Is this true? Why or why not?

6.   Jessie feels that to enter into a relationship with Michael would be unfair to him. What makes her think this? Would it be unfair?

7.   Mr. Huffman describes going to great lengths to find Jessie. Did he do enough? Why or why not?

8.   In the opening chapter of the book, we are led to believe that Lindy was a neglectful mother. By the end of the story, did that perception of Lindy change? If so, how?

9.   Nora questions which is most important in determining the personality of a child: nature, or nurture. In your opinion, which has the greater influence on a child? Why?

10. At the end of the novel, Jessie states that she has learned a great deal about herself during the week, not only about her past, but about herself. What sorts of things has Jessie learned? Do you think her life will be a more peaceful one as a result?

More Great Books by
Melinda Clayton

Appalachian Justice, Cedar Hollow Series, Book 1

Entangled Thorns, Cedar Hollow Series, Book 3

Shadow Days, Cedar Hollow Series, Book 4

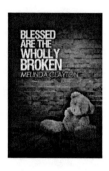

Blessed Are the Wholly Broken

Making Amends

About the Author

Melinda Clayton is the author of *Appalachian Justice, Return to Crutcher Mountain, Entangled Thorns, Shadow* Days, *Blessed Are the Holy Broken,* and her latest novel, *Making Amends.* In addition to writing, Dr. Clayton has an Ed.D. in Special Education Administration and is a licensed psychotherapist in the states of Florida and Colorado.

CPSIA information can be obtained at www.ICGtesting.com
Printed in the USA
LVOW08s2250280616

494507LV00002B/212/P